PROLOGUE

N OW, I AM DISMISSING THE immediate from my mind! Things are whirling about in my head in a continuum of blinding flashes. It just seems easier to not focus on the present. No, I am not having a nervous breakdown, nor do I have serious psychological problems, anxiety aside. I think I am about to lose my job and my "perfect" life may be unraveling. It is very important to me that I understand what might be happening. I want you to understand too. Getting the unvarnished truth down on paper might get us to that point. If nothing else, the process will be cathartic, I hope.

My Perfect Life

FRANK FARRELL

NEWMAN SPRINGS PUBLISHING
320 Broad Street
Red Bank, NJ 07701

First originally published by Newman Springs Publishing 2024

An Invitation is an original poem by the author

ISBN 979-8-89061-511-4 (Paperback)
ISBN 979-8-89061-512-1 (Digital)

Printed in the United States of America

To Janet, my wife of sixty-three years and best friend.

CHAPTER 1

LET ME BEGIN BY INTRODUCING my family and sharing with you my early experiences growing up. Brian, my father, had been a medical doctor, specializing in cardiology. Dad was six feet tall and very trim, with a full head of curly black hair and a touch of gray. His eyes were very blue; he had an engaging smile and a wonderful laugh. A bright and kind Brian Murphy, Boston born and raised in the Catholic faith, was a very observant member of the church. Margaret, my sweet mother, trained as a nurse, migrating to a stay-at-home mom as the children arrived. Peggy, as she was known to all, was a tiny woman of five feet, two inches. She had auburn hair and, like Dad, had striking blue eyes. She too was Boston born and a practicing Catholic. My family is 100 percent Irish on both sides. My parents were third-generation offspring of families who enjoyed early and considerable success. We made our home in Brookline, Massachusetts. A comfortable suburb of Boston, near the Ocean and Cape Cod, with great cultural, social, athletic, and eating venues.

The extended family of grandparents, aunts, uncles, and many cousins enjoyed each other's company. Family events and casual gatherings were frequent, raucous, and fun-filled. I was the last born of three children. Patrick, the firstborn, follows our father, being six feet tall and trim. He also has Dad's curly black hair and the Murphy blue eyes. We never tell him, but he is one handsome fellow. Patrick was everything a little boy could want in an older brother, always there to pick me up, dust me off, give me a needed pep talk, and send me on my way. Patrick was off to Princeton when I was twelve years old. Usually, I would find my big brother in the audience or bleachers for my performances or games. I remember so clearly the overnights at Princeton, the fishing trips, the Red Sox games, and other boys-only events. Pat was and still is my best friend! The second Murphy child is my dear sister Kathleen a.k.a. Katie. She has been my second mom and is the love of my life. Not just providing a shoulder to cry on, but a trusted confidant with whom I could share my deepest feelings. Katie favors our mother, with auburn hair and bluish eyes. She, too, is petite at five foot four. Katie is very bright and was off to Columbia as I was in the throes of becoming a full-fledged teenager. As with Brother Patrick, Katie has always been there for me.

Growing up in a happy, comfortable, and supportive household with loving parents, great siblings, and with an extended fun-loving family shaped me in so many ways.

My family regularly ate dinner together, with dialogue around the table always informative, sometimes edifying, sometimes humorous, covering a full spectrum—politics, the economy, current events, religion, family news, our individual experiences and challenges. Opinions were expressed freely, sometimes vigorously challenged, but always with respect. Our parents were supportive, fostering independence and self-reliance; they were also strict and made clear their expectations of how we should lead value-driven lives. My siblings and I enjoyed growing up in Brookline, relished our college experiences, and managed to all graduate with high honors and debt-free, thanks to scholarships, grants, and awards.

Patrick found early and enormous success in the world of high finance. Sadly, for the family, that took him first to California and two years later to London, England. Despite his work schedule, extensive travel, and the time difference, we all made a concerted effort to stay in touch.

Sister Katie, the most academically inclined of the Murphy children, having earned a BA and an MA in Literature from Columbia University, encamped to Dublin, Ireland, to pursue a PhD in Irish Literature. As the runt of the litter and upholding the family tradition of academic excellence, I earned a BA in Humanities from Penn University and graduated with the highest honors.

So there you have briefly, a snapshot of the wonderful and supportive environment I enjoyed as a child and young adult. With that, let me move on to my story and my terrible sense of foreboding. Let me set the stage. Armed with a newly minted degree, I left the cocoon of college life, a four-year run at drinking too much, eating too well, trying a variety of drugs, and enjoying an active sex life with a range of young ladies. By the way, I cannot explain this somewhat off-the-wall behavior, given my strict Catholic upbringing, perhaps a bit of rebellion. I arrived in New York City, after an intense round of interviews and with five offers, ready to enter the real world of work. I had accepted an offer from Peters & Wells (P&W). The company is small but considered one of the best adult-fiction publishers with a roster of award-winning authors. I am now an editorial assistant to a junior editor. Both the company and the job were considered prestigious, meaning the pay is meager. To this day, I do not understand that reverse equation: the better the company, the less you are paid. Consider yourself fortunate! So there I was, earning $450 a week and living in a 250-square-foot closet, euphemistically called an efficiency studio, on the fifth floor, a walk-up, meaning no elevator! My degree is not in accounting, but it didn't take too long to grasp the fact that the math was not quite right, income vs. expense. I tried for sympathy from my well-off folks, a subsidy, or a loan. No luck! Time to grow up, self-reliance, be independent—those were the marching orders. I was too proud to ask either Patrick or Katie for a helping hand. With my quick turn of mind, the answer was clear.

Seek a higher-paying job and leave P&W or find a side job to provide the needed supplemental income. Pride simply wouldn't let me leave P&W. I turned to reading the Help Wanted ads. Hospitality, the bar and restaurant business, is hot and apparently pays very well. Modesty aside, I present a polished manner, particularly good conversational skills, good looks, and always well-dressed. Within a few weeks, I had several particularly good offers. The prospects were excellent, making as much as $1,000 per week by working part-time weeknights and/or weekends.

My gig, as it has been called, is a bartending job, working from 7:00 p.m. to 1:00 a.m., Friday, Saturday, and Sunday evenings. With extraordinary luck, the Dove hired me. The establishment has multiple $$$'s in all the guidebooks and holds a Michelin Star! The first several weeks were intense, even frantic. The money started to roll in! I must be good, or the world had suddenly gone mad. I was attentive and had an excellent memory for names and drinks preferences. I was a good conversationalist/story-teller, very much up on the Broadway scene, the music hot spots, and skilled at getting an "impossible" reservation or ticket. The out-of-town people were particularly grateful for the assistance. Regulars warmed quickly to my affability.

Initially, I was concerned that I might be wiped out on Monday mornings. Everyone seemed slow on the uptake with the start of a new week. Too many parties, working side jobs, too much sun on the beach out in the Hamptons, etc.

My real job at P&W was going just fine. I was getting along well with my boss, a stunning and very bright woman of near thirty. Anne Hopkins, known as Annie, had been with P&W for nearly six years. With a BA and MA in Literature from Smith and Harvard respectively, she was an incredible editor. I found my boss most attractive! To my disappointment, Annie was, it seems, in a long-term relationship with another woman. However, as time would have it, the three of us developed wonderful personal relationships that could not have developed otherwise.

Enter now Henry Smithe Weathersbee, managing editor of P&W. Mr. Weathersbee, universally known as HSW, had been with the company for twenty-eight years. A graduate of Princeton, he was considered and acknowledged as the finest managing editor in the business. Imagine my amazement, being summoned to his office on the third day of my employment. Annie explained that HSW was known as a committed mentor to new arrivals in the editorial operations. The managing editor, a portly, short, and nearly bald man, had a continental style of dress and manner. HSW had certainly done his homework. He knew more about me than any personnel department could have gathered with the most rigorous background check! It was a bit curious. His questions and probing were both to the factual and to highly personal and subjective matters. We got into questions that I thought were prohibited by law, but I was too intimidated to object. Did I attend church and which one? Do I drink, smoke, or enjoy recreational drugs? On to my friends, male and female. HSW didn't ask how often I masturbated, but he came close! HSW apparently sensed that I was growing uncomfortable and moved the dialogue to my job and career path. The information and advice were informative and helpful. After the better part of an hour, we ended our meeting. I thanked HSW sincerely. He, in turn, offered to make himself available as a mentor/adviser anytime I wanted to chat or needed advice.

CHAPTER 2

WITH THE STAGE BEING SET and several key characters introduced, with more to come, let me fast-forward, about six years. I was now happily established at P&W, with increased responsibilities under the skilled direction of Annie Hopkins. HSW, true to his word, had proven to be a great mentor. He had introduced me to the movers and shakers in the publishing business with invitations to events, conferences, award ceremonies, and the like. Beyond that, it turned out we are both opera buffs and frequently enjoyed each other's company at performances and dinner.

Annie Hopkins was now a senior editor and considered the best of the best, reporting directly to HSW. Modesty aside, my rise through the ranks had been nearly meteoric. In six short years, I had moved from an editorial assistant to a junior editor to the position of editor, being paid $54,000 per annum. I would like you to believe that my rapid advancement had been wholly due to my extraordinary talents and hard work. In truth, I had been the beneficiary of many fortuitous events! I had reported to Annie directly since joining P&W. In addition to personally being a dynamite editor, she was the absolute best teacher and mentor. We had become remarkably close personal friends. Our personal rapport had allowed me no slack at all, quite the contrary. Annie was always fair but demanding. That was, very demanding! HSW's mentorship had been constant and worth more than words can say. He had shared his experiences and given me a perspective that can only come from his many years in the business. Being the proverbial right person in the right place at the right time also played into my quick movement up the career ladder. Working with fast-track associates and subordinates, aligning with editors who have quickly emerged as outstanding, all contributed to my personal success. I had worked very hard to develop and hone my knowledge and skills. My greatest strength had been as a developmental editor, finding emerging talent and collaborating effectively with those established authors already in the P&W stable. All this now had top agents seeking me out with book proposals, manuscripts, and introductions to promising authors.

In my other world, as bartender extraordinaire presiding at the Dove, my gig was now Saturday nights and working frequent private parties. I was sought out by regular customers with whom I have developed a personal rapport, planning and managing their special occasions, significant anniversaries, a daughter's engagement, hosting important business clients, etc. I now could take home $800-plus, for a busy Saturday night. A private party would easily generate a $500 gratuity. Beyond my gratuities, management now paid me a retainer of $1,500 per month. Life was good! No, more correctly, *life was perfect!*

I was very busy with my P&W job, required travel, and my involvement with the Dove. But I did manage to enjoy a small but interesting circle of friends. I had my gym friends, my poker group, my golfing partners, my music-loving buffs, interesting business friends, my fraternity brothers, and several young women. New York City did certainly have an enormous pool of prospects as life companions. With a mature approach to relationships, I had enjoyed the company and a sensible sexual relationship with a small number of young ladies. However, for the last year or so, I had been seeing one young woman exclusively. We were in a committed relationship. More on that later.

On a Monday morning, Annie came into my office and was obviously excited.

"HSW will be calling you, exploring an assignment that could be a major career opportunity. Good luck."

The call came about thirty minutes later. HSW's administrative assistant was on the line.

"Kevin, would you please join HSW in his office for a chat, with lunch to follow *upstairs*."

I had never been to the executive dining room, referred to as upstairs. Fifteen minutes later, settled in comfortable chairs in HSW's office, he asked if I knew of Larry O'Neil? Of course, I did. O'Neil was the hottest author to come on the scene in the last several years. He had *two* books on the *New York Times* list of best-selling books, his first and second novels! HSW told me confidentially that movie rights were under discussion for his first novel. Smith & Holbrook Publishers had brought O'Neil's two novels to market. S&H was a major publishing house and an important competitor to P&W. Again, in confidence, HSW outlined the situation. S&H had offered O'Neil a new contract with a substantial advance for three additional titles. The author had *not* signed the contract. It seemed O'Neil had serious issues with his assigned editor and an ongoing personality conflict with several senior people. HSW allowed that O'Neil could be difficult. He then outlined a proposition. O'Neil would leave S&H and sign a three-book contract with P&W. The specifics had already been negotiated, and O'Neil was ready to sign. *However*, signing was contingent on O'Neil having complete control over the selection of his editor. While not unusual for a major author to have serious input as to the assignment of the editor, O'Neil's demands were well outside standard practice. HSW said the company was willing to make the concession.

"I have known Larry for a few years through a mutual friend. We are confident O'Neil will find you acceptable as his editor, and you will work well together."

HSW rose, patted me on the shoulder, and ushered me to the door.

"Are you ready for lunch and to meet Larry O'Neil?"

I was stunned!

The executive dining room was super-exclusive and reserved for the most senior company executives and their guests. Coming off the elevator, we waited for O'Neil to arrive. We were casually greeted by several executives as they arrived for lunch. My head was spinning! The elevator door opened, and an attendant escorted a young gentleman over to us.

"Your guest has arrived, Mr. Weathersbee."

O'Neil was tall, better than six feet with longish blond curly hair, and a neatly trimmed beard. His eyes were gray, and he sported bushy eyebrows. He had the look of a man who worked at staying trim. He had a very deep tan. Larry O'Neil was a handsome young man. He dressed in a British Bond Street style, which suited him quite well.

The young gentleman turned to HSW, gave him a warm smile, and shook hands. HSW turned toward me. "Kevin, I would like you to meet Larry O'Neil, and, Larry, I would like to introduce Kevin Murphy, the young man we have been discussing."

O'Neil offered his hand. "I've been looking forward to meeting you."

We were escorted to our table, given menus, and offered the wine list. The view, décor, the menu, and the wine list were all first class!

The next two hours were an admixture of intense and, at the same time, relaxed dialogue, largely between me and O'Neil. We covered a broad spectrum of subjects. Larry was quite skilled at getting down to the essence of the matter. HSW seemed to enjoy the exchanges, occasionally adding his own observations. Lunch was just fine. Larry seemed pleased with my assessment of the wine list and my recommendation.

Over coffee, Larry asked if I might be free for dinner Sunday evening. I quickly accepted his invitation, glad he had not suggested a Saturday night. Handing me a card, "Here is my address, six thirty if that works for you."

We would be having dinner at his apartment. HSW suggested we adjourn and asked Larry to join him in his office. We made our goodbyes at the elevator.

I hurried down to Annie's office. She asked a stream of questions. "Who, said what to whom? What did I think of O'Neil? Did I know how fortunate I was to have HSW as a mentor?"

After chatting for nearly an hour, I returned to my office. The phone rang. I literally jumped out of my chair; it was HSW on the line.

"The luncheon went quite well. Larry was impressed with your comportment and ease of conversation. Your command of the wine list was a pièce de résistance. Larry is a very serious wine connoisseur. I have assured him your editing skills were top drawer, and I would be available should you need advice."

Of course, HSW was familiar with O'Neil's book proposal and assured me I will find the topic and Larry's approach to be intriguing. He wished me well. "Dinner should be most enjoyable."

For the next several days, I was completely focused on Sunday night. The big day arrived. I was up at 5:30 a.m. How should I dress? Should I bring wine? White or red or both? Arrive early, a few minutes late, just on time? Would there be other guests?

CHAPTER 3

I WAS NERVOUS. I SHOWERED, ATE a light breakfast, read the *New York Times*, and was out the door by 7:00 a.m. I wanted to do a dry run to O'Neil's apartment to establish the needed travel time, deciding that an arrival promptly at the appointed time of six thirty was the correct thing to do. Back in my apartment, I was ready to do the rest of my prep work. I checked my limited but excellent wine collection; great, I had a bottle of red that would do nicely, a 2000 Chateau La Lagune Haut.

Next, I laid out several potential outfits for the evening. The first wasn't quite the right style. A suit was nice, but a bit too formal. The last, a blue blazer with slacks, seemed just right. A white button-down shirt with a regimental striped tie pulled it all together.

As a matter of course, I regularly read all the trade publications, book reviews, and such. I am comfortable presenting myself as an informed editor/publisher. I had always been a voracious reader across a broad spectrum and was well informed on contemporary issues, politics, the economy, and the arts. I had read both of O'Neil's two books as they came off press. Blessed with excellent recall, I decided to, nonetheless, quickly scan both titles to refresh my recollections. I also would scan the major reviews. I also needed to do a bit of deeper research on the person, Larry O'Neil.

With my afternoon well planned out, I opted for a long, hot, relaxing soak in the tub. Dressed in a comfortable robe, I put my feet up, checked my emails and phone calls, then dealing with any that required attention. Then I called my girlfriend, Natalie. We chatted for a bit; she wished me good luck with my O'Neil meeting. We agreed on dinner Monday night and, with that, said goodbye. I had a light lunch of yogurt, blueberries, and toasted almonds.

My next order of business was who is Mr. O'Neil? Larry was about thirty-four years old, single, and a native of California. The only child of a socially prominent San Francisco family, both his parents were deceased. With an undergraduate degree from UCLA, majoring in English literature/creative writing, Larry came east to New York City / Columbia University. He earned an MA in Creative Writing. He followed his master's degree with enrollment in a doctoral program in Literature. He also worked as a teaching assistant. With the demands of his studies and the teaching assignment, Larry still managed to write his first novel, amazingly done in just about two years! Continuing as an adjunct, he produced his second novel in a span of two years. Larry did not finish his work for a PhD.

O'Neil seemed to be a very private person. Despite being out on the New York social scene and involved in the arts, very little was known of his personal life; frequent foreign travel was a part of his life. Besides an apartment in the city, he maintained a cottage in Provincetown, Massachusetts. It was assumed he is gay.

I gave each of his two novels a fast, selective reread. My initial impressions were confirmed. Reviews were generous and quite positive. Larry was widely recognized as an emerging important major author. The writing style was crisp and moved the reader along at a good pace. Characters are few, a device used in both his novels. The character development was rich, and the reader was given intimate insights, which can be intense. The plot is seemingly uncomplicated, not so! Character intentions were just below the surface, lending a deep dimension to the story. The reader is engaged both mentally and emotionally. Wow! I could be collaborating with this author on his next novel!

The afternoon was drifting by; I was prepared! I shined my shoes, put the bottle of wine in a gift bag, and made myself a cup of tea. I was dressed and out the door at 5:45 p.m., arriving, as planned, at Larry's building on the West Side with time to spare. I took a walk around the block, entered the lobby, and took the elevator to the sixteenth floor. I pushed the apartment bell at exactly six thirty. The door opened immediately; I jumped back!

"I knew you would be super-punctual," my host said with a smile. He extended a hand and invited me into his home.

Now before I go on, I want to make a point. With my emphasis on planning, you may get the impression that I am borderline compulsive or suffer from anxiety. Not so! I could be and mostly would be quite relaxed about most things. I am known to be a bit forgetful and a little careless. In truly important matters, however, such as dinner with a major author, I was *totally* focused and meticulous in every detail. I am competitive, and this dinner was the *biggest*, single, most important event thus far in my career!

Larry O'Neil's apartment was quite large and extremely well-done. I first noticed the artwork. Obvious quality older pieces, mostly European in style and theme, mixed with several stunning contemporary pieces. The shelving and side tables displayed many, many books, small pieces of Asian statuary, and several interesting glass pieces. The furniture was muted in color, even subdued, and looked very inviting. Your eyes quickly went to a fireplace with a fire burning, despite it being mid-August! It made the room. I offered Larry my gift of wine. He knew the vineyard and complimented me on my choice.

"If you wouldn't mind, I would love to have this with our dinner tonight. It is the perfect complement to the roast pheasant."

It seemed that I would be the only guest this evening. Larry suggested a drink before dinner. I would enjoy a very dry, straight-up vodka martini with a twist of lemon.

"Splendid, that happens to be my favorite before-dinner cocktail."

Larry pushed some type of discreet button; a servant immediately appeared. Larry ordered our cocktails, and we settled into a pair of armchairs in front of the fireplace. The conversation was light and relaxed, and Larry showed great interest in my background. We shared family information, college experiences, and interests outside work. He had a very good sense of humor and laughed easily. Our drinks arrived, along with a plate of interesting-looking hors d'oeuvres. We were getting to know each other; he wanted me to know him, and he wanted a good reading on me. With our second martini served, Larry shifted the conversation and asked me to comment on his writing.

I started with my sense of his writing style, technique, character presentation, and plot development.

"There is a deep richness to your storytelling, while it remains sparse in many ways. I find the intimate relationship you establish with your reader to be powerful."

My host did not interrupt with comments or questions. I then moved on to discussing his first novel in greater detail within the framework of my analysis of his style and technique.

I was careful to not regurgitate the reviews, although several points made by noted reviewers coincide with my assessment. Larry's first novel was set in Paris, 1998. The author's familiarity, appreciation, and love of the city were evident. The primary character was Paul, a twenty-two-year-old American, enrolled as a graduate student at the Sorbonne, focusing on eighteenth-century French poetry.

A graduate of Harvard with a concentration in French literature, Paul spoke French with a native fluency. Raised as a Catholic, the character was deeply religious, although not a practicing member of the church. While urbane in most ways, Paul's sexual experience was very limited.

As was the author's technique, there are few supporting characters. Agatha, also a graduate student at the Sorbonne, a doctoral candidate in psychology, was twenty-six years old and originally from Paris. Agatha had earned degrees from the University of Padua and the University of Chicago. In addition to speaking her native French, she was fluent in English and Italian; the character is an outspoken atheist and considered herself sexually liberated.

Professor Francois Belange was a full professor of psychology at the Sorbonne. Francois was forty-six years old and had earned degrees from Louvain University, the University of Padua, and Oxford University. The character was native to Paris and fluent in both English and Italian.

Claiming to be an agnostic, he had little or no interest in religion. Alcohol was a controlled issue in his life. Francois is bisexual and also a recognized sexual predator among both students and faculty.

William was British and the third son of an English earl, as such, not the heir to the title. The character was twenty-two, a recent graduate of Oxford University. He had been gifted a year in Paris, all expenses paid, to acquire polish and maturity. He dresses well and was quite handsome, spoke French marginally well, was sophomoric, abused several substances, could be very manipulative, and is gay.

The plot laid out simply, our characters met, and relationships began to develop: boy meets girl. First, Paul and Agatha literally bumped into each other on the street, Agatha dropped a bottle of wine she had just purchased. Paul admitted to being at fault and offered to replace Agatha's wine. A visit to the nearby wineshop allowed Paul to continue to demonstrate his excellent French fluency but also his deep knowledge of French wines. Both were taken with each other; however, Paul was late for a class and must rush off. They enjoyed a laugh; Agatha was in the same situation. They agreed to meet that evening for a drink.

We find Professor Belange encamped at the George V bar, having just ordered his second martini. For several years, the bar has been his favorite hunting ground, looking for sophisticated foreign visitors interested in exploring a French sexual experience, heterosexual or homosexual. As the bartender served the professor's drink, he nodded toward a young man seated two seats down the bar. Jean Paul, a longtime employee, knew the professor quite well and had been a spotter for him over the years; he rarely missed the mark. The young gentleman was young and quite attractive; he was clearly English. Belange, in too loud a voice and speaking English, summoned Jean Paul and berated him, "This martini is not acceptable, make another and use good English gin!"

The young man smiled. Belange motioned for him to join him. Several hours later, after a few more drinks at the bar, an excellent dinner with wine and a few cognacs, our two characters were somewhat intoxicated but in control. They had clearly recognized a mutual attraction and were off to William's suite.

Francois, as a full professor, taught only a limited number of graduate-level courses. His student interactions were more in his role as a dissertation adviser to the brightest and most promising Doctoral candidates. Agatha, in her second year of her doctoral program, had approached Professor Belange with a request to serve as her dissertation adviser. Francois knew her from one of his classes. He did a review of her academic record and her written work and read her dissertation proposal. Her work, dealing with sexual ambiguity, would be original and was a subject of particular interest to the professor. Following a long inter-view, he accepted her dissertation proposal and informed her he would be pleased to serve as her adviser. Agatha was delighted. He was intrigued. Agatha was, in every way, desirable, bright, and projected a vibrant sexuality. With his long-standing practice, student seduction will be slow, carefully planned, and always discreet. Agatha was on his agenda!

As the plot unfolds, Paul and Agatha, finding each other attractive, had come to the very edge of having an affair. With an active libido and having had more than a few sexual experiences, Agatha was more than ready to sleep with Paul. His initial hesitancy caused her to wonder if his strict Catholic upbringing was getting in the way, or were Paul's sexual persuasions ambiguous? Agatha chose to discuss the relationship with her adviser. The situation was within the scope and focus of her dissertation. Francois was titillated at the opportunities presented and immediately saw a plan.

A very robust relationship had developed between William and Francois. The English lad's sexual appetite was insatiable! William operated at a very primal level and was easily manipulated. He thought himself clever and enjoyed trying to manipulate people and situations. The plot unfolds. The Professor suggested Agatha establish a controlled experiment to gauge Paul's sexual inclinations, assessing the prospect of ambiguity. He offered the suggestion of an introduction to a young gentleman, the son of his friend, an English earl. The young man was in Paris on an extended holiday. He was handsome, witty, and gay. When told of the plan, William was excited at the prospect of seducing Paul, and he hinted at possibilities of a ménage à trois. William took the bait—intrigue, manipulation, sex, and totally new experiences! As the professor and Agatha spend more time together, their focus and the dialogue were heavily sexually based. Paul had been relegated to the role of the study subject. Let the seduction begin!

Raw passion and what appeared as simple manipulation engaged the reader at several levels. With strong and weak characters, manipulative intentions were, in fact, complex; we saw the vulnerability of human nature.

I spent about an hour sharing my thoughts, assessment, and judgment of the author's work. Larry had never interrupted. More from nervousness than desire, I asked for another cocktail. Larry rose, excused himself.

"Time to see to dinner."

Had I overdone it? Larry reappeared after a few minutes and announced dinner. My host led the way into an artfully arranged dining room. The table setting was well-done, with an interesting floral arrangement. Dinner was excellent, the pheasant roasted to perfection. As Larry had suggested, the La Lagune Haut was a great compliment. Our conversation during dinner was animated and across a wide range of topics. As the table was cleared, Larry suggested returning to the living room for coffee and a brandy. I checked myself. Heads up, you have had enough to drink. We were now going into act 2.

Once comfortably seated in front of the fire and with coffee and brandies at hand, Larry began. He was impressed with my overview of his first novel. I had avoided self-serving flattery and had seen very clearly his approach to plot, character development, and reader engagement.

"Did you discuss your thoughts with HSW prior to our meeting?"

Seeing my immediate flinch, he apologized for the question. There was an awkward pause.

"I would like to share with you what I am working on for my third novel. I invite your aggressive probing and straightforward comments."

Larry's first novel dealt with human frailties, sexuality, and manipulation. His second novel dealt with man's incredible strength in the face of adversity, in the face of the pure horror of the Holocaust. He had used the same basic methodology for plot reveal, character development, and reader engagement as used in his first novel. The storyline took the reader where he did not want to go. To see and to hear the unthinkable. Reader engagement was painful and provocative, but one could not put the book down!

"Human nature offers such a range of approaches to difficult or challenging situations and to other people. We are capable of incredible cruelty and, on the other hand, wonderful self-giving compassion." Going on, "What underlies choices made? Is it what it appears to be? Cruelty is easier to understand. I am intrigued by compassion. Mother Teresa, now Saint Teresa of Calcutta, as canonized by the Catholic church, is seen as a model of compassion and self-sacrifice. Why did she do what she did? Did God inspire or direct her? Did she have a burning desire or need to be recognized on the world stage? I look at Saint Francis of Assisi, giving up a life of wealth and position and all that it entailed for the opportunity to wear rags and beg for his food. His vows of poverty, chastity, and obedience are the perfect trifecta of self-sacrifice. Why would one voluntarily take all of that on board?"

Perhaps knowing that I was at least a nominal Catholic, Larry was looking to me for answers. I did not offer, couldn't offer what I didn't have!

"I want to take possibly four characters, such as Saint Teresa and Saint Francis, possibly all saints as declared by the Catholic church or possibly others drawn from history, people known for their extraordinary compassion and sacrifice for other human beings. I want to look at each person, their lives, stripped, if possible, from mystery, imagination, politics, maybe lies, or fulfilling the need for institutional heroes. I will strive to get at what motivated their self-sacrifice beyond comprehension. Look at Mahatma Gandhi. His life was straightforward, and his motives were beyond reproach. His sacrifice walked with him, to the point of his violent death."

Again, a very deliberate and invitational pause. I broke the silence.

"Beyond simply rocking the boat, this could and most likely will provoke, and I use that word deliberately, both negative and widespread public reaction and a strong global institutional reaction from the churches, most particularly the Catholic church. The risk is the approach being perceived as an attack. I think it well and good, *if* you can establish clear justification for the acclaim accorded an individual. It's the what-if that worries me. Suppose the individual's life story is questionable, created to serve a purpose as opposed to being factual? Suppose the attributed motivation becomes suspect. Suppose the institutional need for role models creates a fictional life?"

Larry gave me a small smile and lifted his brandy glass in a toast.

"Thank you. I think the evening was most enjoyable and informative. I now know Kevin Murphy."

The evening ended. Where we were going next wasn't clear to me. Except I sure wanted to work with this man on his next book.

CHAPTER 4

SSUMING LARRY WOULD DISCUSS THE evening with HSW, I expected a report card on my performance. Annie contained her curiosity and didn't bring the subject up for conversation. I did tell her over lunch on Wednesday, the meeting had gone well, and O'Neil's book proposal was most interesting and could be a real winner! I never received a call from HSW.

I did a bit of research on Saint Francis and Mother Teresa. Francis, being centuries removed (died 1226), presented more of a challenge in probing the human being and to dealing with the awe in which he has been held. Francis is a *saint*! On the other hand, Mother Teresa is a contemporary who died in Calcutta in September of 1997. Her canonization was noteworthy for the unusual speed with which her life was examined. She was canonized (declared a saint in 2011). Of interest, she was awarded the Nobel Peace Prize in 1971.

In contrast, the long-running examination of the worthiness of the late Pope Pius XII as a candidate for sainthood invites commentary. Highly regarded in many respects, pause has been taken due to his evident disinclination to condemn Germany's treatment of Jews of Rome, the very evident and rampant German anti-Semitism, and the realities of the Holocaust. Pope Pius's hesitancy had been attributed to political concerns. The very deliberative consideration of his cause speak well of the Catholic church's process.

I find Mahatma Gandhi, assassinated in 1994, an excellent example of self-sacrificing commitment centered on the betterment of his countrymen. Gandhi was aware of the real possibility of violence against him personally and, nonetheless, moved very openly and unguarded in promoting the cause for India's independence. I will research for more ordinary mortals who achieved unquestioned greatness with personal sacrifice and a heroic commitment to others.

The week moved by quickly, and I looked forward to my Friday night gig at the Dove. The bar was hopping, as they say, and I was on top of my game. Pierre, the maître d', stopped by the bar and asked if I could hold two seats open for around nine. We did this for valued customers who asked to have drinks at the bar prior to dinner. It was a busy night, but I knew the pattern of my regulars and was comfortable, two seats would open. At nine ten, Pierre escorted two gentlemen to the open seats I indicated. To my amazement, one of the gentlemen was Larry O'Neil. Deeply engaged in a conversation with his companion, he didn't recognize me.

"Good evening, gentlemen, what can I serve you?"

Larry's head shot up.

"Kevin, what are you doing in back of the bar?"

"If you tell me your drink preference, as the bartender, I'll serve it up directly. As I remember, vodka martini, dry, olive, straight up."

Larry laughed. "Make that two."

When I served their drinks, Larry introduced me to his companion, an older gentleman.

"Kevin, this is my dear friend, Peter Cordillion, and, Peter, this is Kevin Murphy, who when he is not tending bar, is an editor at P&W."

Mr. Cordillion gave me a curt "Nice to meet you."

Larry's companion was, I'd guess, in his fifties, tall, trim, and sporting a great tan. I busied myself tending to my other customers. Always attentive, I noted that Larry and his companion were close to finishing their drinks.

"Can I get you another round?"

"Just the check," I was told.

They stood to leave, and Larry said, "If you would, give me a call Wednesday afternoon."

Peter Cordillion left a generous tip.

With the encounter, Larry was hopefully alerted that I have a commitment on Saturday nights. The rest of my weekend was busy. I had a private party Sunday evening, with a $500 gratuity from a very pleased regular customer. The new week at P&W was unusually busy. As requested, I called Larry O'Neil Wednesday afternoon. With apologies for short notice, he asked if I could join him for dinner at seven. He explained, Peter Cordillion has surprised him with a birthday gift, a trip for ten days to the beaches in Greece. They were flying out Thursday evening. Assuring him that it was not a problem, he gave me the name of an Italian restaurant near his apartment.

Conversation during dinner was all business! Larry wanted my considered thoughts on his proposed book. I weighed in with my first point: "Ancient saints, as in Saint Francis of Assisi, will prove difficult to deal with, given the centuries that have passed since they walked on this earth. We will be dealing with very little, hard, verifiable facts and a lot of conjecture and even suspect or manufactured information filling in voids. On the other hand, the more contemporary holy ones, such as Mother Teresa, would afford considerable life details, verifiable independent of the church. Speculating on the motives of a particular Ancient Saint could or would be viewed as pure conjecture. A real issue, *if* one were to appear to be questioning the integrity of the holy one's motivations. I would see that as a potential land mine."

As was Larry's style, he didn't interrupt. I continued.

"I would have a balance of holy ones with laypeople. As I mentioned last week, Mahatma Gandhi is very plausible. I would recommend being openly more speculative, inviting the reader to form their own opinion, rather than taking a hard stand on a point per se. This is inviting the reader to weigh the facts while considering any conjecture offered. It will be important to clearly establish two levels of conjecture, asserted and that which is based on some verifiable information. There would be important 'they say points' from credible and respected sources, and then of course, there would be the author's point of view. I'd suggest a somewhat unusual element, the addition of selected graphics. These can add a level of poignancy not achievable with words alone. Lastly, I would use a chapter format, dealing with the challenge of thematic continuity. We need to assist the reader in digesting what can at times be very heavy material."

I hesitated for a moment.

"I have a question for the author. Why this book?"

After a long pause, Larry responded, "I have never been asked that question."

I started to talk, but Larry held up his hand to stop me.

"Integrity, personal or institutional, if treated lightly or with disregard, can undo the very fabric of our society. If there is a lack of integrity due to manipulation of fact to achieve institutional objectives, we invite, with such discovery, cynical and negative reactions. Your point, on contemporary versus ancients, is well-made. However, it is in the deeper history, we might find fact/motive being engineered to serve a purpose. The message presented, being compatible with the times and recognizing the past, with its lack of literacy, education, media, etc., and the easy mix of religion and superstition. Your structural suggestions are interesting, a bit off-putting. I will need to reflect on all of that."

We both retreated to a studied silence. Larry spoke in a slower and deliberate tone.

"Kevin, you have a quick mind, and you read me quite well. My reservation in working with you is the danger of your falling in love with your own ideas. To be blunt, the project is *my* book, not ours! We would *not* be collaborating in creating the work. Your role would be that of a midwife. The book is *my* child! The editor's role is to help me through what can at times be a difficult, painful process. The role is of immense value, and I will respect it and will be grateful for your support. *However*, at the end of the day, it is solely *my* book! Can you understand and accept all of that?" Holding up his hand. "Don't try to answer that now. Think about it. We will talk again when I am back from my holiday in Greece."

I spent many hours agonizing over Larry's very pointed comments. I had clearly overreached! I remind myself, O'Neil was measuring my suitability and compatibility as his editor, *not* as a collaborator. I reviewed the evening. I was comfortable with my thoughts on his first book. I was spot on and thought he would agree. Taking Larry's presentation on the proposal for his third book as invitational, I jumped in! My thoughts, on reflection, in dealing with the historically removed ancients, were valid. However, my follow-on thoughts and suggestions, in retrospect, were heavy-handed and presumptuous. The graphics addition and chapter structure were, in fact, patronizing. Larry, without question, drew the line, putting me bluntly in my place! The evening ended with "Let's think about it." Too ominous!

The next two weeks were agony, an eternity. There was an inexplicable silence on the whole subject from HSW and no probing at all from Annie. Did they know something? After what seemed like an eternity, Peter and Larry were back from Greece. The gossip columns picked up on their return; Peter was a well-known wealthy playboy, always in the company of handsome young men. I waited for Larry's call. The phone did not ring! By now, I had pretty much concluded that I had not made the cut. HSW stopped by my office late on Friday afternoon, with an invitation for the following Tuesday's Met performance of Verdi's *Rigoletto*. I wanted to decline, avoiding any discussion of the situation with O'Neil. Before I could decline, HSW offered Larry O'Neil and Peter Cordillion would join us for a late-night dinner. With controlled delight, I accepted!

As a side note, I do not want to create the impression that my whole life is wrapped up in my job at P&W and my gig at the Dove. For sure, they were both central to my economic life, my career, and my sense of accomplishment. With all of that keeping me busy, I do have an active social life. As physical fitness had always been important to me, I belonged to a gym and regularly worked out several times a week. Over the past years, I had developed great friendships and enjoyed their company with musical performances, sporting events, exploring interesting restaurants, trips to the beach, or just enjoying a few beers. Backgrounds vary, which added much to the relationships. We had a mix of family backgrounds, enjoy a multiethnic diversity, and come from a range of states and even other countries. There were frequent poker games with beer, jokes, and of course, a lot of bluffing. Added to the richness of my social life, I had established several good friendships with peers both at P&W and in the publishing industry. We saw each other at a broad range of industry events. I had learned so much from these contacts in addition to keeping up with industry gossip. I had also developed a warm personal relationship with Annie Hopkins, my supervisor at P&W.

As I had been aware early on, Annie was gay and had been in a long-term relationship with her partner, Helene Weinstein, a practicing psychiatrist, native New Yorker, from a very wealthy family and known for her philanthropic generosity; she is often in the social columns. I am very fond of the two women, and they had made me a regular on their list for all kinds of events, including frequent, casual threesome pizza nights at their apartment. As I had mentioned, Annie was striking. She was tall, slender, with mesmerizing blue eyes and blond hair. In the office, Annie was the consummate professional and all business in her dealings with people. Socially, another side emerged: warm, engaging, with a quick wit and ready laugh. Helene was the older of the two at forty-three. A bit on the short side at five feet, four inches, and somewhat heavyset, she reflected her Ashkenazi roots with her hazel-green eyes. Helene was prematurely and attractively gray-haired, in fact nearly white. She followed Masorti Judaism, with a relaxed observing of traditions and the holidays. In contrast to Annie, Helene was quieter and less outgoing. Obviously quite bright, she had a sharp and very quick wit. The two women were an endless joy to be with, and I treasured our friendship.

The weekend was relaxed, spent with my feet up and feeling so much better that I might not have blown it with Larry O'Neil. Saturday night was hopping at the Dove; my regulars were, as always, great to be with and generous, even more than usual, a sign that things were going my way. I slept in Sunday morning, did my housework, got organized for the week, called my folks, and enjoyed an early dinner date with a young lady, Natalie Hewitt; more about her later.

I was really looking forward to pizza with my friends, Annie and Helene. Their apartment was on the Upper East Side, a high floor with an incredible view. Given their financial and social status, the apartment is quite large, beautifully furnished, and designed for entertaining. The pizza arrived, and we opened a bottle of wine and settled down for an evening of catching up, sharing news, and laughing. We covered the full landscape, the social scene, the latest in deaths, marriages, affairs, and divorces, the publishing industry gossip, and world affairs. I gave the latest from the Dove: private parties, news from the bar, additions to the menu, etc. With a second bottle of wine opened, I anticipated where the curiosity of my friends would take the conversation. I had not mentioned having met Peter Cordillion at the Dove. I told them of the planned dinner following the opera. Both my friends knew Larry O'Neil, and it turned out, Peter Cordillion.

"Not that it matters, but what is the relationship between O'Neil and Cordillion? Are they an item?"

They both howled with laughter.

"That expression went out twenty years ago," said Helene.

"Do you mean are they sleeping together?" asked Annie. "Peter Cordillion is gay, known the world over for being with attractive, usually younger men. He is very wealthy and is a globe-trotter. He is bright, can be quite charming and witty. He has a major fault: he is an alcoholic. However, he usually exercises good control. It is known that when he has had too much to drink, he can be extremely aggressive and mean."

Helene was very candid!

"Our Mr. O'Neil, while being quite private, does not hide the fact that he is gay." Annie went on. "Larry has a house in Provincetown on the Cape. He spends a great deal of time there, writing and enjoying the beaches, the music, the restaurants and the vibrant gay community and a circle of straight friends, several of whom we know quite well."

What a comprehensive answer to a simple question. I wondered aloud as to why Cordillion would be at a business meeting. Helene offered her opinion.

"Peter can be possessive and jealous. I am sure he wants to observe the interaction between you and Larry. Are you gay? Are you potential competition for Larry's affections?"

We ended the evening with my promise to debrief them on the upcoming meeting.

*****

Tuesday was a busy day at the office, and when I answered the phone, it was already 6:00 p.m. HSW was calling to suggest meeting for a quick drink before the opera. We met in the lobby and walked the short distance to the Bull and Bear at the Waldorf. We chatted over the great excitement and the favorable reactions to the completely new staging of *Rigoletto*. As usual, HSW had arranged the best seats for what was a superb performance. We took a cab to La Grillade, a small but very well-rated French restaurant on the West Side. HSW was recognized as a regular. Larry and George had already arrived and were at our table. Warm greetings were exchanged all around. Both Peter and Larry were sporting great tans. Drinks were ordered, arrived, and are consumed during a lively conversation around the table. With a second drink ordered, we addressed the menu. Our waiter suggested two chef's special dishes for the evening: a poached striped bass or grilled baby lamb chops. We had two for the fish and two for the lamb chops. Larry and I consulted on the appropriate wines. With our order placed, a third round of drinks was ordered. I hope it hadn't been noticed, I wasn't finishing my drinks. I needed to be on my toes for the conversation that was to follow.

Conversation continued at a relaxed but lively pace through what proved to be a fine dinner. Peter was most interested in my life story, my interests, my work at the Dove, and my career at P&W. HSW afforded me accolades, praising my professional development over the years. He especially made note of the rapport I had with my authors.

With after-dinner coffee and brandies, the conversation moved to a discussion of my assessment of the opportunity to work with Larry. I was direct and succinct.

"The opportunity to work with Larry would be frankly, a major career opportunity. It would allow me to demonstrate a deep understanding and appreciation for the creative process. The opportunity would be mutually beneficial"—careful to avoid overreaching—"I would hope to ease the author's discomforts that accompany the process of creating a great novel. I would approach this with respect for the author's perspective and an understanding of my supportive role."

Larry spoke up. "Kevin and I have had several lengthy conversations on my writing approach, dealing with plot as the overarching structure, character development, pace of the story, and my focus on creating an apparent simplicity in all of that. We discussed my first novel. His insights, well beyond what reviewers had to say, demonstrated a keen insight into me as a writer. In this, he avoided regurgitating what others thought or had written about my work. We have had an in-depth discussion on my proposal for a third novel. I went into detail as to my focus and how I would approach developing the narrative. Kevin quickly grasped the idea and offered perceptive commentary on where I proposed to go. His intense focus, particularly on character selection, was very much on point, and I spent a good deal of time reflecting on his thoughts and suggestions. Later in the conversation, his analysis and commentary moved into areas where he was assuming the role of a collaborator. I found this overreaching, not the role of an editor."

I was now extremely uncomfortable, quite sure the guillotine was about to fall!

Larry continued, "I was forceful, perhaps too forceful, in rejecting the relationship between author and editor as being a collaboration. We left it with the situation very much up in the air. I promised to think about it while I was on holiday in Greece and suggested that Kevin reflect on our conversation."

Continuing, "Peter and I have had more than a few discussions on the matter. I shared with him my appraisal of Kevin's assets and HSW's high regard for Kevin, both professionally and personally. I also shared my reservation, squarely on the issue of Kevin's perception of his role as my editor. Peter helped me to accept that I *need* to work with not only someone who is bright and knows his or her craft, but a person with the ability to know me and understand my approach to being creative. Despite his youth and being in the early years of his career, Kevin reinforces the flow of my creative juices, with insight and great perception. Peter, knowing me as he does, understands and agrees."

Peter nodded as Larry talked.

"As HSW knows, Larry and I have been very close for several years. In that time, we came to know each other very well. Larry *needs* to work with someone who can relate to who and what he is all about. Having the greatest respect for HSW's assessment of Kevin's personal and professional attributes coupled with Larry's needs, I am very comfortable suggesting that Kevin is absolutely the right person to work with Larry on his next *great* novel."

I was sure I had a silly grin on my face. Larry reached over and patted my hand.

"Kevin, please accept the assignment to be my editor. I look forward to working with you, and developing not only a productive relationship in the years ahead, but also finding a personal rapport and friendship."

HSW and Peter both smiled.

"Thank you all for your support. I am overwhelmed with your kind assessment and confidence. I share your hopes and expectations as we move ahead."

We left the restaurant; everyone seemed greatly pleased with the evening. In the cab, I thanked HSW for his support. He assured me his support was in the best interests of P&W, so signing a rising star author was a major part of his job. On a more personal note, he explained, my career advancement/successes reflected on him as the managing editor and on his role as a mentor.

Larry called early the next morning.

"Could you possibly get away for a long weekend in the next week or two? I am anxious to begin our planning."

I would need to clear it with the Dove, but I was comfortable that with advance notice, it would not be a problem.

"Let me clear the date, I'll be back to you within the hour."

I called Pierre and explained the situation. No problem at all. I got back to Larry, and we settled on the date.

"I have a cottage on the Cape. It's my favorite getaway place and I have always done my best work there. The weather this time of year is great. How about we drive up

Thursday afternoon and plan on coming back to the city midday Monday?"

We settled a few particulars. I was really looking forward to the weekend. Just as I hung up, Annie bounded into my office.

"So tell me!"

I gave her a detailed synopsis of the dinner meeting and the just-planned working getaway to Larry's cottage on the Cape. She could not contain her joy! She jumped up and gave me a huge hug, rare for her.

"Oh, wait until we tell Helene the news at dinner tonight."

In the excitement, I had forgotten our date; we confirmed seven.

I called HSW's office, but he was not available. At eleven thirty, his administrative assistant called. Would I please join HSW for lunch upstairs at one thirty? The executive dining room *again*! I arrived at one twenty, gave my name, and said I was joining Mr. Weathersbee. I was immediately seated at a choice table with a great view of Central Park. Within a few minutes, HSW appeared at the entrance to the dining room. Coincidentally, the CEO of P&W, Tom Clarkson arrived about the same time. The two shook hands and started toward my table. Oh my god! I had met Mr. Clarkson on several occasions, company gatherings or industry affairs, one of dozens of underlings basking in his presence. I had the good sense to rise.

"Tom, you might remember this young man, Kevin Murphy?"

Mr. Clarkson offered his hand.

"Of course I do, please sit down, Kevin."

I remained thunderstruck and concentrated all my mental and physical strengths on *not* wetting my pants!

"HSW gave me the great news. Larry O'Neil has signed our contract for his next three books. As I understand, O'Neil had specifically and contractually stated his wish for you to be assigned as his editor. This great contract came to closure, according to HSW, as a direct result of several extensive meetings you had with O'Neil to discuss plans for his third book. I've met Larry, but don't know him other than through his published work and his reputation. His writing is brilliant! P&W is fortunate to add him to our growing roster of distinguished authors. I foresee a healthy contribution to our bottom line in the years ahead. Reputation-wise, O'Neil is known to be difficult to work with, requiring more care and feeding than even the most senior and successful authors. Have you seen any of this, Kevin?"

I looked at HSW; he gave a slight nod.

"Larry O'Neil is both bright and can be very intense. He's emotionally, heavily invested in his work. He is, in my opinion, capable and willing to listen to well-thought-out suggestions and even constructive criticism. I believe Larry sees me as a midwife, an intimate relationship to be sure.

He needs to be comfortable exposing the pain, suffering, even the anxiety of giving birth to his novel. I believe the root of his issues with past editors rests in their attempts to be a collaborator with the author. O'Neil absolutely rejects the very idea! If I were to have any difficulties with the author, it would be in keeping up with his intellectual pace. I believe this potential shortcoming will be overlooked by my steadfast and faithful presence as the dutiful midwife."

Mr. Clarkson turned to HSW.

"We have a situation here, proposing the assignment of a junior editor to a top-rated and newly signed author. I find that questionable!"

I suddenly felt physically ill. HSW looked stumped by the CEO's apparent challenge to my appointment.

"Mr. O'Neil has, as you know, requested Kevin by name and was contractually given that prerogative," offered HSW.

After a pause, Mr. Clarkson spoke. "Well, the solution becomes apparent. Let's promote Kevin to senior editor."

Neither gentlemen could hide their amusement. They had pulled off an agreed-to ruse! Mr. Clarkson, laughing, offered his hand as did a widely smiling HSW.

*****

Helene had made dinner reservations at one of our favorite restaurants in Chinatown. When I arrived, my two friends were already seated. Drinks were ordered, and Helene said, "Okay, now let's hear, blow-by-blow, what happened last night."

I chuckled and launched into what I knew had to be a detailed "who said what to whom" narrative. There were frequent interruptions and many questions. After a good forty-five minutes, we were ready to pause and order dinner. As we ate, Helene made the comment, "Frankly, I'm surprised Larry was able to sort out any reservations he might have about you. There is a dynamic between Larry, Peter, and HSW that is clearly to your advantage. I had expected Peter to be wary of a threat to his relationship with Larry. Again, the time in Greece gave them a chance to deal with any issues Peter might have had. HSW's support of course was what 'closed the deal,' so to speak."

Over coffee, I told them of the plans for the Cape Cod working session. With a planned pause for effect, I went into detail about the lunch with HSW that afternoon and the surprising presence of Mr. Conroy.

"Mr. Conroy personally promoted you? That simply does not happen," exclaimed Annie.

We ended the evening with my friends extracting my promise to take notes and give them a full report on the Cape Cod getaway.

*****

First thing in the morning, I stopped by HSW's office and found him free. I thanked him for his mentorship and support.

"The luncheon with Mr. Conroy was over-the-top! You had me nearly wetting my pants."

That got a huge laugh from HSW. I knew the promotion was his idea. He wanted me to know that the ruse was Mr. Conroy's doing. Our CEO, it seemed, has a great sense of humor. I explained the arranged planning getaway with O'Neil. HSW could not have been more pleased and suggested we have lunch prior to the weekend so that he might offer his suggestions. I, of course, welcomed his continued mentorship.

Returning to my office, I found the manager of facilities waiting for me. Word had traveled fast!

"If you have a few minutes, I would like to discuss your thoughts on your new office layout and see if we can get the move on the calendar."

I guess senior editors warrant more space and a host of amenities: a higher floor, private conference room, upgraded furniture, etc. I told him Jane would coordinate the planning and the move.

Annie called to discuss her suggestions for turning over some of my workload. She had a candidate to suggest, Mary-Ellen McKnight, a senior editorial assistant. The new position would report to me. We agreed to an interview for Mary-Ellen the next afternoon, giving me time to think through how I would go about rearranging my personal workload.

I was ready to get back to work. I had a full basket of mail, loads of emails, twenty-five phone calls to return, manuscripts to speed read, book proposals to review, a meeting with the art department on a cover design, and I needed to do a lot of thinking on my upcoming getaway with Larry O'Neil. With enthusiasm, I dove into the work-load. The day evaporated.

Jane, my secretary, told me she had scheduled the personnel manager, with various paperwork requiring my signature, for five thirty.

"I'll be working late, please order a Caesar salad, roll, and coffee for around eight."

It was five thirty in a blink and the personnel manager arrived.

"Congratulations on your promotion! I was notified directly by Mr. Conroy's office. If we could, there are several routine forms to be filled out and signed and a few decisions you need to make."

We sat down at my desk, and she quickly and very efficiently moved the forms along for my signature.

"There are two forms relating to payroll deductions/elections based on your new base salary of $78,000 per year. I'll leave booklets on the stock option plan and the incentive compensation program. You will be eligible for both at year-end."

I tried not to act surprised! I was currently drawing $54,000 per year and had not been eligible for stock options or incentive compensation awards. I studied the various forms and signed, having made the necessary elections.

"That does it. Thank you. Again, congratulations and best wishes. I thought you might like to know, you are the youngest person I can remember, promoted to senior editor *and* the only one ever directly promoted by the CEO."

I thanked Mary for her help and good wishes and went back to work. I planned to connect with my folks and my siblings, Katie and Patrick, as I ate dinner at my desk. All the great news on compensation and the uniqueness of my promotion recharged my batteries, and I worked at a fast and efficient clip. My light dinner arrived at eight thirty as ordered; the in-house service was great! I texted the good news to Katie and Patrick in detail. I knew they would be so proud of their little brother. Next, I called home. Dad answered, and I asked him to have Mom join us on the line. I told them I would be working with Larry O'Neil on his next book. Both, being avid readers, knew the name and had in fact read both his novels. Larry's first book could have offended their strict Catholic views, but subject matter aside, they acknowledged O'Neil was a skilled novelist. My parents were aware that I had moved from being an editorial assistant to junior editor in a relatively short period of time. I then casually mentioned, the CEO of P&W had just promoted me to senior editor; I was the youngest person to ever reach this level of responsibility! I had never discussed compensation with my folks, other than my meager starting salary a few years back.

"I will now be making $78,000 per year, and I will be eligible for stock options and incentive compensation awards."

They were impressed and offered their best wishes. Mom asked if I would be home for Christmas.

"You bet I will."

Mom was beside herself, knowing her three children would be home for the holiday; we had not been all together in nearly three years.

I was back to work by nine fifteen and reduced my paperwork and email/phone messages to almost nothing. I turned to planning, some serious thinking, and a bit of research. When I next looked at the clock, it was almost midnight. While I was still alert and focused, I decided a good night's sleep would keep me on my game far better than grinding out any more hours in the office. I closed shop and headed home. A hot shower, a small brandy in bed, and sound asleep by 1:00 a.m.

Friday morning found me back at my desk and working around 6:30 a.m. I had picked up a bagel and coffee, which I enjoyed as I organized my day. Thinking about my afternoon interview, I recalled Mary-Ellen McKnight was bright, not particularly attractive; however, that's not a job requirement. She was a graduate of Skidmore College, with I think, a BA in Liberal Arts. My thoughts on realigning my work came together more smoothly than I would have expected. Aside from the nuts and bolts items always requiring attention, I would give up three of my junior authors, retaining my two senior well-established authors, with whom I enjoyed great personal rapport. Despite being a rapid reader, the combination of book proposals, sample manuscripts, suggested advertising copy, and the more mundane correspondence, all took up a substantial block of my time. Mary-Ellen will be my filter, doing first readings/reviews. We would develop a system where she would pass along her evaluations, suggestions, and ideas in three-per-week meetings, each scheduled for one hour. What has been consuming at least two to three hours per day of my time could be managed in three one-hour meetings per week.

Cover design was something I greatly enjoyed. Our art department housed several gifted artists/designers. I firmly believe that the cover design of a book was integral to the marketing success of a title. Without hard data to support my contention, the shelf appearance of a book, coupled with promotional literature and optimal display, contributed importantly to the successful sale of a novel. I would ask Jane to schedule a meeting with Art and Design for the end of the day.

I had several calls to make, which I organized and would attend to as my first order of business. I had two author conferences scheduled for the afternoon. I needed to finalize my notes for review, as we would be discussing their latest manuscript submissions; both works were nearing completion. I had worked with both authors for several years. It would be a third novel for each. We have developed productive working relationships, and we very much respected and liked each other. These are the two authors I would retain as we begin shifting my workload.

Jane, my super secretary, soon to be my administrative assistant, arrived well ahead of everyone else. She had coffee and a sweet roll for me. We had worked together long enough and to the point where I believe Jane could read my mind! Jane is in her mid-fifties, in a constant battle with too many pounds on her five-foot, three-inch frame, dressed with great care, had a great sense of humor and a quick mind. Her husband passed away several years ago, leaving her with two daughters, both of whom are now in college. She and the whole staff were aware of my promotion. Straight out, I asked her to consider joining me with a promotion to administrative assistant to the newly minted senior editor. She gave me a hug.

"Congratulations, boss. I would be thrilled to continue working with you, and thank you for the opportunity."

With her pad in hand, we went through the day. I gave her my list for returning calls, asked her to confirm the time for my two authors' conference calls, confirm my time with Annie and Mary-Ellen, and schedule the meeting with Art and Design for around five thirty.

"Jane, I want you to coordinate our move to our new quarters. I would like to get that done ASAP. Secondly, Annie suggested Mary-Ellen McKnight as your replacement with expanded duties. A new secretary will support Mary-Ellen, a person we will also need to hire. I would like you to sit with Mary-Ellen after she and I talk. I want your take on her. Be candid with her about how we work."

At nine, the business day began, and we were ready to roll! I attacked my call list with gusto. I tried eighteen calls, connected with twelve, and had thirteen more to try later in the day. At ten thirty, Annie and Mary-Ellen arrived. With introductions made and a few kind words of endorsement, Annie withdrew and left a somewhat nervous Mary-Ellen with me.

"I have had an excellent rundown on your background from both Personnel and Ann Hopkins. I want to take some time in laying out what I see as the responsibilities of the position."

I took great care to talk through what has been on my desk and what would be new as I assumed the position of senior editor. Focus would be on what I needed to delegate to the person filling the new position. Mary-Ellen, with her background, very quickly grasped where I was going. She relaxed as we talked. Her comments and questions were excellent. She was not only bright and quick but could be quite engaging. After forty-five minutes, I was sold on the young woman, assuming Jane did not see any negatives.

I suggested, I thought it would be a good idea if she and Jane were to spend a few casual hours together, perhaps over dinner.

"Jane has the advantage of knowing me quite well, the good and the bad. The position would be coordination between the three of us. You will have domain over areas that are familiar and new challenges, important to your continued professional development."

"Thank you for considering me for the position. I certainly would appreciate spending time with Jane, understanding the expectations, and getting to know her."

I ended our meeting.

"I would like you to take the weekend to ponder all of this, and Monday afternoon, we will see where we are."

I excused myself and sat down with Jane. I reported, "She is bright and quick. I outlined the major aspects of the position, my needs and expectations, and made it clear that the position is a key member of the team. I suggest the two of you spend a few hours together, dinner sometime this weekend, if you can arrange it. I want your take on the young lady, before I make a final decision. I have scheduled a meeting with her for late Monday to see where we all stand. If you are okay with her and she asks for the order, I am ready to make her an offer."

Jane replied, "I will sit with her for a bit when you are finished, and I will set up a luncheon or dinner meeting over the weekend. You will have my candid assessment first thing Monday morning."

I took Jane back into the office and suggested that she and Mary-Ellen spend some time together.

My phone rang, and Jane buzzed through with my brother Pat on the line.

"Congratulations, little brother," he boomed from London. "I couldn't be prouder. You talk about coincidences. I am sure he will not remember, but I met your author last year. It was one of those very busy cocktail parties for a Saudi prince at our embassy in London. O'Neil seemed to know a lot of people. I recall he spoke French fluently and is very comfortable hobnobbing with the rich and famous."

Knowing that I would be eligible for stock options and incentive compensation, Patrick told me, "I've reviewed

P&W's last several annual reports. The balance sheet is very clean, and the company is in great shape. The earnings are impressive and growing. The company should do well in the years ahead. I did a bit of research on your CEO. Mr. Conroy is very well regarded in the publishing world. At fifty-two, he has a few years ahead of him before retirement. The Board of Directors is strong, with a good balance of skills and experience. So, my friend, you should do very well in the years ahead. I've talked with the folks, and they were more effusive than I ever remember, so proud of you! I haven't caught up with Katie, but I sure she is super proud of her baby brother."

We talked a bit more about my new job and assured each other, despite being super-busy, we will all make time for a true family Christmas.

I moved into my afternoon schedule. The calls with my authors were productive as we had a long-established and very efficient modus operandi. Both were happy for me as I told them about my new responsibilities. I assured them, at my insistence, they and I would continue to work together. I was pleased both projects were right on track and will be in prepress as scheduled.

My favorite designer, Paul, from the art department arrived as scheduled. Of course, like the rest of the world, he knew about the signing of O'Neil and my promotion.

"Way to go lad, O'Neil is a huge feather in your cap. My friends at our competitor report their management is pissed! Also, the word has it, O'Neil can be a handful!"

I laughed. "He can be a bear on cover design, so sharpen your pencils, clean your brushes, order new boards, and do whatever else you need to do to keep the savage happy."

Laughing, we got down to business. We had gone through several passes at this cover design. There wasn't a disagreement, but more a sense, we just were not there yet. Paul, as he always did, listened to my comments, asked questions, and floated several ideas for change. He concluded at our last meeting; we needed a completely new approach. His new design was on the table. In my experience, artists could be heavily invested in their own creations. Paul had that rare ability to step back and try a different approach.

"Bingo, my friend," I said. "I don't want to overinflate your already-huge ego, but you are a wonder! You and I truly appreciate how much a great cover design adds to a book's success. I thank you, as will the author!"

I had shared some detailed notes with HSW on the upcoming getaway meeting with O'Neil. He in turn sent back my notes with annotations and suggestions. My mentor's advice was worth more than words can express. I called HSW to check in. He was in a rush but assured me all should go just fine; I was well prepared. As the day went down, I realized I had beaten the world into good order and could look forward to a rare, relaxed weekend.

CHAPTER 5

I HAD A DATE FOR DINNER and some music in the Village. The young lady, Natalie Hewitt, and I had been seeing each other for over a year. Our relationship was warm, and we shared many interests. The fact of the matter, as I thought about it, we are in a serious relationship that had really become exclusive. I knew that Natalie was not seeing anyone nor was I.

Natalie was just a few years older, very attractive in an almost exotic way. She is half-Chinese through her mother and biracial, black/white, through her father. She was on the taller side at five feet eight inches and quite slender. Her hair is a rich dark-brown, worn long, and often braided. Natalie favored her Asian roots, with deep brown eyes and a light tan-like complexion. Growing up in Chicago, she had a charming and relaxed Midwestern way about herself. Her dad is a lawyer as is Natalie. Both were graduates of Harvard Law School. Her mother managed a range of family interests, both in the US and abroad. Natalie was an only child. Prior to Harvard, she had earned a degree in Asian Studies from the University of Chicago. Natalie modestly and reluctantly shared that she graduated from the university as magna cum laude and graduated with highest honors from Harvard Law School. She had also earned the high honor of serving on the prestigious Harvard Law Review. With her graduation from Harvard, she had been approached with many great job opportunities, including a clerkship at the Federal Appeals Court level.

Money apparently was not a concern, allowing Natalie to follow her great interest in cross-cultural pollination. She, without difficulty, sought and was offered a position with the United Nations in New York City. In addition to being obviously bright, Natalie spoke several languages fluently: Chinese (Mandarin and Cantonese), Japanese, and French. She was now the senior adviser to the vice president for Asian Affairs.

We both enjoyed a broad spectrum of music, from classical to rock. After our usual date for dinner, we often attended the opera, an outdoor performance in Central Park, or visited one of several popular jazz music bars in the Village. Natalie would sometimes cook a Chinese dinner at her apartment, which I very much enjoyed. She was an excellent cook! For the last six months or so, we usually were back at her lovely apartment for a nightcap, and I would sleep over. Our intimate relationship had developed gradually, comfortably, and was mutually satisfying.

Natalie and I had agreed to meet at the Bull and Bear for cocktails. We had reservations for dinner at an outstanding but largely unknown dim sum shop in Chinatown, to be followed by a musical experience in the Village. We had heard that a new group were playing outstanding bebop jazz. We both loved the fast tempo, complex harmonies, and improvisation. Over drinks, we caught up on our lives since our last date a week ago. Natalie shared her news first; she had been offered an opportunity to lead a six-month NATO-sponsored study on Chinese-American mutual cultural interests. The assignment would require her to spend extended periods of time traveling in China. I sensed this was being floated as a probe on the state of our relationship. I of course allowed that I would miss her greatly but recognized that it was a wonderful opportunity career-wise. A look of disappointment briefly crossed Natalie's face. She, I surmised, wanted/needed some type of commitment beyond a promise to miss her. Natalie quickly changed the subject with "And what's happening these days at P&W?"

With relief at the change of subject, I spent half an hour going over my situation, my promotion, wonderful salary-increase, etc. Natalie reacted with questions and the requisite compliments.

It was time to move on to dinner. In the cab ride downtown, Natalie was withdrawn. With brief reflection, it occurred to me that I would really miss Natalie and everything about her.

"When will you have to leave for China?"

Natalie hesitated. "I haven't accepted the assignment as yet, so it is up in the air."

"Do you have reservations?" I asked.

"Frankly, I wanted to discuss it with you before I made a decision."

So there it was!

"I answered your question as to what I thought about the China opportunity with the comment on the benefits to your career. Promising to miss you, in retrospect, was a bit lame. Natalie, we have been seeing each other for just about a year. In that time, we discovered a great range of common interests and, more importantly, have a growing bond between us. I guess I've allowed the pace of my business life to override my personal life. In that, I have inadvertently taken you for granted, and for that, I apologize. The bond between us has developed to a point where we have a mature, comfortable, and warm emotional connection. Said in a few simple words, I am suddenly aware that I am very much in love with you!"

Natalie started to cry very softly.

"I hear what you've said, but I'm not sure I know what you're trying to tell me. For that matter, I'm not sure you truly know what you are trying to say."

Arriving at the restaurant, we had twenty minutes before our reservation.

"Let's walk," I suggested. "I think what I am trying to say is, as a sudden awareness, I care more for you than I have recognized. It has taken this turn of events to let me see that and put our relationship in perspective. I love you very much! And I need and want you in my life, now and forever! Presumptuous, but I hope your feelings and sense of our relationship may be the same."

Natalie stopped walking.

"You're a little slow on the uptake, my dear!"

We embraced and kissed, much to the amusement of the passers-by. We could now sit down to eat!

After a great treat of the finest dim sum, we agreed to skip the music and go back to Natalie's apartment. We both knew we had more to discuss.

We did not talk a great deal during the cab ride to Natalie's apartment. We held hands, and Natalie rested her head on my shoulder. Her apartment is large, well put together, and in a very good building, within walking distance to the NATO building. This meant that it cost an arm and a leg.

We settled down on the cozy couch, and I embraced Natalie and said, "I love you."

This brought tears to Natalie's eyes again, the second time I caused that reaction.

"I am not sure why it has taken me so long to recognize what you mean to me. I can claim being too caught up in my day-to-day life, but that is neither a reason nor an acceptable excuse. I told you earlier that in part, it was a case of just taking our relationship for granted. For that, I apologize again. I admit to being emotionally immature."

Natalie started to interrupt.

"No, let me finish, recognizing my lack of maturity in dealing with our relationship is something we need to deal with and discuss."

There was a long silence. Natalie, in a soft voice, said, "I am guilty of taking you for granted. I assumed that we were in a serious relationship, maturing toward a longer-term commitment to each other. The China offer forced me to put our relationship into a tight focus. It hit me that you had never said you loved me or that you had never really made any type of commitment as to where we were headed or where you wanted our relationship to go. I am guilty of the same offense. I have never said that I loved you nor I have made any commitment to our relationship. Our reasons differ. I think you need to know, I was simply afraid to run the risk of you not reciprocating! I want to correct that now. I love you and want to spend the rest of my life with you. I accept your self-analysis of emotional immaturity, and I accept your declaration of love. What you have not addressed, and it's okay, raises the question of do you want to spend the rest of your life with me?"

Natalie got up from the couch and suggested, "Let's take a breather and have a cup of coffee."

While she was in the kitchen, I thought about Natalie's comments. Specifically, on her comments having to do with commitment and the absence of mine. I was truly comfortable with my declaration of love for her, just very sure of my feelings. The next admittedly logical step, a commitment to spending the rest of our lives together, made me very nervous. As I thought about it, the newness of it all, the enormity of it, simply needed time for me to digest. Quite suddenly, an idea struck me just as Natalie came back into the room. I jumped up, hugged her, almost spilling the tray she was carrying.

"Can I tell you again that I love you?"

She laughed. "As many times as you like, my dear."

We settled down on the couch, and Natalie poured the coffee.

"I've thought about your very reasonable and logical question: do I want to spend the rest of my life with you? The question is so new to me and so enormous that I must answer, I really think I might."

Natalie leaned over. "Kevin, I don't want to push you to answer the question unless and until you have thought deeply and long on it and are sure of your answer."

I kissed her on the forehead.

"I have an idea, the China proposal is huge in terms of your recognition and professional status. Additionally, I know your love of your heritage and how important it is to you to expand an understanding of mutual cultural interests. A six-month separation would be painful for want of a better term. So here is my idea, hear me out. I want you to accept the assignment. I want you to use your best negotiating skills to get approval for at least two R&R trips to somewhere. I will, without fail, negotiate the time away with P&W and join you in somewhere."

I paused and could see Natalie digesting my suggestion. After a few moments, she said, "On the theory that absence makes the heart grow fonder, your idea just maybe a good approach. I am comfortable that my boss will be open to the idea, and I really want to take on the project without the risk of losing you."

At this point, we were both emotionally spent, and without saying a word to each other, we moved into the bedroom. Natalie went into the bathroom, and I took my overnight bag out of the closet and began to undress. I suddenly laughed aloud. I realized that bringing an overnight bag to Natalie's apartment several months ago was a subliminal commitment and recognition of the depth of our relationship, not a logistical convenience.

The bathroom door opened, and Natalie emerged, dressed in a flowing and gorgeous nightgown. This was a distinct change from her simple T-shirt she always wore.

"You are gorgeous," I said as I passed by her going into the bathroom.

My shower was hot, but not my usual long soaking. I dried off and put on my pajamas, experiencing a very serious erection! The bedroom was dark, but I easily found the bed and Natalie.

"What have we here?" as she felt my erection up against her derriere.

She rolled over, and we locked lips in a deep and passionate kiss. We, of course, had been intimate any number of times, but somehow, this was something very different.

"Kevin, that was wonderful. I love you."

"There is a very good chance that I love you more!"

We were at a new and wonderful point in our relationship. We very soon settled into a deep sleep.

We were both early risers and found each other just as the sun was peeking through the shades. Neither of us had put our nightclothes back on. Our sex had always been good, but we seemed to have reached a new level. We both recognized the magic that came from acknowledging and happily accepting our mutual love.

Natalie rolled out of bed, slipped into her nightgown, and suggested, "Roll over and snooze while I fix breakfast."

I quickly drifted into a light sleep. With a kiss to my cheek, I was awakened. I jumped out of bed and embraced Natalie.

"That was a very special evening, and I want to tell you that I love you!"

"Breakfast is on the table and getting cold. Get dressed and join me!"

We had no plans for the day, so after a leisurely breakfast and reading the papers, over a second cup of coffee, I said, "We have so much to talk about."

"Yes, we do," agreed Natalie, "you go first."

I thought about it for a minute, "What are your thoughts on children?"

"That's an easy one," laughed Natalie. "You know, I am an only child, and while my parents were great in every way, I always resented that they hadn't given me siblings. So I most definitely want children, not sure how many, but more than one. How about you?"

"Being the youngest of three, spoiled by my older siblings, and enjoying the hustle and bustle of our home, I could not imagine not having children. Like you, not sure of the number but certainly several."

She asked, "How will your family react to my being biracial?"

I paused before I answered, "My folks are intelligent people, somewhat liberal, devout Catholics, but it will take time for them to adjust to the whole idea. I would not see them opposing the union and cannot imagine their not coming to not only accepting you but also loving you and our children. I see my brother Patrick and my sister Katie totally accepting and embracing you without a single reservation. You will come to love them as I do. Bottom line, you will be a beautiful and wonderful addition to the Murphy family, accepted and loved by the whole damn family! My turn: the same question, how will your Chinese mother and African American father react to your being in love with an East Coast, Irish Catholic, younger, white man?"

Natalie also paused before she spoke. "My parents in their marriage, accepted biracial unions. Would my father favor a black American son-in-law? Alternatively, would my mother favor a Chinese or Asian partner for me? I honestly don't know. In the past, I have dated fellas across that whole spectrum, with nary a comment from either parent on racial/ethnic backgrounds. They will have many questions about education, work, earnings, family, values, political orientation, etc. To be honest, I would guess they will be okay, with some reservations. The racial/ethnic part I do not see as ever being an issue. Being from the East Coast and liberal, from a Catholic, probably Democratic family, religion aside, would be a minor issue for my father who is the essence of a straitlaced Midwestern conservative, church-going Protestant, and verbal Republican. My mother is the personification of the Asian/Chinese soft acceptance of all God's creation. She delights in my deep understanding and love of the Chinese culture and her heritage. Whatever turns my life takes, she knows that I will always carry these with me. Any reservations would be based on her personal assessment of you, vis-à-vis what she believes are my sensitivities and vulnerabilities, she is a mother."

Natalie, of course, knew of my Saturday night gig at the Dove. As it was now nearly 11:00 a.m., we decided on a celebratory lunch at Tavern on the Green. Sunday would be a dinner date with the music we had missed Friday night.

"It sure is wonderful being in love," I said with a huge grin on my face.

Following a great lunch at the Tavern on the Green and a long leisurely walk in the park, Natalie and I parted with a hug and kiss. I would sleep in at my apartment Sunday morning, after a late night at work, not disturbing Natalie sleep.

As I walked to the Dove, I thought about how much longer I could/should continue my Saturday night and frequent party gigs. The money, of course, was incredible. With my retainer plus gratuities, I now would easily make $1,000 to $1,800 a week. I live frugally, and because of that, I had nearly $350,000 in my savings accounts! With my P&W increase in salary, stock options, and incentive compensation awards, I could continue to live quite well and save, absent the Dove income. That was one side of consideration. The fact of the matter is, I really enjoyed my time at the Dove. I looked forward to both my time behind the bar and working private parties. I had developed several very good contacts across a wide spectrum of industries, businesses, and even countries. True friendships had developed with a very enjoyable group of people, younger and older. The long and short of it, I would dearly miss the Dove. I pretty much concluded that retaining my Saturday night gig for another period could be manageable. The lack of predictability of the private parties, however, could quickly become a problem. It was clear I needed to have a sit-down conversation with the management at the Dove.

As was my practice, I arrived at five thirty. My shift beginning at seven gave me time to check the bar stock, order needed supplies, change into my uniform, and check the reservations listing for the evening. Another fully booked night promised to keep me busy at the bar. Reservations had more than a few of my regulars, an enjoyable and profitable night in the making! I managed to have a few words with my maître d'.

"Peter, could we get together for a chat after closing?"

A look of apprehension came over his face; he might have anticipated the purpose of the meeting.

"Of course, Kevin. I shared your good news with staff and customers, everyone is so proud of you. The boss gave me this envelope to give to you."

As it was coming up to opening time, we both went off to our workstations. We opened at exactly seven. The early diners were the older folks who tended to have their drinks at their table. Everything was spit and polished. I remembered and opened the envelope Peter had given me. Enclosed was a card with a handwritten note and, to my amazement, a check.

"Kevin, you have been with us at the Dove for nearly six years. The owners, staff, and our customers truly value your skills behind the bar and, more importantly, your wonderful interpersonal magic. We are all so proud of your career advancement at P&W. The check enclosed is our way of saying *thank you* and all the best."

Peter, the general manager, and the owners of the Dove had signed the card. I could not believe the enclosed check for $5,000! After the conversation with Peter, I will certainly give the check back!

The night began with two couples, both regulars, arriving for their usual hour at the bar before dinner. The Connellys, he was a retired senior judge and the Borgs, he was a retired corporate CEO. Handshakes, hugs, and kisses across the bar.

"Kevin, we are so proud of your promotion at P&W."

Without the need to order, I quickly put together two vodka. Stolichnaya Elit, martinis, dry, one with onions for the judge, the other with a lemon twist for Mrs. Connelly. A bourbon. Woodford Reserve, Manhattan, very light on the vermouth, with a cherry for Mrs. Borg and an eighteen-year-old Scotch, Bowmore, neat, for Mr. Borg. These folks know what they liked, and price was never an issue. They of course loved my knowing *exactly* how and what they would have, no need to order!

Another couple appeared; I did not know them. She was stunning and a good ten years younger than her partner.

"Good evening and welcome to the bar. What can I serve you this evening?"

The gentleman smiled. "We are celebrating our engagement, I think champagne might be in order. What do you recommend?"

"Congratulations to you both. Do you prefer a dry champagne or something a bit on the sweet side?" I asked.

"Definitely not sweet," said the young lady.

"In that case, might I suggest, a 2008 Piper Heidsieck Cuvee Brut? It will be from the first cut grape, always the best and moderately dry and definitely not sweet, 2008 was a wonderful year. I think you will enjoy it."

"Splendid, young man, we'll have the Piper Heidsieck."

I quickly put that all together, and the young lady clapped with the cork popping. The gentleman was pleased.

"Great recommendation."

Another couple had taken seats at the bar and waited as I served up the champagne. I remembered them from several weeks ago.

"Nice to see you again, Mr. and Mrs. O'Connor."

They were so pleased that I remembered them. This was one of my many tricks. In checking the reservations list for regulars, I would also look for other names that I recall. It frequently worked. If Peter was free, we would jointly go over the list, combining of our excellent recall abilities.

"What is your pleasure this evening? Gin martinis as I remember."

It was a guess. Bingo! They were delighted I had remembered their drink preferences!

This Saturday night played out like most others, a full bar until around eleven thirty. Great dialogue enjoyed with both my regulars and the new folks. The O'Connors came back to the bar after dinner, as did my champagne couple. The gratuities were much better than usual. My regulars added more than a few extra dollars, along with their con-gratulations on my promotion. I must remember to thank Pierre for his great job getting the news out.

The dining room was wrapped up by eleven, and I could shut down the bar by twelve. I closed the register, a very good night! I checked the bar stock and left notes for replenishing. Pierre came over to the bar area and sat down at one of the tables. He had brought coffee for both of us. As I was grappling with where the conversation should go, Pierre spoke.

"Kevin, I've been thinking all evening. Your promotion and greatly expanded responsibilities at P&W may begin to set up conflicts with your work here at the Dove. We all recognize that your career at P&W has to be your highest priority. As I thought about it, you have two important contributions here at the Dove, behind the bar and as our private party maestro. In support of the private party busi-ness, the Dove has it all: our Michelin Star, outstanding food and service, a great ambiance, our wine cellar is one of the five best in the city and we have a large following of loyal regulars. You are the proverbial frosting on the cake, with your attention to detail and easy rapport with people.

"Kevin Murphy, the bartender, has created a setting with a warm ambiance, a place where our customers spend money and time enjoying each other's company. Looking at the bar receipts for Saturday nights over the years clearly demonstrates your management skills, the warm ambiance, and the customer rapport you have developed. Putting it simply, you are a huge draw in and of yourself!

"In your role as the private party maestro, you have greatly lightened my workload. However, I see the potential for conflicts as being greater with this role as compared to you tending the bar. As folks approached me about scheduling an event, they often asked if you could be available. I must say we have never lost a booking where you were not available. So weighing the two roles, your greater value is being behind the bar on a Saturday night and the potential for conflict with your job responsibilities at P&W will be much less. I would think, on occasion, a conflict could develop, as with your upcoming trip to Cape Cod. We recognize where your priority needs to be! As you know, we have an excellent group of bartenders, most of whom you have trained. All of whom would mind the store quite well in your absence. They would fall over each other to pick up your gig.

"I suggest, and I'm sure management would support the idea, of you continuing as our bartender extraordinaire on Saturday nights. A particular private party event scheduled can be your choice, as your time permits. We will bring a replacement on board to handle the bulk of the private affairs business with your tutelage. We will have a clear understanding that instances are going to arise where you need to be attending to P&W business. What do you think?"

"Pierre, I have known you to be many things, as a good friend being the most important to me. However, I didn't know until now that you are a mind reader! Aside from the money involved, which has always been great, I thoroughly enjoy my time at the Dove. I guess in part, it is the thespian in me. I love to perform for an audience. I find the dialogue with both with my regulars and the new people to be a source of amusement, informative, an opportunity to sometimes provide empathy or encouragement. I am enriched by hearing their life experiences and being supported in my life endeavors. Your analysis of the potential for conflict in each of my two roles is spot on! I've been wrestling with the issue for some time. Your suggestion is brilliant, not only doable but in the best interests of Kevin Murphy and the Dove. Thank you!"

Pierre smiled. "Sometimes, I can see something coming down the pike, giving me time to think and maybe sort it all out. Thank you for accepting me as your friend.

I, along with the management, recognize you as a valued employee. I also value you as a person of integrity with whom I am honored to share a friendship."

"Pierre, I need your advice on another issue. I am troubled accepting the overly generous check enclosed with my congratulatory card. I believe it assumes an indefinite and unchanged commitment to the Dove going forward."

Pierre reached over and patted my hand.

"You are wrong on both counts. The amount of the check is meant to be generous, as we choose to define generosity. Secondly, the check is meant to reward you for the nearly six years of great service to the Dove. There are *no* assumptions as to your continued or longer-term relationship. Lastly, as I have pointed out to you, we see you as a valued asset and positively impacting our bottom line. So, young man, off to your bank and enjoy the well-earned fruits of your labor."

CHAPTER 6

AFTER A GREAT NIGHT'S SLEEP, I got up, showered, and had a quick breakfast. I called Natalie. We both had a list of things to do: groceries, laundry, and other mundane matters. I read the *New York Times* and had a second cup of coffee. It was time to get moving. I pulled out the vacuum and gave the apartment a good cleanup. I changed the bed linens and bathroom towels and put together other laundry for my pickup service. Next, I emptied the dishwasher, cleaned up the kitchen, made up my grocery list, and called it in for delivery. Boy,

I was organized! With my domestic chores done, I opened my briefcase to get organized for the week ahead. Just as I sat down, the phone rang. It was my sister Katie in Dublin. We had exchanged emails but hadn't talked in a while. She had been in the midst of midterms, and there was always the time difference. An hour later, I had shared all the news, including my maturing relationship with Natalie.

"I can't wait to meet her. Will we be able to get together when we are all home for Christmas?"

"I hope we can work all of that out," I replied.

"Please do," said Katie. "I'll be bringing a fine Irish lad home for you all to meet."

I am taken aback! "Serious?"

With a laugh, Katie replied, "Serious, yes! I'll write to you all about it. Must run, I have a class in fifteen minutes. Love you, my little brother."

I managed a good several hours of work, getting ready for the upcoming week. It would be a short week. Larry and I had agreed to get away from the city before the rush of outbound traffic. A rental car had been reserved. Larry would pick it up and then would come by the office for me. I was really looking forward to the getaway and working with my new author.

I was in the office by seven, joined by Jane with my coffee and a bagel. She reported that drinks and dinner with Mary-Ellen had gone very well.

"She asked a good number of probing questions on job specifics and how we worked together. She wanted a rundown on current staff and asked many questions about you. I answered all her questions with absolute candor. Mary-Ellen is quick, bright, enthusiastic, and has an excellent grasp of the editorial process. She's going to be just fine. I look forward to working with her. I rescheduled her for a brief meeting with you at nine. I will have the office layout, furniture, and the move date scheduling ready for your review and sign-off before you leave Thursday. That's it for now. I'll let you get to work."

What more could I ask for in an administrative assistant?

"I'd like for you to sit in on my briefing with Mary-Ellen as I go over what I will be turning over to her and how we can efficiently share the workload."

"That's fine," said Jane. "She will have a lot to absorb. I'll be her backstop."

My personnel plan, promoting Jane to administrative assistant and hiring a new secretary, needed to be reviewed with Personnel. I called Mary Martin in Personnel, with questions on salary levels for the new positions, job descriptions for review, candidates for the opened secretarial position, etc. She gave me the established salary range for the admin assistant position and promised to get back to me with the other information, within the hour. I wanted to quickly get together with my finance people and review the budget for any needed adjustments. I jotted down my notes for my meeting with Mary-Ellen. That seemed to cover the waterfront for the moment.

I gave Annie a quick call. She had already heard back from Mary-Ellen and said the young lady was super-excited with the prospect of joining our group and hoped she has passed muster. Annie asked, "I know you have a short week before getting away, can you do our usual pizza get-together Wednesday night?"

"I wouldn't miss it for the world, seven as usual" was my quick reply.

I called HSW's office to schedule a brief meeting to go over his thoughts/suggestions for my weekend planning session on the Cape. HSW was out of the office; his administrative assistant was aware of the topic and suggested a thirty-minute session for 6:00 p.m. on Wednesday.

"Thanks, I'll put that on my calendar."

I returned half a dozen phone calls and responded to nine emails. The clock struck eight forty-five. I took a quick break and was now ready for Mary-Ellen.

Jane buzzed to announce Mary-Ellen's arrival. Mary-Ellen came into the office, very nicely put together, and gave me a small smile, a bit nervous and, I am sure, apprehensive.

"Well young lady, how was your weekend?"

"To be honest, I hardly slept. Jane laid out a full plate for me to digest. I am very grateful for her insights and her candor. The weekend flew by as I tried to visualize working with you, Jane, and the rest of the team. I want to tell you straight out, I would be delighted to join your team, and with your good patience and Jane's support, I promise to quickly earn my keep."

"That's great!" I said, "Now let's talk about my ideas for work sharing. I want you to ask as many questions as come to mind and be very frank, particularly if something is not clear or causes you some anxiety. Okay? I've asked Jane to join us, and she will chime in from her perspective."

Mary-Ellen smiled. "That's great. I am ready."

We had a productive one-hour meeting. Mary-Ellen's questions were focused and well thought-out. Jane, for her part, offered more than a few suggestions, all of which were spot-on. Mary-Ellen had only one reservation: dealing with well-established authors. I reminded her that I wasn't stepping off the planet and would always be available. Also, I told her I knew the authors quite well and I was comfortable that she and they would mesh just fine. Jane also assured ME, as we had named her, she too was readily available. As we were about to wrap things up, I said, "ME, I am pleased that you have asked for the order and you are ready to join our team. The past hour has been very productive and re-reinforces our initial impressions that you were the right person for the job. So unless you have changed your mind, I would like to extend the offer to you to join our team. You will be moving up to the position of junior editor with an annual salary of $29,750, with a six-month salary review."

Mary-Ellen let out a small scream! "Oh my god! Thank you."

We agreed on a starting date, one week hence.

I spent the rest of the morning in conference calls with two authors. The first had reached a mental block on his storyline. The second of my authors would be reacting to annotations I had made on his latest segment of manuscript. The greatest joy of my job has been these types of situations. Interacting with truly creative minds was challenging and stimulating. I am very focused on staying in the role of midwife, in practice for working with Larry O'Neil. As I thought about my first scheduled conversation, I had no suggestions or thoughts on the storyline per se. Ted McGowan, my author, had in my opinion, simply gotten lost in his own narrative. I suggested taking a long weekend away from his desk, then reconnecting by going back and reading the seven chapters he had already written. I told him he just needed to regroup. Ted was relieved and promised to take a brief break, as I suggested, and to regroup!

Frank Lazzo, my second author, presented a much more complex and challenging situation. My extensive annotations on his latest manuscript installation focused on what I saw as a pronounced language problem developing. The major character had taken on a sense of superiority and condescension, neither of which were consistent with earlier character presentation and didn't seem pertinent to the plot or storyline. I saw this as a major drift away from what had been a very promising novel. My concern centered on the author's intent. Where was he going and why? Did he intend the shift? As it turned out, Frank's shift was very intentional! He, in fact, was pleased that he had pulled it off. My author went into detail as to where he was taking the storyline and asked me to wait until I could read the next installation of manuscript. He assured me I would understand and might even applaud the impact of the shift in storyline.

"I can't wait for it to arrive."

We left off with laughing at his enjoyment in surprising his editor.

Jane buzzed, with a question as to luncheon plans.

"Soup and a sandwich will be just fine, surprise me."

Not wanting to let Katie's cat out of the bag, I texted my brother, asking if he had been in touch with our sister lately. I was surprised; he was on the phone with me almost immediately.

"I had a business meeting last week in Dublin and got to spend a great weekend with Katie. She had been pestering me to come for a visit. Our dear sister was marvelous, totally in love with all things Irish: the food, the climate, the humor, and most of all, the people. We may have lost our sister to our fatherland. Speaking of people, we had lunch with a young man, a fellow student. A redheaded Irishman with the name of Shamus O'Leary. Mr. O'Leary is a tall lad with an athletic build. He originates from Castlebar, County Mayo. He is about Katie's age, bright, and charming as all get-out. The lad is gifted with a wicked sense of humor. Shamus is just finishing a PhD in history. He hopes to deal with the presentation and defense of his dissertation next month. Your obvious question, what's going on? Katie didn't volunteer, but I would guess they are in a serious relationship. As I was leaving, Shamus said he hoped to see me again. If I were to venture a guess, Christmas in Brookline is going to be very interesting! Got to run. I'll catch up this weekend." I told him I was tied up all weekend but would be in touch. "Love you, brother."

Lunch arrived, lentil soup and a grilled cheese sandwich along with a nice cold bottle of milk. I attacked my mail as I ate. Jane was a master at sorting and organizing my mail, attaching backup documentation along with explanatory notes where needed. I dictated several notes, emailed responses, comments, answers to questions, suggestions, inquiries where I need more information, etc. I always found lunchtime at my desk to be highly productive. I wrapped up with returning several phone calls. Jane came in with several questions on the new office layout. I begged off, saying we could do that at around 5:00 p.m. I want my ducks lined up with the administrative assistant job information I needed from Personnel. I turned my attention back to the planning for the working weekend with Larry O'Neil. I was very interested to sit with HSW and hear his thoughts and suggestions. My phone was busier than usual. I called Natalie at her office. She was delighted with the call, but it was obvious she wasn't free to chat.

"Just called to say I love you."

She laughed. "Right back at you, thanks for the call."

Jane buzzed. She had Pierre LeClair on the line; she of course knew Pierre.

"Just a quick call to tell you I discussed your situation and our conversation with management. The boss was very pleased. I don't exaggerate how highly senior management regards you."

With real sincerity, I tell him, "Pierre, I can't thank you enough for the call and for being such a great friend. I'll see you when I am back from Cape Cod, be well."

At four thirty, Mary arrived with the promised job information. As was her way, she handed me a small package and said, "Let's walk through this, starting with Jane's promotion. Excellent move on your part, I have had several probes on her availability for promotion. This is the job description, you can give it to Jane. The salary for the position begins at $45,500. Jane is, as you know, currently paid $38,900 per year. I'd suggest moving her to $42,500 initially with a six-month review. If she is fully meeting all job requirements, you can bump her up to the full $45,500."

That seemed reasonable to me.

"As you know, in reading my performances appraisals on Jane, she has always shown outstanding performance."

Next, Mary had three possibilities for the secretarial slot.

"Here's the job description and salary range. I have a good appreciation of how you run your shop and the personality dynamics of your staff. You'll see I have ranked my recommendations. I either know the candidates personally and/or have researched their backgrounds and experience. They are all fully qualified, so it essentially boils down to chemistry."

"I'll review these and have Jane schedule interviews next week. Appreciate your good help."

I buzzed Jane. "We can do the office/facilities now if you like."

Jane came in with an armful of paperwork and diagrams.

"Before we get into this, I need to tell you that we will have a couple of significant staff changes and additions to staff that will affect your planning."

A surprised look passed over Jane's face.

"First, is the appointment of an administrative assistant, and we will be hiring a new secretary."

Jane now looked confused.

"Could you recommend anyone for the critically important position of administrative assistant?" I asked in a very serious tone.

Without hesitation and with her usual self- assured manner, she responded, "You bet I can! Jane A. McFarland would be the perfect administrative assistant!"

I could not contain myself. Laughing and embracing Jane, I said, "Of course, you are the perfect candidate!

Would you please accept my formal offer to become my administrative assistant?"

Absolutely deadpan, she replied, "I am either going to kill you or just accept your offer. I've decided to let you live. I am delighted to be your administrative assistant!"

I gave her the job description and salary details. She was extremely pleased.

"I will give you no reason to not bump me up in six months," she assured me with a serious face.

I gave her the list of the three candidates for the secretarial position and asked her to do screening interviews over the next few days.

"I know all three. Mary's number 1 would be just fine, assuming the chemistry is right."

We put off the facilities review to give Jane time to review and revise with the staff changes and expansion.

CHAPTER 7

BEFORE GOING UP TO HSW'S office for our six
o'clock meeting, I reviewed my notes for the
upcoming meeting with Larry O'Neil. Arriving
promptly, as I always do, I was ushered right into HSW's
inner sanctum. Cordial as he always was, he nonetheless
seemed a bit stressed.

"I just had a long call with Peter Cordillion. He very
much wanted to join you and Larry this weekend on the
Cape. I told him I didn't think that would be a good idea. I
explained you both need to be intensely focused and with-

out distractions. Peter took exception to being labelled a distraction. I explained further, the two of you need to develop a game plan for working together, and this would involve many technical publishing matters, which I was sure would bore him. I suggested that he and I spend the weekend at the beach in the Hamptons. He thought that might be a good idea."

Hoping to alleviate HSW's concern that I might find Peter's periodic involvement troublesome, I said, "I enjoy Peter's company, he's bright and certainly knows Larry well and has his confidence, going forward, I don't see a problem."

I could see a look of relief on HSW's face. We spent the next forty-five minutes going over my thoughts for the planning session. HSW, being the superb editor that he was, had more than a few excellent suggestions. We worked well together, something that would be important as I assumed the work of a senior editor.

As we were wrapping up, HSW asked if I had plans for the evening.

"Planning an early dinner, some paperwork, and early to bed."

HSW suggested, "Let's grab a bite at the Shark's Tooth, it's on the way home for you. We can have a fast dinner, and you can be home at a reasonable hour."

The restaurant was off the beaten path but noted for fine seafood. I enjoyed a Dover sole, baked scrod for HSW. Dinner was enhanced with a good bottle of wine. Our conversation was relaxed with a bit of industry gossip. Skipping coffee, I thanked HSW for his advice and a great dinner and walked the fifteen minutes to my apartment.

I rang Natalie. "How did your day go?"

I could hear the excitement in her voice. "So well, I just can't believe it! I was able to get my boss aside for lunch. A bit of good luck, he is usually booked solid, weeks in advance. We talked at length about the China assignment.

I told him I was honored to be offered the assignment and very excited, recognizing the potential contribution to be made toward bettering relations between the US and China. Dr. Nu picked up the hesitancy in my voice. I was very open, and to the point about our being in a serious relationship, neither of us being happy at the prospect of a six-month separation. Before I could even bring up our idea of a periodic rendezvous somewhere, he said, 'I am so happy for you and understand. We are confident that you are the right person for this important assignment, recognizing your educational training, your family-based connections to China, your fluency in both Mandarin and Cantonese, and your known commitment to the concept of cross-cultural appreciation. We are placing the complete management of this project in your good hands. You and your Chinese associate will develop the specifics, and I assure you of full budgetary support. I would guess that whoever the Chinese appoints as your associate will want to spend a good block of time here in the States as you will want to spend time in China. I see both of you working at your home base, making good and heavy use of our excellent advanced technical abilities to comfortably arrange remote one-on-one or group meetings and site visitations. I see you periodically traveling, spending perhaps a week or two at a time in China with a good portion of your time here in the US, working independently or in conjunction with your visiting Chinese associate. As a last thought, I personally know the leading candidate being considered by the Chinese government. I am sure I will be consulted. The person is preeminently qualified. I will give you a full briefing on the final choice once it has been finalized.' Dr. Nu gave me a smile. 'I hope this clears up any hesitancy you might have.'"

Natalie's voice was filled with joy.

"What could I say? His understanding, his confidence in me, and his generosity took me aback! I accepted the assignment. The sun is surely shining on our parade."

"Bravo, sweetheart! Do you know when the assignment will begin?"

Natalie, thinking out loud, said, "I have to develop a preliminary plan, arrange a number of discussions with my appointed Chinese associate, and start developing a budget. I say we could kick off right after the first of the year."

This was the right moment to invite Natalie to Brookline for the Christmas holidays. "It is few months away, but I would very much like to have you come to Brookline for Christmas. My folks, of course, know that we are an item, to use their term, and are so anxious to meet you. My brother Pat will be home from London and my sister Katie is coming from Dublin. She will be bringing her significant other. I think they will be making a *big* announcement. The family hasn't been together for a while.

Of course, Katie is anxious for us to all meet her Irish beau. I would like to make it a doubleheader by introducing you as my significant other!"

Natalie was quick to say, "I love the idea. Thank you for the invitation. I have never done the 'meet the parents' thing nor have I ever brought a boyfriend home. My folks will recognize this and know that I am/we are, very much in a serious relationship. It fits well from another point. A New Year's Eve get-together with my folks would work just fine. Christmas has never been a big thing for us. The folks are in New York frequently for both business and pleasure. They love the city. Mom and Dad have been very curious about you. I am sure they will think the idea is great! There's time to pull things together. The Waldorf is their New York home away from home, so a reservation will not be a problem."

I offered to host a New Year's Eve dinner at the Dove. The festivity was particularly well-done at my restaurant.

Natalie was really pleased with the idea. We discussed more ideas and took on different responsibilities for pulling it all together. We planned a quick dinner for the evening and signed off with "I love you." Natalie knew of my standing pizza date with my two girlfriends on Wednesday evening and the plan to be off to the Cape Thursday afternoon.

The next days were busy. I was in the office by 6:30 a.m. and worked until nearly 10:00 pm. Jane had done the screening interviews for the secretarial position and recommended that we go with Mary's first choice. Adamma Bhengani, a twenty-nine-year-old African American, having arrived at age five, with her parents in the US from Ethiopia. With a little research, I learned, most Ethiopians consider themselves as Habasha, a nonblack ethno-racial category, emphasizing their Semitic origins, although it is more a language matter in the present day. Ada, as she preferred to be called, had been with P&W for nine years, joining the company following graduation, with honors, from a very good two-year secretarial/business school in the Bronx. Ada was single and lived with her parents. I scanned her performance appraisal file, rated consistently superior in all categories.

"Jane, please schedule Ms. Bhengani for an interview right after lunch."

Jane had a few quick questions on office layout and then went about her business.

HSW's administrative assistant called and asked me to join HSW upstairs for lunch, Wednesday at one thirty, no reason given. I was curious but didn't ask. I called Annie's office. She was always in the know. She was not available, tied up in a long meeting. Ann Hopkins was now thirty-five, soon to be thirty-six, and had been with P&W for just about a dozen years. She was the most senior of the editors and had been reporting directly to HSW for the past three years. I was fortunate to have been reporting to her for the six years I have been with P&W. As a boss, she was demanding but always fair, a great teacher, and always available. There had been a bonus: we had become the best of friends outside the office.

The company editorial organization chart was not that clear on working relationships. Clearly, HSW was on the top so to speak, as managing editor. Directly reporting to him were two senior editors (of twelve), the art director, the manager of finance, the manager of planning, personnel administrator, his administrative assistant, and several minor functionaries. The two senior editors each had five junior editors reporting to them. Annie also had two junior editors reporting to her. I was one of the two. There were thirty junior or assistant editors reporting to the senior editors. The remaining troops, nearly one hundred people, were spread out, reporting through various managers. Is that clear?

I had decided that the upcoming Wednesday luncheon had to follow the good luck of my first experience upstairs.

I put idle speculation aside and got back to work. A long email came through from my sister Katie. As promised, she went into a lot of detail regarding Shamus O'Leary. Katie and Shamus had been dating for nearly two years. Their relationship was exclusive, and they had been living together for the past ten months. Shamus had proposed, and she had accepted. Of course, she said, she would be staying in Ireland and had already begun the process of acquiring citizenship. Katie has discussed the relationship in general terms with our folks, although she had not told them the state to which it had progressed. She wanted that to be a surprise! Also, she said that Shamus wanted to formally ask Dad for her hand! I knew the folks would be so happy! With my bringing Natalie home, their joy would be compounded. Next, we need to find a serious involvement for our long-in-the --tooth brother, Patrick.

Jane buzzed to announce the arrival of Ada. As the young lady came into the office, I was taken with both her height and her great beauty. The young woman was at nearly six feet tall, if not a bit more. Her coloration is very light brown, and she had the most expressive dark-brown eyes I had ever seen! Simply but nicely dressed, she was very much at ease. We covered her experience at P&W, what she particularly liked about the editorial environment, her self-assessment and her aspirations. Based on the recommendations of both Mary and Jane and my review of Ada's file, I had thought a relatively short interview would suffice. She was articulate, quick of mind, answering questions with ease. I was very much enjoying our meeting. As we were concluding, Ada boldly stated, "I think I would fit in quite nicely with your organization. With my background and experience, I will hit the road running. Were an offer extended, I would be delighted to accept."

I buzzed Jane to come in and asked Ada to wait in the outer office.

"I think Ada will be just great! Check with Mary and have her extend an offer. Assuming she accepts, clear a reporting date with Personnel."

I walked out to Ada, shook her hand, and told her we would be extending an offer. Mary in Personnel will take her through the particulars within the hour.

"I am very pleased you will be joining us, and we look forward to working with you," I said with real sincerity.

My author, Tim McGowen, called. He had taken my advice and stepped back to regroup. He reported that he was back at his desk and writing with confidence.

"Thank you for your good insight and advice. You have earned your keep! I will have the next three chapters to you, right on schedule."

I asked myself, "Was I really that good?"

The usual business kept me occupied most of the afternoon. I took great pleasure in how well Jane kept me on track and totally organized. I am confident Ada could and would quickly absorb these skills.

The day was moving along so well. I needed to take the time to check in with my financial adviser, something I should do more often. I knew the market was on a roll, and I was probably doing well with my investments. P&W had a great retirement plan, and I contributed the maximum every paycheck. Kevin Smallwood, a longtime buddy from the gym, had been my financial adviser at Edward Jones since I joined P&W. Kevin was low-key, smart, and doesn't chase me to be more aggressive. I gave his office a call.

"What's up?" he asked.

I gave him an update on my promotion, new salary, stock options, and incentive compensation.

"I need to schedule an overall review with you, looking at the current situation on my investments and suggestions for going forward. Also, I am in a serious relationship with a young lady."

Kevin chuckled, "Boy, are you on a roll. Give me a couple of hours to pull things together. How is four o'clock this afternoon for you?"

We agreed on the time, and I went back to my work. Paul, my dynamite art designer, called with a quick question.

"By the way, congrats on your promotion. I guess I'll be seeing a lot less of you in the future."

I laughed. "Don't count on that, my friend. I can't let you go off on your own."

I had several book proposals to review, which engaged me until Jane buzzed through with Kevin on the line.

"Let me walk you through where you are at this point in time. Answer any questions you have on that and then I'll give my suggestions where you should be headed given your new situation."

I agreed. "Sounds like a plan. Over to you."

"To begin with," started Kevin, "overall, you are in great shape. The Roth IRA is right up to snuff with $36,000 in contributions and with the up market, the account now sits at $51,235. Your regular account, over which you have given me trading discretion, is invested toward growth. The account has a good balance of common stocks, some real winners like UPS and Apple. You have 25 percent invested internationally. I like automakers, e.g., Toyota. Currently, I have you in four ETFs, two of which are doing extremely well. For overall balance and a bit more conservative, you have a range of taxable and tax-free bonds, laddered up over thirty years. We have been keeping very little in cash. I like money to be out and working. As I have told you in the past, while the overall approach is aggressive, I do not buy/ sell a lot, with a sensitivity to your income tax exposure and we are not day traders. We are in for the long term."

I liked that Kevin used the term "we." He was my partner!

Kevin continued, "Putting all this in hard perspective in round numbers, you have $59,000 in your Roth IRA;

equities at $200,000; $65,000 in short-term bank repos, high-interest loans to banks, needed to balance their daily cash positions; $56,000 in bonds; $129,000 in ETFs. Putting all of that into the adding machine, the total in your account looks like $450,000! That's a damn good number for a young man."

I knew I was doing well, but the number was a huge and pleasant surprise. I have always lived quite frugally. My earnings at the Dove, amount to, on average, $7,000 per month. I kept too much money, around $20,000, in a savings account. I rarely balanced my checking account; there probably was a several thousand-dollar balance. I carry no debt, have a modest rent, my biggest expense is dining out, and I have a pension for very good wine.

Kevin continued, "Okay, we know you are in great shape, with an excellent income and low operating expenses. These are my suggestions/recommendations going forward," as he led into what proved to be a good and long dialogue. "The current market volatility we are seeing is, I believe, going to continue for a good period. This is a risk to our current holding in terms of fluctuation. However, they are all solid in the longer term. I see opportunity. We will carefully watch industries and companies taking heavy hits due to, for instance, a drop in their earnings per share, resulting in a sell-off of its stock. The sell-off rationale often has little to do with the industry/company fundamentals. We will be opportunistic! I am suggesting that we move judiciously into day trading. We will set up a new trading account. Opening with $50,000 available liquid capital and at least $20,000 from what, I suspect you have sitting around in cash. I am targeting to reach $100,000 to $125,000 by year-end. Having trading control over the account, I will be paid an incremental management fee based on earnings generated. Going forward, we will need to have discussions more frequently. I hope you are comfortable with this approach and this arrangement."

"Kevin, you have done one great job for me. Thank you again. I totally buy into your suggestions. Your guess on cash I have sitting around is too accurate! I would be comfortable in committing a minimum of $10,000 per month from my Dove income and my increase in P&W salary. I see us reaching our goal by year-end. If you get the necessary paperwork to me, we can be in business directly."

Kevin was pleased. Back to work. I planned for an early getaway. Natalie and I were having dinner.

CHAPTER 8

WE HAD AGREED THAT I would pick Natalie up at the UN Plaza. My cab pulled in; there was my smiling dinner date. She jumped into the cab and gave me a warm kiss. She gave the driver an address I didn't recognize.

"Where are we having dinner?"

She chuckled and said, "That's a surprise."

The driver turned off Third Avenue onto Ninety-Fifth Street and stopped at a restaurant, Nagamuru, without a doubt, Japanese. Across the spectrum of our food interests,

Japanese was in our top five. This would be our first visit to the restaurant. Nagamuru opened to rave reviews just a few weeks ago. I was surprised Natalie was able to book a reservation. We were welcomed by Nagamuru-san personally and taken to our table. To my surprise, there sat Annie and Helene!

"What is going on here?"

My three ladies enjoyed a laugh. Speaking up, Natalie laughed. "I, of course, have known of your great relationship with Annie, transcending your work at P&W. I am also aware of your Wednesday night pizza date with Annie and Helene. I decided it was time to check out the competition!"

Another hearty round of laughter.

"I called Annie and suggested we all get together. She thought the idea was spot on. Knowing you as well as they do, they sensed our relationship had reached a new and important point. They were on the verge of suggesting an introduction would be appropriate."

"I have five women who are so important to me," I said. "My mother Margaret, my sister Katie, and the three women sitting at this table. Annie, my boss, mentor, and dear friend, my psychiatrist, as needed, and also a dear friend, Helene, and Natalie, the woman I deeply and profoundly love."

A long round of applause followed.

Nagamuru-san asked to personally take our order. It seemed Annie and Helene had managed to secure seats for the opening night several weeks ago and had been back several times and were now on the list of valued customers. In easy and apparently beautifully fluent Japanese, Natalie spoke with Nagamuru-san.

"With your permission, Nagamuru-san and I would like to put the dinner order together."

Wonderful, we all agreed. What followed was an animated dialogue between our two Japanese speakers, Natalie asking questions and commenting at length. Nagamuru-san bowed and commented, "You are fortunate to have a friend who understands and appreciates all the finer points of Japanese food and its preparation. In addition, your friend speaks our language with perfection. It is a pleasure to have you with us this evening."

Helene laughed and said, "I would guess that you just jumped past us on the list of preferred customers."

Dinner was outstanding with superb presentation of one great dish after another. The sake flowed, providing unneeded lubrication to an already animated conversation. So much for an early dinner! We parted company at around eleven o'clock. The bonding was important to all four of us. Thank you, Natalie!

I managed to drag myself into the office around eight thirty, mildly hungover. Jane, bless her, greeted me with a double coffee and a bagel with cream cheese and salmon. "I am so happy you had a great time last night."

She apparently was in on the conspiracy. Eating the dressed-up bagel and drinking two coffees, I started to come around. I plowed through my well-organized correspondence, answered a lot of emails, and avoided phone calls! I left the office and got myself to my gym, just around the corner. I visited the steam room, took a swim in the pool, a long hot shower, followed by a massage. I was back in the office by one o'clock. I was feeling almost human again.

I arrived upstairs for my one-thirty luncheon. The lobby was busy with corporate VIPs and guests. The maître d' inquired, "Will you be joined for lunch?"

"Mr. Weathersbee," I responded.

I was led into a large private dining room, off the main dining area. HSW and most of the senior editors, including Annie, were already assembled. HSW's other key staff soon joined us. Drink orders were taken and hors d'oeuvres were passed. It seemed we were waiting for someone else to arrive. Shortly, CEO Tom Clarkson and all the senior corporate officers joined us. Using an old opening line, HSW said, "I am sure you are all wondering why I have called you together. I am going to ask our CEO, Mr. Clarkson, to explain."

Casually moving around the room, Mr. Clarkson began, "We are happy when we see P&W personnel growing into new and challenging positions. Our company prides itself on providing ample opportunities for personal and professional growth. It is recognized, continued success of P&W in the highly competitive marketplace begins at the editorial desk. Finding and signing new authors, being in touch with public taste and interests, shepherding manuscripts through the creative process and, ultimately, bringing a new title to the marketplace. Mr. Weathersbee, I'm sorry that is probably a strange name to you, I meant

HSW, as he is known here at P&W and throughout the publishing industry, joined P&W nearly twenty-eight years ago. He is an excellent example of sustained professional growth, reaching the pinnacle of our editorial operations as managing editor."

A long, loud round of applause followed.

"Anne Hopkins, the most senior of our senior editors and the person who has supported HSW with a smooth-running day-to-day operation of our editorial team, has been with P&W thirteen years this fall. Ann started with the company as an editorial assistant, rising through the ranks: junior editor, editor, senior editor, and now *the* senior editor."

Another round of applause.

"Among her many contributions, the one that stands out is her recruitment, nurturing, training, supporting, and challenging the editorial staff, at all levels, to do their very best! Over the years, she has brought nearly sixty editorial assistants/trainees into the company. Of those, forty-nine remain: twelve editorial assistants, fifteen junior editors, twenty editors, and two senior editors. The latest of whom, Kevin Murphy, as you know from the news release on his promotion, joined P&W just six short years ago. Kevin will tell you, he owes his unprecedented advancement to the mentorship of HSW and the tutorial guidance of Ann Hopkins, to whom he has directly reported, for his six years with the company. I had the honor and pleasure to personally bring Kevin's recent promotion forward."

Applause again filled the room.

"As you know, CEOs are not directly involved in too many promotions, however, I so much enjoyed interjecting myself into Kevin Murphy's advancement, and I have decided to do it again!"

There was a stunned silence across the room. Laughing, Mr. Conroy continued, "No, I am not announcing another promotion for Mr. Murphy! Ms. Hopkins's outstanding contributions as an editor, mentor, and manager have earned her our recognition and a promotion. At the suggestion of HSW, with my complete concurrence and support and with the approval of the Board of Directors, I am delighted to announce the appointment of Ms. Ann Hopkins to the position of managing editor of P&W Books."

Yet another stunned silence followed by a tentative round of applause. Mr. Conroy put up a hand.

"I hasten to assure you that our revered and greatly respected HSW is not being displaced nor is he retiring! I have asked our Board of Directors to create a new position, recognizing HSW's many years of dedication to P&W and the ongoing contributions he will continue to make to our company. With the concurrence and unanimous approval of the board, the position of vice president–publisher for P&W Books has been created, and Mr. Weathersbee has been elected to the position! Please join me in congratulating HSW, Ms. Hopkins, and Mr. Murphy with a toast to their continued success."

Champagne was poured, and multiple toasts were offered. Kevin approached HSW with his hand extended. HSW took it and gathered him into a warm embrace. Annie joined them in a group hug; everyone applauded. The buffet luncheon that followed was most enjoyable with lots of good wishes. We adjourned, and I found Annie.

"I am so proud and happy for you, but I will miss not having you as my boss."

Annie chuckled. "No, you will not escape my clutches, dear boy. You will continue to report directly to me, this by the way, was suggested by HSW. I am delighted and warn you, I will be keeping a careful eye on you!"

We both enjoyed a good laugh and a hug.

Back in my office, I gave all the news to Jane. She was happy for Annie and pleased that we would continue to report directly to her. Ada's date for joining us was set for one week, which was great and fit in well with Mary-Ellen's coming onboard. Jane gave me my call log and emails, as always fully organized. I had much to do. I attacked my call log, knocking off several quick calls, handled four more, which were a bit more involved, and left nine messages. Next, I dealt with my emails. I quickly emailed answers to questions, offered reactions/suggestions, and gave two long commentaries. My in basket was the next order of business. I noticed a manuscript file, from Frank Lazzo, my favorite author.

Several weeks ago, he and I had a long discussion dealing with my concern that he was going offtrack. Frank convinced me that what I was seeing was very deliberate on his part. Would I please wait for the next installation of manuscript? I rarely study manuscripts in the office during normal work hours. I preferred to read very early in the morning or at home after dinner. I buzzed Jane and asked her for no interruptions for an hour, and would she please bring me a cup of coffee. I am gifted with great reading speed and comprehension. However, I read Lazzo's manuscript more slowly. This was chapter 8, the seminal chapter, in what could be an incredible novel. The focus was acutely on the main character, engaged in dialogue with himself. The character was very aware of other characters, noting changes in his personality. The author is allowing the reader to share the character's process of introspection. As can often be the case, the process could be painful, even brutal, and was self-inflicted. This provided the means for the reader to get away from the confusion the character had created in earlier chapters. We, the readers, could now recognize what was going on and almost immediately feel empathy. The author had immersed us in the character's deep pain. We, in response to the intimacy of the character's introspection, might feel guilty, having perhaps too quickly judged him. It was now clear to me, the author had set the reader up to be uncomfortable, confused with an unexplained metamorphosis, evolving toward a real dislike for the main character and then in quick turn, causing the reader to feel the character's pain, regret the dislike developed, and be tremendously empathetic.

I finished reading and immediately called Frank. His answering machine picked up.

"Leave a message."

Frank was out of touch for a few days; he was in the deep woods hunting. I knew this was his favorite form of relaxation. I left a message, "Brilliant! Tour de force! I cannot wait for more."

I buzzed Jane and asked that she have a bottle of Frank's favorite wine delivered with a note: "I think we have a best-seller in the making! Enjoy the wine. Your grateful editor."

I called Natalie with all the news from the luncheon. That old saw, good news travels fast! Annie had called Helene; Helene had called Natalie. Helene insisted that we throw together a celebration at her apartment that evening around seven thirty. Natalie had accepted. I told her that I would run a bit late. I wanted to clear my desk. We agreed to meet at Annie/Helene's apartment.

I called HSW to offer my congratulations again and to thank him for his support.

"I truly love putting these little surprises together," he said with a chuckle. "Listen, Peter, Larry, and I are meeting at the Bull and Bear to celebrate, please join us."

"I love to, but I am already committed to a celebration party for my promotion, but thanks and my best to Larry and Peter."

I called Annie and related the conversation with HSW.

"Maybe a crazy idea, how about we invite them to our celebration party at your apartment?"

"Maybe, I'll call Helene and check. I'll be back to you in a few minutes."

Annie was back on the phone five minutes later. "Helene thinks that's a great idea. Being the super hostess she is, it will come together beautifully. She knows HSW and Peter quite well and has met Larry O'Neil. As the hostess, she will call HSW right away. She will also call Peter, extending an invitation. I'll see you around seven."

I called Natalie with an update.

"Guess I'll run home and freshen up. I want to look my best for HSW, Mr. Cordillion, and Larry O'Neil, and you also, my dear."

"I'll try to get to Helene's ASAP to lend a hand," I replied. "Love you."

I had planned a call to Larry to confirm our plans for tomorrow.

"We are all set. I'll pick you up at the P&W main entrance on Thirty-Seventh Street at, say, two thirty. We can beat the traffic going out of town and get over the Cape Bridge before rush hour."

I agreed, "Sounds great. Listen, I know the plan for you, Peter, and HSW getting together at the Bull and

Bear to celebrate. We are just putting together impromptu drinks and dinner to celebrate both my promotion and Anne Hopkins as well. Why don't we combine the celebrations, and you three join us at Helene Weinstein's apartment around seven thirty. Invitations are just now being extended to HSW and Peter."

"Sounds like a great evening. I'm sure HSW and Peter will be delighted."

Back to Helene, "Okay with Larry O'Neil."

I wrapped up work just before six and took a cab to my regular wine store. I had called ahead and negotiated a very good price on six bottles of fine champagne, 2012 Dom Pérignon Brut. With light traffic, I was at Annie/Helene's apartment, with time to spare before the party start time of seven thirty. Annie answered the door, gave me a quick hug, and was off, on the run, toward the kitchen. I gave the champagne to the housekeeper Lu-Ann, with instructions to chill it lightly, three bottles to be served as we sat down to dinner and the remaining three to be served with dessert.

I heard Natalie's voice in the dining room and wandered that way. Several catering people were just putting the finishing touches on the beautifully set table for seven. Helene and Natalie each gave me a peck on the cheek as they rushed off to dress for dinner. With nothing left to do, I found my way to the living room. The room was large and made for entertainment. Low lighting, soft music playing, and fresh cut flowers set an inviting scene. With time to spare before our guests arrived, Annie, Natalie, and Helene came into the living room. In such a short time, they had morphed into three magnificent ladies, each was simply but beautifully dressed, everything just so!

"Isn't this fun? I do love to entertain," said Helene.

"You are an absolute marvel," offered Natalie. "I have never seen anyone put a dinner party together so efficiently, so quickly, and with a wow menu."

Natalie's international background and being senior staff at the UN had her more than used to a social circuit of elegant entertainment and so her compliment was of the highest order.

"You can lend your excellent helping hand anytime, Natalie," said Helene, acknowledging the compliment.

The doorbell rang; Lu-Ann answered and ushered three gentlemen into the living room. Except for Natalie and Larry, everyone else knew each other. I introduced both. With the introductions out of the way, Annie announced the bar was open! Two waiters appeared to take drink orders, and Lu-Ann circulated, offering hot or cold hors d'oeuvres. With amazing speed, drinks were served and the celebrations were underway. The conversations crossed all kinds of topics, were often very animated, and always interesting. Addressing Larry, I asked if he recalled a cocktail party last year at the US Embassy in Riyadh.

"I go to a lot of cocktail parties," laughed Larry. "But I do remember that one. It was a special occasion."

"A birthday celebration for Prince Khalid bin Salman. Khalid is an old skiing buddy I've known since our college days. Why do you ask?"

"I just talked with my brother Patrick the other day. I mentioned that I would be working with you. As it happened, he was at the same party and recalled briefly meeting the two of you. He has had some business dealings with the prince. I guess that proves it is indeed a small world!'

"Natalie, since we've touched on the international world, tell us what you do at the UN," asked Larry.

Natalie very comfortably took center stage and gave an interesting overview of her responsibilities. She went into a bit of detail on her upcoming assignment in China. I had not known HSW included Chinese culture in his wide range of interests. In fact, he spoke to Natalie in Mandarin.

Talk then shifted to the upcoming trip to Cape Cod. HSW and Peter were frequent guests and very much enjoyed Provincetown. All the other people in the room were very familiar with the Cape: the weather, beaches, cultural happenings, and of course, the great restaurants. P-town was, by the group's consensus, the most interesting town on the Cape.

Lu-Ann announced dinner. Helene took the head of the table and had Natalie seated on the left between Peter and Larry. Annie was placed between HSW and me on the left. Two waiters appeared with bottles of champagne, uncorking and serving. I proposed a toast to my colleagues, HSW and Anne, "Congratulations on your promotions. I am personally and professionally pleased to be able to continue working with you. Cheers!"

HSW raised a hand. "If I might, I would like to propose a toast to P&W's newest author, Larry O'Neil, P&W is pleased and proud to have you with us. Welcome aboard!"

Cheers! I turned to my two friends. "I have just two more toasts. To my dear friends Annie and Helene, thank you for your friendship." Cheers! "Lastly, to Natalie, the love of my life."

Cheers! We exhausted three bottles of the fine champagne, with three reserved to accompany dessert.

Helene's idea of throwing something together for dinner would win three stars any day of the week. She would never reveal her caterer, someone who had worked for her for years. Dinner, having been well oiled with cocktails, champagne, and fine wine, found the diners in a joyful mood. The dessert, a decadent chocolate cake, accompanied by more champagne was worth 1,500 calories at a minimum!

I was so pleased that Natalie was clearly enjoying the evening and the company. It was also clear that HSW, Peter, and Larry were smitten by her. Adjourning to the living room, a servant rolled in a bar cart and asked for after dinner preferences.

"I would enjoy another glass of that excellent champagne, if we haven't consumed it all," laughed Larry.

"Toasts not allowed," barked HSW.

Peter and HSW both ordered brandy. The talk turned to jokes and funny stories. Peter ordered another brandy. Larry gave him a concerned look. As the clock struck ten o'clock, HSW stood. "I hate to be the party pooper, but most of us have a busy day on our agendas for tomorrow. Thank you, Anne and Helene, for an unexpected and delightful evening."

With that, we made our goodbyes. I called Uber, and Natalie and I made our way to the lobby.

Natalie snuggled up to me in the car. "That was a wonderful evening. I can now put a face to a name. Helene, Annie, and I have bonded so well and so easily. They are wonderful friends. HSW is very interesting. His Mandarin, by the way, is quite good. Peter is very charming, but there is something about him that is off-putting. You had mentioned he has an issue with alcohol. I saw hints of that tonight. Larry is all that you've said, bright, engaging, and interesting as all get-out."

As we pulled up to her building, we gave each other a long hug and kiss.

"I'll be back Monday around noon. We can have dinner Monday night, and I will give you a full report on the weekend. Love you!"

With the day being cut short with my two-thirty departure to the Cape, I was in the office by 6:00 a.m., with a cup of coffee and a sweet roll from the lobby vendor. I worked at a great pace to clear my desk, emails first, mail next. On to organizing needed dictation, calls I needed to return and calls I needed to make, authors, etc. Jane arrived with my second cup of coffee.

"Want to order a bite of lunch before you leave for Cape Cod?"

I ordered a cup of chowder and a grilled cheese sandwich with my usual bottle of milk.

"Let's have that around one o'clock, and if you're ready, let's get the dictation out of the way and then we can attack the office layout situation."

The dictation didn't take long. As we turned our attention to the office plans, I wasn't surprised with Jane's grasp of the details. Her suggestions were great, office flow, color schemes, etc. The overall layout would allow for great and easy interaction between staff. Jane had specific questions about my office, furniture, color preferences, layout, etc. We were in great shape!

"Great job and I think it's a go! Thank you, Jane."

The next hour was largely devoted to telephone tag. I had a good connection ratio and substantially reduced the call list.

My staff interactions had always been a mixture of brief staff meetings, phone calls, some emails, and a good deal of my just dropping in for a short visit. As a recent innovation, I began to stagger the due dates on required weekly written staff reports. I read the reports with great attention and react often in great depth. As lunch arrived, I called Annie, reacting to several of her comments/questions on my weekly report. With business concluded, I thanked her for what had been a wonderful evening for both me and Natalie.

"I'll see you late Monday or early Tuesday with a full report on the Cape Cod weekend."

I also got a quick call off to Helene, thanking her for hosting a great celebration.

I made time for reviewing several book proposals and three sample manuscripts. I wanted to clear these as I would be tied up all weekend with Larry O'Neil. Of six book proposals, I rated two as promising, three raised several questions for my submitting editors, and the last was dead on arrival. I asked the submitting editor to rethink her suggestion and give me reasons for going forward. I had a practice of rarely turning a proposal down flat out. I did, of course, turn proposals down. The editor submitting the proposal would rethink the submission. Perhaps resubmit or withdraw, accept the final judgment, feeling that it had been given full and fair consideration, in addition, maybe learning something in the process. I made a few quick personal phones. Natalie was tied up in a staff meeting. I called my mother and had a great chat. She was so curious as to the guests being brought home for Christmas.

"We want for you to be surprised."

Not surprised that calls to Patrick and Katie found both not available. I got a quick email off to both.

"Everyone on this side of the pond is super pumped-up for the Christmas holidays. Call when you come up for breath. I am away for a long working weekend, back late Monday."

I packed up my briefcase and laptop and asked Jane if anything else needed my attention before I left the office.

"You are good to go, boss, enjoy the weekend and take time to hit the beach."

My private line rang. It was Natalie.

"I saw your call and just ducked out of the meeting to say I love you and wish you a great and productive weekend."

I promised to call when I could. I was out the door and down on the curb waiting for Larry. Right on schedule, he pulled up, we loaded my bag and other paraphernalia, and we're on our way!

CHAPTER 9

TRAFFIC WAS LIGHT, AND WE were out of the city in less than thirty minutes. Larry seemed to really enjoy driving, and while aggressive, he was skilled and cautious. We talked about the weather forecast for the Cape. It looked very good! Friday and maybe Saturday should be warm and sunny. We moved on to discussing restaurants. Larry was clearly very familiar with all the best places in Provincetown. He knew I very much like seafood, promising I'd not be disappointed with the choices or the quality. Larry expounded on his love for the

Cape. He had inherited the cottage from his parents; his paternal grandparents built the cottage before Larry was born. He had the fondest memories of time spent there with his grandparents, several months each summer. Larry described the cottage as comfortable, set on a private piece of land with a great water view. Larry had a very evident appreciation for all that Provincetown had to offer: the art, the music, theater, and the great and diverse restaurants. He suggested, there was uniqueness to its culture, influenced, to a degree, by the gay community and the visitors from the world over. Larry said that he does his best writing at the cottage; he enjoyed the coming alive of spring, the vibrancy of the summer months, the beauty of the fall, and the quiet solitude of the winter months. Larry told me he had a small but wonderful group of friends in Provincetown, and I would be meeting them. Some friends were year-round residents, others enjoyed Provincetown with their second homes. As an aside, Larry said most of these dear friends were straight.

The conversation turned to what we hope to accomplish and our individual objectives for the weekend. Larry began by laying out his work habits, practices, needs, wants, expectations, and preferences. We melded this with the general modus operandi of P&W and my approach to working with an author. I discussed the staff supporting the project, assuring Larry that they were the best in the business. We enjoyed a healthy give-and-take. A good hour of discussion found us on the same page. I was the note-taker, promising to summarize and report to Larry and my staff. We quickly agreed, the first order of business would be for Larry to spend a block of time, thinking out loud, with the dialogue focused on developing a more definitive approach to the book. I had studied Larry's original pro-spectus. I also shared this with my staff. The fundamen-tal concept for the work was clear. Larry and I both recognized the need for the author to flesh out the plan for development of his underlying assumptions: the author's reservations about the process of examining the life of a long- deceased person and questions and research needs the author had for his yet unnamed advisers. All of this would be essential for the editorial team to understand. This piece of work, as developed, would be circulated to the editorial staff for comment.

Next, it was agreed, we needed to develop an overall timeline for the project. The front end of this involved discussing what research support the author would require. I had given the subject some very serious thought and had a few suggestions. Father Aloysius Murphy SJ, in residence at Fordham University, was a resource I had known for several years. We were not related. Father Murphy worked with me on two projects. Aloysius held BA/MA/PhD degrees in history, from Yale, the Sorbonne, and the University of Chicago. In addition, he held advanced degrees in theology and is a doctor of canon law from the Pontifical Gregorian College in Rome. Father Murphy was the author of many scholarly works including *Why Saints* (2016). He was the Vatican-appointed advocate for the cause of Archbishop Fulton J. Sheen, a candidate proposed for sainthood. The good father was bright, energetic, and extremely well connected, both in the US, worldwide, and most particularly in Rome. To the point, Father Murphy knew the process for recognizing a person as a saint and can arrange informative interviews in Rome and with people close to a chosen candidate/situation elsewhere in the world. Father Murphy would be an excellent resource for research, as a critical reader, and provide a unique entry to the Catholic church.

I also recommended a Dr. Thomas Harwood, BA/MA/PhD in history from Fordham, Columbia, Harvard. Harwood was currently a full professor at Harvard. As with Father Murphy, I had worked with him in the past. He was meticulous, energetic, and reliable. Tom is both an extremely skilled research resource and an excellent critical reader. Coincidentally, Harwood and Murphy had worked together over several years and are close friends.

Both gentlemen will require contracts, retainers, and hourly rates of compensation, expenses, etc. Travel to selected sites will add to the author's knowledge and feel for a subject. With Assisi and Rome, Italy, for Saint Francis; Calcutta and Kolkata, India, for Saint Teresa; New Delhi for Gandhi. Murphy and/or Harwood would accompany Larry on these trips. With visits to Rome, Father Murphy would be able to gain unique access to those closest to the process of creating a saint.

The master timeline will flow from the author's production of manuscript and P&W's processing, fact-checking, editing, design, etc. A carefully choreographed process from day one to the day the book came off the press.

We took a needed rest stop, and each ordered a large coffee. We agreed that the time spent in the car had been most productive and a break had been earned, a great idea! Back in the car, we relaxed to classical music. We approached the Bourne Bridge onto Cape Cod just ahead of the usual rush hour traffic. The traffic on the Mid Cape Highway, which was mostly only two lanes, wasn't too bad, and we approached Provincetown after an easy hour. I could sense Larry's positive vibe and shared the same, with an added sense of excitement. The approach to Larry's cottage, on the ocean side of the thin neck of land, quickly changed from a paved road to a dirt but well-maintained road, clearly marked as Private Property. The landscape was wooded with pine and various hardwood trees. You could just make out a few homes well back from the road. A good half mile in, we came to a crest and a side road; driving a fair distance into the property, we came up to a clearing and the cottage. Wow!

Larry parked the car, and we gathered our bags and walked along a pathway to the front door. Rosebushes abound, still in bloom. The cottage appeared to be antique, done very much in the Cape style with clapboard siding. The property seemed extensive. Larry said as we walked, "I had told you the cottage was originally built by my paternal grandparents before I was born. I am the only child and only grandchild of very wealthy grandparents and parents, all of whom have passed away. My inheritance from them has allowed me to live an independent and very comfortable life. I want to explain this, which I very seldom do, so you do not wonder how all of this is possible. I have had a full-time couple in residence, Tomas, and his wife Semmi. They have been with the family for a number of years. Between them, they care for the grounds, keep the house in order, keep the pantry stocked, cook, and serve meals and generally make my life on the Cape worry free. They have a very comfortable apartment over the garage, I know you will enjoy meeting them."

As we approached the front door, it opened, and a couple welcomed us. Larry gave them warm hugs and made the introductions.

"Kevin, here we have Tomas and Semmi. They have known me since I was a teenager, spending weeks here with my grandparents. They are my Cape Cod family."

The couple were both short with gray hair and ready smiles. Tomas was from a long line of Cape Cod Portuguese and Semmi is also Portuguese, although her name was oddly Islamic in origin.

The cottage opened into a large foyer, with a living room visible to the left and a dining room to the right. A staircase to an upper level was braced on the side wall. It was apparent, the external look of the cottage is deceptive; it was much more extensive than it had appeared. Straight ahead is a large family room. First impressions, throughout, are of understated quality in every sense.

"I'll give you the grand tour after we get settled in," suggested Larry. "Let me take you to your room."

The guest room was large, with a king-sized bed, a sitting area in front of a fireplace, and an en suite full bath. The room had extensive east-facing windows with a partial view of the water through the trees. With a knock on the door, I opened to Larry.

"Let's do the grand tour. You'll see, I have kept my grandparents' and parents' wonderful antique pieces, accumulated over many years. I've judiciously mixed these with a few contemporary pieces."

The flow of the house was designed for relaxed living and, I would guess, entertaining on a large scale. There were more fireplaces in the living room, dining room, and in a book-lined study/library. Larry said that on days when the weather cooperates, he would work on the extensive deck, on the rear of the house. With inclement weather, he would work in the study with a fire burning. The deck,

I noticed, with its partial view of the water, had a Jacuzzi, ample seating, and a firepit. The kitchen had every convenience you could imagine. Larry said Semmi was more than a cook, a chef beyond compare! My parents would flip over the antique Orientals. They had collected over the years on a modest scale. Along with the fine carpets and antique furniture, the walls displayed a superb collection of both antique and contemporary art. Larry gave a summary: there are five bedrooms, three with en suite baths; two other full baths; two half baths; six fireplaces; a finished basement with a small home theater and a wine cellar. The living room, dining room, study, family room, and professionally equipped kitchen took up the downstairs. The three-car garage also has a small gym and a large apartment for Tomas and Semmi. Who wouldn't love to spend time in this setting?

Larry announced, "I've made dinner reservations for seven thirty at the best seafood restaurant on the Cape. That gives us time for a cocktail before dinner."

I had given Larry a couple of bottles of wine as a house gift. He said, "Your 2018 Pouilly-Fumé Cuvée d'Eve would be just right."

We sat on the deck, enjoying the briny breeze and the fine wine. Life was *good!* We left for dinner. Traffic was predictably heavy as we came into town. Larry demonstrated his knowledge of P-town and maneuvers through back streets to the restaurant, the Impudent Oyster. Parking looked impossible! Larry pulled into a driveway marked Private. My host was not only knowledgeable but also apparently well connected in town. There was a long line at the front door. Larry took my arm and guided me to a side door. A waiter greeted us, "Good to see you, Mr. O'Neil, your table is ready, right this way."

The seating was choice, with just enough daylight left to see Provincetown Harbor. The maître d' came to the table. "Good to see you, Larry. The lobster you ordered is a beauty, ready for your guest to choose how he would prefer it prepared. For you, Larry, I have your favorite, a nice-sized striped bass, just off the boat. The kitchen is offering clams fra diavolo as a starter tonight. The clams on the half shell would also be excellent. George will be over for your drink order. Enjoy dinner!"

The sommelier came to the table. "Mr. O'Neil, my special order came in just this afternoon. I have one of your favorites, a Margaux Pavillon Blanc 2018."

"Wonderful, George, we'll have that with dinner."

Our waiter came and asked if we were ready to order drinks. I would have a vodka martini dry, a lemon twist, and straight up. Larry held up two fingers and said, "Make that two, mine with an olive."

With drinks in hand, we ordered dinner. Larry would have the clams fra diavolo and the striped bass grilled. I ordered the lobster steamed, with clams on the half shell as a starter.

The food was, as Larry promised, simply outstanding! Dinner unrushed, we enjoyed the wine, a second bottle in fact. Larry talked a good deal about his personal life.

"I rarely, if ever, mix my personal life and my professional/business dealings. As I told you, I have a wonderful circle of friends here on the Cape, several of whom also live in the city. George and I travel and have many acquaintances around the world, although very few real friends. I want to tell you how greatly I envy the relationships between you, Natalie, Ann, and Helene. You obviously care deeply for each other. The simple joy you find in each other's company is so evident. The range and dynamics of your conversations and your hedonistic love of good food and wines makes for such a marvelous group of people. You and

Natalie are at ease in accepting the relationship between Ann and Helene and my relationship with George. I am drawn to you all and would very much like to develop a friendship with you individually and with all of you as a group."

I paused before I reacted. "Personally, I am flattered and pleased with your invitation to be more than work associates. I think it important that we both acknowledge, there simply can never be any conflict between us as author/editor and us as friends. I am comfortable that we recognize that delineation and can smoothly inhabit both roles. I would be delighted to be your friend! I know each of the ladies will be pleased with your suggestion, and I would encourage you to approach each individually, extending that invitation."

We toasted the idea with an excellent brandy!

It was now past our bedtime, and we had an early start on what would be a busy day. Larry settled the check. We were home safely, and we are off to our bedrooms. My bag had been unpacked, the bed turned down, and my pajamas were laid out. Such luxury, I could quickly learn to love this lifestyle!

Hoping Natalie might still be up, I dialed her number.

"Hi, sweetheart. How was the drive, the Cape, and how are you and Larry getting along?"

I gave her a full report: the productive time in the car, the incredible cottage, our excellent dinner, and how very well Larry and I were bonding. Natalie gave me an update on the China project. Plans were jelling nicely, and the timing could be moved up. It now looked like her first trip to China would be the first part of September for about two weeks.

"That's great. I am excited for you. We have an early start on the day planned. Larry and I are both early risers. I love you, Natalie, sleep well."

The sunrise was beautiful! I showered, dressed, and wandered down to the kitchen. Larry served coffee.

"Semmi is preparing a Cape Cod breakfast, blueberry pancakes, and bacon, I hope that appeals to you. The weather is great, why don't we eat outside?"

We moved out to the deck where a table had already been set. Within a few minutes, Tomas brought out orange juice, a coffee tureen, and maple syrup. Semmi followed a few minutes later with a platter of pancakes overlaid with crisp bacon strips. Finishing our breakfast, we decided to work outside, enjoying the sunshine and ocean breeze. We brought our laptops and briefcases and set up shop; Tomas cleared the table and left fresh coffee.

"I've been thinking about your suggestion of Father Murphy as a consultant and critical reader. His background is impressive, and it will compensate for my admittedly sparse understanding of the whole sainthood business. Additionally, as you said, he has unique access at the highest levels in the Catholic church. I find his role as the advocate for Fulton Sheen to be very interesting. Sheen could be a possible subject, a saint in the making. I am moving toward the possibility of adding ordinary mortals to my list of possible subjects. As we have discussed, Mahatma Gandhi could be an excellent candidate."

I thought about Larry's comments. "I'm glad you are considering Father Aloysius. I think Fulton Sheen, as a widely known contemporary and active candidate for sainthood has great possibilities, however, it could be a bit tricky. The focus would need to be confined to the process per se, not the attributes of the candidate for sainthood. It would be a 'half a loaf' situation. Father Murphy could find himself in an awkward position, one he simply would have to avoid."

Larry was typing furiously as I talked. He was thinking as well as recording some of my thoughts/comments. I continued, "I very much like the idea of looking at ordinary mortals alongside the holy ones, as we call them. It will allow you to consider two very different pathways to greatness and differing objectives and perhaps different motivations."

Again, Larry was pecking away.

"Excellent observations, but you look concerned. What's on your mind?"

"To be frank," I hesitated, "I'm concerned that I am flirting with violating our author/editor relationship. Have I gone beyond being the midwife?"

With great emphasis, Larry said, "No, your observations and suggestions are certainly helpful to this author as I refine *my* sense of the work I am undertaking. Your thoughts and reasoning are excellent. I couldn't be more pleased! Rest assured, I will always be frank with you, and hopefully, you will be equally frank with me."

The morning literally flew by, and we moved on to developing a broad calendar, dealing with a host of logistical matters. My stomach called out a need for lunch. Magically, Tomas appeared and announced lunch, to be served in the kitchen. Larry, the perfect host, had preordered. A traditional Cape Cod chowder, followed by a cold seafood salad, warm homemade corn muffins, and an excellent well-chilled white wine. As we enjoyed lunch, Larry smiled.

"As I recall, you are fond of French food. We have a sterling French restaurant in town, Les Poissons. It is small, and the owner/hostess is a very dear friend. We have a dinner reservation for this evening."

Again, the perfect host.

We finished our luncheon with strawberries over vanilla ice cream. Taking our coffee back out to the deck, we returned to our work. The calendar needed to be refined. We both recognized Larry's need to meet with both Father Murphy and Tom Harwood and determine if he and they could work together. I would then need to put together time commitments, availability, compensation, travel schedules, etc. Larry would need to outline specific research projects and his information needs.

The plan was to finalize the book's cast of characters and the shape of the plot by the end of the summer. This assumed both Dr. Harwood and Father Murphy being on board and available for consultation. Critical next step would be establishing who were to be seen/interviewed, where, and when. A heavy travel schedule would ideally be developed for late fall through early spring of the next year. Retainers, hourly rates, etc., also need to be addressed.

I proposed calling both Fr. Murphy and Tom Harwood and outlining the project and suggesting a meeting with Larry, if possible, within the next two weeks. Larry agreed and I went to the den to place the calls. Neither Tom nor Aloysius were available. I left messages to get back to me at their earliest convenience. I took the time to check my emails and phone calls. I answered most of the emails, made referrals to several to staff, and then addressed my call list. Both my major authors had called, reporting that writing was going well; in fact, both said, "Very well," and each thanked me for being one super editor! I called both and enjoyed basking in our mutual regard for each other. Each had a few points which we comfortably dealt with, and we made our goodbyes. Other calls: Kevin, my financial adviser, to clear several transactions, dealing with a tax issue and, most important, according to him, to confirm my hosting our next poker game! Katie had called, asking for information on my Christmas guest; what was going on? Both HSW and Annie had called; no need to return their calls, each hoped all was going well. I gave Natalie a quick call, no answer, left a message: "Miss you."

Returning to the deck, I saw Larry in the den on the phone; he waved. I found a pitcher of iced tea and a plate of interesting cookies on the table. Larry joined me.

"George sends his regards and wishes he were here."

The next order of business focused on an overview of the author's concept for the book, elaborating on Larry's earlier proposal. I would use this to roundtable with my staff, drawing together comments, questions, and suggestions for Larry's information. Larry suggested that he participate in the staff discussions.

"Not a good idea. The staff would be too guarded in their comments."

"The book concept is very straightforward on first appearance but is in fact inherently complex. With an evident and needed lack of cynicism, you are striving to understand the commitment and heroics of a selected group of people. People who have been accorded the highest levels of esteem. You are looking at the purity of their lives, validating the absence of any ulterior motives. Have the accolades afforded to them been given to further or serve institutional interests?"

There followed a long silence.

Larry got up from his seat and walked to the railing. He seemed to be just staring out to the sea. Without turning, he said, "Kevin, I have never had the experience of another person who can so precisely understand my creative thoughts. George, as you know, is very close to me emotionally and intellectually. Yet he doesn't see and understand the process of my thinking, feelings, and intellect as I translate those to words on paper. Those words on paper bring the whole of me to something called a novel. You understand that!"

I got up and walked over to Larry. I offered my hand; he took it, and we gave each other a hug.

Both our phones rang. Larry went back to the den as I took a call from Aloysius Murphy. After exchanging pleasantries, I explained the purpose of my call. He, of course, knew who Larry O'Neil was and had read both his novels. I sensed an initial coolness. I took time to deal in some depth with the author's concept for the book. I assured Aloysius it *is not* an exposé.

"Kevin, on the face of it, the concept intrigues me. However, I need to assure myself I am not put in an unacceptable or compromising situation and my connections in the church could not, in any way, be embarrassed or inadvertently misused."

"Father, I completely understand. Aside from my reassurances, you need to sit down with O'Neil and put your concerns on the table."

"That's a great idea, Kevin. I would like to do that. I am in the city Thursday and Friday of next week. I could do dinner either night if that fits Mr. O'Neil's calendar."

"I am with Larry at the moment, give me a minute and let me check his calendar."

I rushed into the den, explaining I had Father Murphy on the line with two possible dates for lunch or dinner. Larry reached for my phone.

"Father Murphy, this is Larry O'Neil. I'm free for either lunch or dinner Thursday or lunch on Friday. If your schedule is tight, we can meet for a drink at your pleasure. I am really looking forward to meeting you and discussing my book concept."

"You are too kind, an early dinner Thursday night would be just fine."

"That's great. I will put something together and give you a call with the particulars."

Larry ended the call with a smile on his face!

We were back on the deck.

"Great and productive day, time for cocktails before dinner."

Larry buzzed for Tomas, who appeared in a flash. "Two of your finest vodka martinis please, one with a lemon twist, and mine, as you know, with an olive."

We were both dressed in shorts and, after our drink, went to change for dinner.

Just as I was leaving my room, the phone rang.

"Aloysius Murphy here, I just wanted to thank you for the introduction to Larry O'Neil. I must tell you, I am intrigued with the subject matter and his concept of the book, but to be honest, I have reservations having to do with my personal involvement. I will need to get my superior's okay. I am looking forward to meeting with Larry next week. Again, thanks, Kevin."

I reassured him that he will find the man as interesting as the book proposal. We agreed to talk after the dinner meeting. I told Larry about the phone call; he was pleased. He asked if I would join them for dinner. With no need to be involved, I declined.

"The conversation will need to be very focused, and the two of you need to connect on several levels. You will be each taking the measure of the other person. I think a third party would interfere with that process."

"Point well made," agreed Larry.

The drive to dinner took us through downtown P-town out toward the beaches. It was a weekend night, and the town was jumping! The evening was just great with a light ocean breeze. As we approached the far end of town, we turned into a lane that could easily have been missed. Sitting at the end of the short lane is Les Poissons, with a million-dollar view of the water. Our arrival coincided with the sun setting, the water ablaze. The restaurant is quite small and sat in a still, flowering courtyard, more like a charming private home than a commercial restaurant. The door opened to a foyer with a view of the dining room, small and very intimate with only ten or so tables. A woman, obviously well on in years, beautifully dressed, greeted us, smiling, "Bonne soirée mon cher."

She greeted Larry with a kiss on each cheek. Kissing her hand, Larry smiled. "Tu es magnifique, ma chérie."

I was introduced as a dear friend, warmly welcomed by our hostess, Madam Fontaine. To demonstrate my fluency in French, I commented on the charm of the dining room setting as madam led us to our table. She was pleased. Our waiter greeted Larry. Apparently, Mr. O'Neil was a valued regular. We ordered our usual martinis and studied what was a very interesting menu, with so many tantalizing seafood dishes. For starters, the evening menu offered moules marinières, a classical presentation of mussels. My eye locked on a main course offering of coquilles Saint-Jacques. My favorite French seafood dish! Scallops baked in a decadent sauce of butter, shallots, mushrooms, and white wine, topped with a fine Gruyère. My choice was made! Larry selected the sole meunière. We both ordered the mussels to start. Our drinks arrived with an offering of cheeses, a pâté du maison, and olives.

Larry asked if he might be excused for just a few minutes. He traversed the small room, stopping at several tables for brief chats. P-town was a place where Larry was well-known, and he is so much at home. He apologized for leaving me alone, "I truly love New York City, but when I am here on the Cape, I gear down to a level of peace and contentment I've never found in the city or elsewhere in my world travels. There is chemistry here between the ocean, the dunes, the change of seasons, the vibrancy of the summers, the invigorating fall weather and the storms at sea, the tranquility of the winter months in front of the fireplace, and then the colorful emergence of spring. Add to all of this, there is always interesting admixture of people, the artists, commercial fishermen, the amateur anglers, writers, and poets, musicians across the spectrum, classical to hard rock, the tradesmen and working folks, the lost souls, the young and the old, the mixture of gay people and straight people. The gay community of P-town and visitors from around the world have a sense of joy and community that is rare. Putting aside the wilder, uninhibited behavior of some people acting out, usually under the influence, we all quietly and simply enjoy being ourselves, accepting and being accepted, for who we are!"

We placed our dinner order, and the sommelier came to the table and greeted us in French. After a lively discussion, we settled on a Margaux Pavillon Blanc 2019, the same wine I had brought as a house gift. Words fail me in describing dinner. It was truly outstanding from start to finish! The presentation, the pace of service, the attention of the serving staff, and the ambiance were simply beyond compare. Madam Fontaine came to the table and asked to join us for an after-dinner digestif. The sommelier presented a tray with calvados, cognac, Armagnac, and cut-glass snifters. It turns out Madam has a somewhat outrageous sense of humor. Compliments were offered on my French fluency.

It was observed humor in any language is often highly nuanced. After too many excellent cognacs and with hugs, we left Les Poissons. The air as we drove back through town was literally throbbing, Friday night in P-town! Back at the cottage, we bid each other good night, with breakfast planned for 7:00 a.m. My bed was turned down and my pajamas laid out! I must remember to tell Natalie.

Ready for bed, I called Natalie. She was still up and waiting for my call.

"We had a productive day and capped it off with another super seafood dinner. I could really get use to this lifestyle."

I told her of Larry's outstanding role as a host, the service of the staff and the vibrancy of P-town. We agreed, the Cape would have to be on our near-term, short list of getaways. Natalie said she had an excellent long Zoom meeting with the woman who had been chosen as her China-based collaborator. Dr. Hu, her UN superior, was pleased with the selection. It had been his first choice. He was very familiar with the individual's qualifications and experience and had briefed Natalie in depth prior to their first Zoom meeting.

"Her name is Chu Hua, which means 'chrysanthemum.' Her English is excellent. Chu Hua studied abroad and earned a PhD from Oxford with a focus on world cultures."

She is a few years older, Natalie guessed, and single.

"Chu Hua is a full professor, teaching world cultures at Tsinghua University in Beijing. The university is ranked number one in China and seventeenth, worldwide. Dr. Hua is highly regarded in China and internationally. Looking at our individual calendars and commitments, we have both committed to an early September startup, with me initially spending about two weeks in Beijing for detailed planning. We have also agreed that I would speak either Mandarin or Cantonese to her and she would speak English or French to me. I am so excited!"

We chatted for a few more minutes and signed off with my promise to call Saturday night.

*****

Saturday morning: breakfast at seven o'clock and then to work. It was a rainy and somewhat chilly day, we decided to set up shop in the den. Tomas started a fire to take the chill out of the air, as we settled into comfortable, oversized chairs. We began by discussing Larry's familiarity with saints in general and Saint Francis of Assisi and Mother Teresa of India in particular. We also talked about the Catholic church's approach to recognizing/creating saints. We shared what we each knew of two additional candidates currently under consideration, Archbishop Fulton J. Sheen and Pope Pius XII. Mahatma Gandhi continued as a prospect if Larry were to choose to include ordinary people in his list of subjects. Having been raised Catholic, I had a fair understanding of how the church goes about considering candidates for sainthood. I was also familiar with the lives of Saint Francis and Mother Teresa. Larry's knowledge was more generalized. We both know of Pius XII and were quite familiar with our contemporary, the TV personality, Fulton Sheen; his reruns are still being aired.

We focused on Dr. Thomas Harwood. I suggested he would be excellent researching and preparing concise briefs on potential candidates, adding a deep historical perspective on their times. I knew Tom to also be an excellent critical reader/fact-checker. I recommended we follow the same approach we had taken with Father Murphy. When Tom Harwood returned my call, I would outline the project, detailing the needed support, the timelines we were working with, discuss his calendar and commitments, the business arrangements, and his initial interest. If it appeared it could come together, Larry would call to schedule a meeting and determine mutual interest. We agreed on the game plan. We spent the next hour developing and fleshing out what Larry would need in the background briefs we might ask Harwood to develop.

My phone indicated that Harwood had returned my call. I went into the office and dialed his number. After exchanging pleasantries, I launched into a discussion of the project and our need for his support.

"As you know, Kevin, Aloysius Murphy and I have worked together on a number of projects, including several with you. We are also personal friends in addition to being colleagues. Without violating confidences, Aloysius called to discuss the project. I told him it was interesting, *but* I could see tripping over assumed intent versus fact in looking at the church's process of creating saints."

"That is an insightful observation, Aloysius has raised the same point. As I have explained to our mutual friend, the author has absolutely no intent of writing an exposé or in any way attacking the Catholic church and its process of creating or acknowledging a person as a saint. Given Father Murphy's position in the church, we recognize this is critical to his decision to join the project or not! O'Neil's focus is on the why questions, in terms of choices made, the verifiable facts separated from and isolating conjecture. In dealing with conjecture, which in cases of subjects long removed in time, will be the challenge. The acknowledgment of any bit of critical conjecture must be transparent and rationalized. Harwood accepts the approach as reasonable, likening it however, to the task of threading a needle."

"With your call, I checked my calendar and longer-term commitments. I am just wrapping up my latest book within the next weeks. As already planned, I will have a reduced teaching load over the next several semesters, with just several PhD candidates for whom I am serving as their dissertation adviser. As you know, I use my assistants on a number of research projects in addition to handling part of my classroom hours. It happens, I have an unusually brilliant young lady close to wrapping up her PhD. She could be an excellent asset to the project."

"Larry O'Neil and Father Murphy have a dinner meeting scheduled for Thursday night. This is an opportunity to frankly discuss the project, any reservations or problems, and decide if the personal chemistry is right."

I suggested taking the same approach.

"How is your calendar next week?"

"Lunch would work for me, either Tuesday or Friday," offered Tom.

I was aware of Larry's calendar/commitments.

"That would work for Larry. How about lunch Tuesday say one o'clock at the Dove?"

We agreed on the date, time, and place.

"We'll talk after your luncheon. Call me if you have questions before. Thanks, Tom, for getting back to me."

I went back to the den.

"The call from Tom Harwood went well." I would respect Tom's confidential conversation with Aloysius. "He raised several points and reservations as had Father Murphy. He finds the project uniquely challenging, carefully threading a needle. He would welcome the opportunity to meet with you, discussing the book concept in depth, and allowing each to assess personal chemistry. His longer-term calendar is fairly well open, and he has extremely good support on the research side. Knowing your calendar, I've booked lunch with Tom, one o'clock next Tuesday at the Dove."

Larry laughed. "My god, Murphy, you are superefficient!"

Tomas served lunch in the den. We worked until around three thirty and agreed on a break to catch up with the rest of the world. As the weather was clearing, Larry suggested a relaxing soak in the hot tub before cocktails and dinner. We agreed to meet on the deck around five thirty. Dinner was to be at our usual seven thirty. My host had not indicated our dinner plans. He did say it was a surprise! I went up to my room and got to work on my emails and calls. I talked briefly with Annie, covering several business issues and updating her on the progress with Larry. The boss was pleased. She told me, Helene, Natalie, and she were having dinner Sunday night.

"Give my best to Helene, and thank you both for including Natalie."

I called my folks and had a long chat with both online. Mom asked if I had plans for Thanksgiving.

"Natalie and I have tentative plans to spend the holiday on Cape Cod."

I reported that Natalie and I had finalized the plans for our families' get-together for New Year's Eve. Reservations had already been made, at the Waldorf, for both sets of parents. Dinner, black tie, would be at the Dove, details to follow. Dad said they had chatted with Patrick about a visit to England, and it looked like Thanksgiving might work.

I called the office. Jane had a few questions about the office layout, budget, and my future commitments. All was well. She is worth her weight in gold. Mary-Ellen had lots of questions and several issues. She is proving to be very much on top of her game. I was particularly impressed with her review of sample manuscript and book proposals. I talked with my two favorite authors, both of whom had called. They each had several questions. They reported the writing was going very well. I so enjoyed these interactions.

I had plowed through my work list with great efficiency. The clock showed four thirty. I put away my work and took a thirty-minute nap. I saw a bathrobe, slippers, and an oversized towel had been laid out.

"Thank you, Semmi."

I was off to the tub! I stripped down, pulled on my bathrobe, slipped into the comfortable slippers, hung my towel over my arm, and was off to the hot tub. Good rule of thumb: restrict alcohol consumption when going into a hot tub! We allowed ourselves a miniature martini, one only! Tomas had a plate of hors d'oeuvres set up on a side table.

"You are not only efficient, Mr. Murphy, you are also super punctual! Are you ready for the hot tub? It's just at one hundred degrees."

Larry stood up and moved to the ladder, removed his bathrobe, and went straight in. Larry was super fit and tan all over, save for the important family jewels. I disrobed and gingerly entered the tub.

"My god, Kevin, you are way too thin, and you absolutely need to spend more time in the sun."

As we soaked, I asked, "I am really curious about dinner tonight, any hints?"

"You'll know all you need to know as we arrive," Larry said with a chuckle.

The hot tub was the perfect way to step down from a productive but intense workday. I could not be more pleased with the progress we've made and the great rapport established between author and editor. After about forty-five minutes, we exited the hot tub, pulled on our robes, and reclined on the comfortable chaise lounges. After fifteen minutes, our heart rates were back to normal, and we could enjoy a full martini; Tomas saw to that immediately.

"I have to tell you, Larry, I could adjust to this lifestyle very easily. Thank you for being a great host. We have accomplished all that I had hoped for and then some. I have fallen in love with the Cape and P-town. Natalie and I have tentative plans for getting away for Thanksgiving, the Cape is now number one on our short list."

Larry rolled toward me. "From a work point of view, like you, I am very pleased at what we have accomplished. We work very well together. On a personal note, while I am social, I am very slow to make friends and can be very private. I've found it comfortable, sharing personal thoughts and feelings with you. The bonus of our working together is, I hope, we may be finding a friendship. As I had said at dinner last night, I also hope I can add Helene, Annie, and Natalie to my small list of special people."

Finishing our drink, it was time to dress for dinner.

"Any particular dress code for this evening?"

Adding to the mystery, Larry laughed, "Come as you are will be just fine."

After dressing, we met in the foyer and walked to the car. We took the main road away from town. Just as we were about to cross out of the town of Provincetown, Larry took a paved road to the right, leading down toward the Bay. There were several significant homes on the road, all with great views of the Bay and outer Provincetown. Nearly to the water's edge, Larry turned into a dirt road and approached a very large, much older traditional Cape Cod with a widow's walk and a wraparound porch, giving an unobstructed view of the Bay and, I'd guess, even the lights of Boston on a clear night.

"This is the home of my dearest Provincetown friend, Allen Templeton. He is an artist and very highly regarded internationally. Allen travels worldwide and frequently, but this is his primary home and his studio. We will be joined for dinner by six of our close friends, some living here year-round, others, like me, spend as much time here as we can manage. I wanted you to meet them all, giving you an evening off from listening to me ramble."

I knew Templeton by reputation. I have enjoyed viewing several of his works in the collection of MOMA. He was indeed known worldwide. His works generally were very large abstracts and sold for a great deal of money. Coincidentally, Natalie was a *huge* fan of Templeton. She would be so envious of my evening!

All the makings of a rare evening, the setting, the art on display, and an unusual eclectic group of people as it turned out. Allen Templeton, an attentive host, introduced me around the room. I was pleased to see Madam Fontaine.

We greeted each other almost as long-lost friends. Tom Hopper, a black man, was a musician, singing and playing the piano with a popular band in P-town. The young man was very outgoing. In chatting later in the evening, I learned, in his off-Cape life, he was a professional cellist playing with the Boston Symphony. Tom frequented weekends on the Cape and longer visits when the Symphony was on holiday. He is not just *a* cello player, one of several—he is *the* number one. Tom is internationally recognized and had several recordings to his credit. A couple, Theresa and Sergei Soldatov, both with ready laughs, were New York City folks, who like most of the others, have second homes in P-town and were here frequently throughout the year. Theresa is British, a published poet. Sergei was older, with a heavy accent, and is a well-known international financial maven. The couple were attractive, both with a studied presentation. I recognized the name from the social columns and knew of their involvement with several major art museums. Larry introduced me to a young woman with striking green hair. Alina Alberto, it seemed, was now a tattoo artist. Reportedly, she changed occupations each year. She lived in P-town year-round, with frequent international trips. Alina was from Italy and had a delightful accent. Her family, I was told later in the evening, are very old Italian nobility, with substantial land holdings, including several vineyards of note. Alina was fascinating. She spoke several languages fluently, was a gourmet cook, and could discuss economics, politics, religion, world affairs, art, music, contemporary issues, sports, wines, and much more with ease and with a deep understanding of the subject! I learned later the name Alina was both Greek and German, meaning "truth and noble." She is the self-appointed property guardian for all the friends in the group. Alina checked their properties whenever they are off the Cape. Everyone, of course, had a caretaker; it didn't matter! She was an extremely unusual and interesting young lady!

The last guest arrived a bit late. There had been an awfully bad accident on Route 6, and traffic was backed up. Phillip Arenstein was a middle-aged, very tall, and thin man with very little hair. Phillip wore the thickest glasses I have ever seen. The gentleman is a practicing psychiatrist from New York City. He had a profound and serious look about him. Phillip lost his wife of twenty-five years to cancer some two years ago. P-town was his home away from home. The bonds of deep friendship are so apparent between the people gathered for dinner.

The cocktail hour, more like cocktail hours, in addition to readily replenished drinks by an attentive staff also had exotic hors d'oeuvres passed, each more interesting than the one before! All were in a jovial mood as dinner was announced. The dining room was large but made an intimate setting for our dinner party. I was seated, with Madam Fontaine to my left and Phillip Arenstein to my right, joined by Theresa Soldatov to Phillip's right.

Opposite found Alina between Larry and Tom, joined by Sergei. Allen hosted from the head of the table.

Dinner was a served buffet. Bountiful fails to describe. Food, both cold and hot, baked, stuffed lobster, poached salmon, shrimp larger than any I had ever seen, a standing rib roast, a wide choice of vegetables and sauces. There was more, I just do not recall. Serving were two very attentive, well-trained staff. The wine choices were absolutely the very best! Conversation was animated, well lubricated by the cocktails and wine. English is spoken, most of the time, but there were side conversations in French.

Larry had said that he was slow to form friendships, but over the years, he had certainly managed to put together a fine group of friends on the Cape. Being a small world and so many of us being from the city, it turned out we had a number of friends or social connections in common. Phillip Arenstein knew Helene quite well, both being practicing psychiatrists on the Upper East Side. The Soldatovs travel in the same social circles as Helene. HSW, with his passion for the opera and being out on the cultural/social scene, saw the Soldatovs quite frequently.

The evening rolled into the proverbial wee hours of the morning. I was glad I had broken away before dinner for a very quick call to Natalie. She thought I was kidding when I told her who was hosting dinner. Around 1:00 a.m., with handshakes and hugs exchanged, we took our leave. I thanked Allen for a wonderful evening. On the drive home, Larry commented, "We both agree that we have had several highly productive days and are in great shape going forward. I checked the weather, and Sunday is a definite beach day. We need to work on your pallor! Let's really break training and sleep in, with breakfast at say eight o'clock, and then off to the beach."

We arrived safely back at the cottage. I thanked Larry again for the great evening and the introduction to his friends. I was really looking forward to the beach.

I did not manage a sleep in; old habits prevailed. I was up, showered and dressed by seven fifteen, and called Natalie. We had plenty of time to rehash last night's surprise dinner, the house, the guests, the food, the great conversations, and of course, the artwork on display. Natalie was particularly interested in Allen Templeton. She had met the Soldatovs a few times, on the New York City social circle.

"I am having dinner with Annie and Helene tonight. I am sure Helene will know Phillip Arenstein, and they will certainly know the Soldatovs. I will give them a full report on your wonderful evening."

We covered her developing China plan, as we had begun to describe the project. Each time the subject came up, she was so excited and enthused! Our plans for Christmas and New Year's Eve were beginning to come together nicely. Her parents were excited to meet my parents *and* me.

"Time for breakfast. The weather is spectacular, and the beach should be fun. Give the girls my best, love you."

I joined Larry on the deck as Tomas served breakfast.

"Natalie sends her best. She is so taken with my report on your surprise dinner. Templeton is, by far, her favorite artist, and she has met the Soldatovs several times. I hope we can visit with Allen when we are on the Cape for Thanksgiving."

Larry smiled. "It would please me immensely if you and Natalie will use the cottage for your visit to the Cape. Peter and I will be in London for ten days, so the house is completely available, and Tomas and Semmi will take good care of you. I know Allen will be in Provincetown for the holiday, and of course, Madam Fontaine will be at Les Poissons. Don't know the other folks' plans, but that will develop."

I was taken aback by Larry's generosity. "Larry, you are a superb host, an editor's dream as an author, and a wonderful friend. Your generosity knows no bounds. Natalie and I would be delighted to enjoy the cottage for our Thanksgiving visit to the Cape."

"Good that is settled, we can work the details out later. Kevin, I have shared with you that I have been greatly blessed with material gifts, and I cherish the few good friends that I have acquired. Nothing pleases me more than to share my good bounty with friends."

After a great breakfast, we were off to the beach. Tomas had put a picnic basket, cooler, and beach chairs in the truck.

"We have two choices for the beach. The dunes beach is very popular and bathing suits are required. The other is far out on the neck and is bathing-suits optional, the second is less crowded. The water is somewhat colder and the waves bigger. If you're not uncomfortable, Kevin, I prefer the second beach."

I was dressed in shorts. "I'm okay with your favorite beach, I didn't pack a bathing suit, so I will just lay out in my shorts."

"No problem, I have a couple of suits in my bag, and we'll find one to fit you. I start out in my bathing suit, get several hours of sunbathing, with frequent swims in the buff. You can borrow a suit, which will be better than your shorts for sunbathing and for the water." Laughing as he did. "I assume you may not be ready for total public nudity."

The drive to the beach took forty-five minutes with the heavy weekend traffic. Larry found a great parking spot within easy walking distance to the beach. We saw a good spot and set up our chairs and an umbrella. The beach was well populated but not crowded.

"We can change at the beach house. There are lockers, a john, and showers."

Larry led the way, a short distance. As we walked, several people greeted Larry. I would say the people on the beach were 70 percent male and 30 percent female. Although a good number wore bathing attire, many were nude or partially so. At the beach house, we went into the locker room and to adjoining lockers. Larry opened his beach bag, sorted through it for a minute, and handed me a bathing suit.

"That's actually a bit small on me and maybe too big for you, but it should do."

I could only say it was light blue and the smallest Speedo-type suit I have ever seen. Oh well, when in Rome!

Back out to the beach and our chairs. Stripping off his bathing suit, Larry announced, "I'm ready for a dip. Race you to the water."

Larry took off at a run to the waves. I followed suit and, naked as the jaybird, took off at a run. The water was bracing and the waves manageable. Growing up near the ocean,

I loved swimming in salt water. Larry was hailed by several people in the water. Provincetown, as I had already noted, was a place where Larry enjoyed warm recognition. After a good half hour in the water, we went back to our spot. Larry spread out a large towel, pulled on his bathing suit, rubbed on lotion, and laid down to enjoy the sun. I pulled on my mini bathing suit, also lathered up, and joined Larry on the blanket. We both dozed off and enjoyed a brief but enjoyable nap. I was being careful with the sun and went under the umbrella. Larry turned over to expose his back to the sun. We were both pretty much into our own thoughts, so conversation was limited. After baking for about an hour, split between back and front, Larry joined me in his chair under the umbrella. We chatted casually about a range of topics, just enjoying the company. Occasionally, someone would stop by with introductions made and an exchange of pleasantries and news. I surprised myself that the nudeness was not bothersome or awkward. Having spent many hours in the gym/locker room and common showers, I had mentally neutralized the naked male body. The occasional nude/partially nude female was a bit of another matter!

We enjoyed another of Semmi's lunches, with a chilled bottle of Pouilly-Fumé. The afternoon went by with a bit of business talk, several more swims, and sunbathing. Around four o'clock, we packed up, showered, and drove back toward town.

"I thought we might have a relaxed dinner tonight at home. Semmi is, as you know, a superb cook, and I have asked her to prepare one of her specialties, a bouillabaisse. I'm surprised you didn't catch the aroma, as she started the dish yesterday."

The perfect host, with such careful planning and attention to detail.

"I have not had bouillabaisse in a great while. Will your surprises never end?"

"I have been looking for an occasion to open a 2018 Château La Mission Haut-Brion, it has been resting in my wine cellar. The Pessac-Léognan gives us such wonderful whites and reds," said Larry. "After dinner, I've invited Tom Hopper to join us and give a petite cello recital. Allen Templeton, Theresa and Sergei Soldatov, Madam Fontaine, and Alina will also join us. Theresa will give us a reading of several of her just-published poems."

I needed to pinch myself; this was just too much. In my wildest imagination, I could not conceive of such an evening! I only wish I were sharing this with Natalie.

Back at the cottage, we agreed to have cocktails at five thirty, dinner at six fifteen, guests arriving for dessert/ drinks at seven thirty, and the entertainment to start at eight thirty. The evening weather promised to be perfect. We would gather with our guests on the deck with a fire to create a warm and inviting mood.

I quickly dressed for dinner and gave Natalie a call. She laughed at my beach experience. I shared the evening plans and Larry's offer of the cottage for our Thanksgiving getaway.

"Larry is just extraordinary. I am so happy that your time on the Cape has been so productive and exciting. Please tell Larry how appreciative I am of his generous offer. I'm sure the girls will be green with envy. Looking forward to your coming home. I'll do a relaxed dinner at my apartment."

"We plan to get away early tomorrow and should be back to the city around noon. I'll call you from the office. Love you."

I made my way downstairs. The aroma of the bouillabaisse was now pleasantly evident. I could see the dining room table was set for after-dinner dessert with our guests. I popped my head into the kitchen.

"I can't wait for dinner. It smells absolutely wonderful."

This brought a huge smile to Semmi's face. The kitchen table was set for two. I joined Larry on the deck, Tomas was faithfully preparing his excellent pre-dinner martinis.

"No appetizers per Semmi's instructions," advised Larry.

The weather on the Cape this time of year could be very variable. Sometimes rainy. Fog in the evenings and early mornings was not unusual. We have had, in that regard, the best weather possible. The evening promised a soft breeze with pleasant temperatures in the low sixties. I noticed Tomas had set up the seating for our soiree around the firepit. Alongside Larry's management and attention to detail, having Tomas and Semmi on his staff allowed for entertaining, which appeared effortless and is always top drawer!

"Talked to Peter, I think he is jealous and wishes he had come along on our trip. He sends his best. I called Tom Harwood to confirm our luncheon date. We had a great conversation. I will have a very strong team in place with you, the good Father and Tom. Thank you for your excellent suggestions."

Tomas served our second martinis; dinner would be served in half an hour.

I relayed to Larry Natalie's appreciation of his generous Thanksgiving offer.

"She will be having dinner tonight with Helene and Annie and will be giving them a full report on our comings and goings."

We joked about our three girlfriends, and Larry again expressed his joy at adding our gaggle to his small list of friends.

"Speaking of friends, you know of course that Peter and HSW are the best of friends and, in fact, were in a relationship for a number of years before my time. I mention this only so that you know that Peter will, no doubt, share his jealousy with HSW, and they can get bitchy. Peter worries that our age difference might lead me to stray, as he puts it."

At the time, we both found the situation not to be of great concern; how wrong we were, as time would tell!

Tomas announced dinner, and we moved to the dining table in the kitchen. The aroma was intoxicating. The dinner was in one sense very simple: the bouillabaisse, home-baked bread, and wine. The Haut-Brion, lightly chilled, was simply extraordinary. Rating a dish on pure aroma, the bouillabaisse was one hundred plus! Mussels, clams, and shrimp had been cooked to perfection. We guessed and Semmi confirmed the fish as a mix of cod, sea bass, and haddock. The sauce was presented with grilled slices of bread, spread with a rouille, a mixture of mayonnaise made of olive oil, garlic, saffron, and cayenne pepper. The clams, mussels, and shrimp came to the table in sauce along with leeks, onions, tomato, celery, and petite potatoes. The fish was plated separately, flakey to the fork. Larry and I talked a little and ate with gusto. Hints of bay leaves, thyme, and orange zest were evident in the sauce. I have had a number of truly great dinners, ranging across signature dishes from many countries. Rarely does one experience a meal that can truly be described as magical, utterly simple in content and presentation. Semmi's bouillabaisse transported us to Epicurean heaven! We called Tomas and Semmi to the table and gave them a round of applause.

Larry and I adjourned to the deck, about a half an hour before our guests were to arrive. Tomas had started the fire, which would burn down and be perfect after dessert. Very subdued lighting bathed the deck in a soft glow.

"Larry, what can I do for Tomas and Semmi to thank them for their wonderful care and attention?"

"Your genuine compliments and gratitude are gold to them. You might want to leave a note as we leave. Nothing beyond that is needed or expected."

Tomas announced the arrival of several of our guests. The Soldatovs soon followed Tom Hopper lugging his cello with an assist from Allen Templeton. The last to arrive were Madam Fontaine accompanied by Alina. Tomas relieved Tom of his cello, and we all migrated to the dining room. Tomas and Semmi had worked their magic once again. The table was candlelit, with multiple flower arrangements. Semmi had created a multilayered cake with huge strawberries and whipped cream. Our guests also had the option of either a strawberry/rhubarb or a blueberry pie. The side table offered an array of cordials, wines, and liquor along with coffee and espresso. Tomas solicited drink preferences, and Semmi served dessert preferences. The conversation with the group was lively and ranged over an interesting spectrum of subjects, politics, social issues, the economy, and happenings on the Cape and in Provincetown. The group offered compliments to our host and to Tomas and Semmi; it was obvious they all had had the pleasure before.

With drinks in hand, we all went outside to the deck. Tomas brought Tom's cello out and we all took our seats. Tom introduced his program: a Bargeil Adagio, Myaskovsky's Cello Sonata no. 2, and lastly, Dvorak's Concerto in B minor. For those of us less familiar with cello music, Tom explained, he would be doing selected movements from two lesser-known composers, recognized as brilliant works and the very famous and highly regarded Dvorak work. Playing without sheet music, Tom began. The music was warm, at times very soothing and at other times racing with passion. Tom's mastery of the instrument was so evident; he and the cello were one. An hour or so later, Tom had presented the Bargeil and Myaskovsky pieces. Taking a small break, he explained that the last piece, a Concerto in B minor by Dvorak is his favorite. He had played it for his audition with the Boston Symphony, receiving a rare round of applause from the orchestra. The work was written in 1894 and premiered in London in 1896, Leo Stern playing the cello with the London Philharmonic conducted by Dvorak. Tom took his seat and began playing the second movement, Adagio non-troppo, played slowly, lyrically with moderation. The performance was deeply moving in that Tom's lyrical sense was on full display enhanced by his moderation in pace. We rose to our feet and applauded. We were all so taken with the last hour and forty-five minutes. Tomas made the rounds and refreshed drinks.

Larry waited a few minutes and then introduced Theresa. "Her work combines her poetic skills with her deep understanding of art. Her poetry has been published broadly around the world. Theresa serves on the board of MOMA and finds great inspiration in its collection."

Theresa moved to the chair vacated by Tom. "My work is labelled as ekphrastic poetry, isn't that a mouthful? I work to bring an artist's intent to the forefront with a lyrical style. Some poets have used the device for social purposes, as did American poet Edwin Markham writing on Jean Francois Millet's *Man with a Hoe*, an example of the cruel backbreaking labor of a field hand. I'm sure most if not all of us have read 'Ode on a Grecian Urn' by John Keats. The British Museum of London holds a large collection of ancient Greek artifacts. Keats was a frequent visitor. His work focuses on the interrelation between art, truth, and beauty. I quote Keats, 'Beauty is truth, truth beauty— that is all ye need to know on earth and all ye need to know.' My poetry is much simpler and more direct. I spend a great deal of time at MOMA and, as a director, take advantage of my easy access to the collection. Sergei and I are avid collectors and enjoy sharing our personal collection quid pro quo with other collectors. We all recognize, as does the world over, our dear friend Allen Templeton as one of the world's greatest abstract artists. Allen's work is a unique voice expressed in form, striking colors and a brilliant use of texture. His work is the subject of three of my just-published poems. Important to tell you, I have never discussed these works with Allen from the perspective of his intent. I seem to favor deceased artists. They cannot take exception to my interpretation of their intent! I hope I don't lose a friend with how I have represented Allen's work."

This, of course, drew a good laugh.

"Rather than being presumptive and reading my latest work to you, I am giving each of you an autographed copy of my 'hot off the press' book. Enjoy!"

"Please read one of your poems on my work," asked Allen as he stopped Theresa from sitting down. With some reluctance, Theresa read a poem on a work Allen had done some twenty years ago.

An Invitation

I am drawn to the canvas

there is a magnetism real not imagined

color flows both bright and muted left to

    right and back again

the motion is electric

I have an urge to let my fingers explore

which route do I take

My fingers traverse the textured uneven

    terrain

I feel joy

The journey is short

I am invited to travel again I do

many times many routes

The joy repeats and repeats

For: Allen Templeton

"I promise you this was not rehearsed," said Allen. "Of course, Theresa has an advantage in our having been the dearest of friends for more than twenty-five years. In that time, we attended many art shows, visited museums and private collections, and had endless conversations on art, others and mine. Notwithstanding, in discussing my art, we have focused on the elements of form, use of color, line, tone, and my love of texture. Interesting, she never probed my intent. I guess it is fair to say, she and I focused on the physical aspects of my work and its emotional impact. Her poetry deals with the essence of an artist's work. I must tell you, Theresa's sense/interpretation of my intent in the poem she just read is so incredibly beautiful, insightful, and accurate. I am deeply moved."

"Bravo, Bravo" was enthusiastically offered by the group. We settled into a quiet and reflective enjoyment of the moment. Our guests took leave, expressing thanks for a wonderful evening and the hope that I would "be in touch," particularly in the city and when I visit Provincetown over the Thanksgiving holiday. Larry and I discussed an early departure in the morning and said our good nights. I stopped by the kitchen. Tomas and Semmi were cleaning up.

"I just have to say what a wonderful evening you two put together, thank you."

I laid out my clothes for the trip back to the city and did a bit of pre-packing. Semmi had laundered my used clothing! I sat and wrote a thank-you note to Tomas and Semmi, adding Natalie and I were so looking forward to seeing them for the Thanksgiving holiday. Off to bed.

CHAPTER 10

A S WE HAD AGREED, I was packed and downstairs for breakfast at six forty-five. As we were eating breakfast, Larry said, "Change in plans, we will be flying this morning. There is a plane waiting for us at the Provincetown airport, so we should be back in town by about ten thirty."

We were out the door, with Tomas driving, and we arrived at the airport by seven forty-five. A twin-engine Cherokee was on the ramp with the engines running. As we boarded the plane, Phillip Arenstein was already seated.

"Good morning, great day for flying."

We settled in and were underway. Again, the life-style of the rich and famous was something I could really become accustomed to in a hurry! As it turned out, the plane belonged to Allen Templeton and was frequently loaned out to his friends. The flight was smooth and very quick. We connected with helicopter service to midtown, and with a short cab ride, I was back to the office by ten forty-five. I had set up meetings with Jane, Mary-Ellen, and Ada, with a late afternoon with Annie. HSW was not available until Tuesday morning.

With her usual efficiency, Jane had an agenda for me as we sat down. The new offices were coming along well, and we had a move-in date in two weeks. The new people, Ada and Mary-Ellen, were working out super well; both were quick studies and were completely onboard with the rest of the staff. Jane had basic stats for my weekly report to Annie, along with status on works in progress. Art Design needed a final okay on a cover design, ready to go to press. Jane has the proposed design for my sign-off. Jane handed me a tentative calendar for the next four weeks. She noted commitments/standing meetings/elective events (book signings/industry meetings), travel plans, and critical or time-sensitive items. We added a few items from my calendar, passed on several items, and I asked a few questions needing research.

"That wraps it up, will you want lunch in?"

I ordered a ham and Swiss cheese on rye, chowder, and milk for twelve thirty.

Ada was next. She had my regular mail and emails, pre-read, with data for responding as needed. She had sorted the mail by order of priority. Next, she gave me my incoming call log by date. Again, where needed, she had data for background or response. Ada then suggested a log she created for working manuscript flow, showing status by author and internal status, noting planned pub dates. With the working manuscript control log, there were secondary logs on book concept proposals and sample manuscript submitted for review. I complimented her on the ideas and her initiative.

"I want you to know I love my job and the people on staff. Everyone has been super helpful," Ada said with a big smile.

Mary-Ellen came bouncing in exuding excitement. Her first report was a more detailed look at the status of working manuscripts. She pointed out several smaller issues with authors, all of which were being addressed. She noted a potential problem in copyediting.

"We may be at the point of needing an additional copyediting support. I am working on an analysis and will be back to you on this mid next week."

Her next report dealt with concept proposals. She reviewed six, two of which came up from our editors with high recommendations. Of the two, she was extremely excited with one. She handed me a one-page summary of the proposal. After a quick read, I said, "Yes indeed, I see why you are excited. Let's move forward on this and kudos to our editor." On the second proposal, I gave her a smile. "It's your call."

"Here are my summary reviews of nine sample manuscripts submitted. I think three have very definite possibilities, all from existing authors. With these, I have noted the proposed assignments to our editors for follow-up. I believe all three can go to a contract within six weeks. You'll see a synopsis of the remaining four concept proposals and the six sample manuscripts. My recommendations are noted for your approval."

I asked if she was comfortable with her workload.

"My learning curve is steep, but I am handling the challenges. I would appreciate any feedback, particularly from the editors and staff."

A fast-paced, abbreviated morning but efficient, thanks to the great job being done by my staff. Jane popped in with lunch. I had reviewed the proposed design from the art department and initialed it with my approval.

"Get this back to my best friend with my thanks."

I worked through lunch, dictated my report to Annie, and had time to call Natalie. She answered my call on the second ring.

"So happy you are back in town. I missed you."

Knowing we were having dinner that night, with lots of time to catch up, our call was brief.

"See you around six, love you."

I tried calls to both Pat and Katie. Not unusual, they both went to their answering machines. I gave each a brief update. I had time for a quick call to my folks. My dad answered and called to my mother to get on the line. I reported on my wonderful week on the Cape. I asked if they had heard lately from Pat and Katie. I had missed them on my last few calls.

"We've talked to both of them, over the weekend. Still frustrated by the time differences. Pat is working all kinds of crazy hours and traveling it seems all the time. We know he is doing very well financially, but he does not seem to have any personal life. Katie is, as usual, up to her eyeballs in her studies. She says Shamus's orals went very well, and for all intents, he has his PhD wrapped up. We can't wait to meet what appears to be our future son-in-law."

Mom laughed and asked if they would be meeting a future daughter-in-law at Christmas?

"Natalie is really looking forward to Christmas in Brookline and to a great get-together in the city for New Year's Eve."

"You didn't answer your mother's question," said Dad.

"Got to run, love you."

Using Ada's excellent logs, I spent the next hour working my phone log. With the usual success rate for phone tag, I had several connections and left a few "call me backs." My good friend and broker reported that my account continued to do very well, with his superior management! Ken also confirmed our poker game for Friday night.

"See you at the gym."

Moving on to my email log and thanks to Ada's backup notes, I very efficiently handled the entire list. I must tell Ada how her logs add to my efficiency. Next, I turned to Mary-Ellen's report on concept proposals. As I read, I found it easiest to simply annotate her report with comments/suggestions and follow-up questions. Turning to the sample manuscripts was like an excellent dessert for me. I simply greatly enjoy working with an author's efforts. My annotations on each manuscript were intended for Mary-Ellen, the staff editors involved, and the submitting author. I did not quite finish the manuscripts; I needed a few minutes to gather my thoughts for my four-thirty meeting with Annie.

As the new managing editor, Annie had moved offices. Her new digs were HSW's former office, redecorated modestly to her tastes. I arrived punctually, as is expected by my boss. Our greetings were, of course, cordial but businesslike.

"Tell me how your planning session went."

I reported in detail on the discussions, the work on shaping the book's concept, the great progress on bringing expert advisers on board, and the development of a quite specific over-all calendar. I did not go into any details about the social events nor the development of a personal rapport with Larry. Annie asked several probing questions on the book concept. She quickly saw the potential for problems in dealing with the perception of author's intent and complimented me on suggesting Father Murphy and Dr. Harwood. We covered several other points on budget and schedules. Our meeting adjourned at five fifteen, and I returned to my office. I met with Jane to go over the schedule for Tuesday and the rest of week. I jotted my notes for my meeting with HSW at 9:00 a.m., read the last two manuscript samples, wrapped up the day, and took a cab to Natalie's apartment.

I rang the doorbell, and the door to Natalie's apartment flew open!

"I missed you so much," my sweetheart said and gave me a very long kiss.

We settled on the couch with a glass of wine, and I did a recap of the trip to Cape Cod. The trip had been a huge success purely from a business point of view. I then went into detail on the dining and social experiences. I shared with Natalie how very well the personal relationship with Larry had matured into a budding and true friendship. Natalie had so many questions about the people I had met, particularly Allen Templeton. As I focused on the cottage and all its amenities, not the least of which would be Tomas and Semmi, Natalie expressed her great excitement for our trip to the Cape. We shared several good laughs with my retelling of my beach experience.

After I finished my report, I received a rundown on the Sunday night dinner Natalie had had with Annie and Helene. Yes, Helene knew Phillip Arenstein quite well. He was a well-regarded and competent psychiatrist with an excellent practice. They saw each other professionally and on the social circuit. Both Annie and Helene knew the Soldatovs, having many interests in common. The Soldatovs entertained across a broad spectrum of the international social and artistic communities. Their soirees were one of the most sought invitations in the city. Helene had met Allen Templeton and knew his work. She, in fact, owned two of his paintings in her personal collection. Natalie told me she had shared my visit to a nude beach on the outer Cape. I should be forewarned; it would be the source of a good deal of teasing when we were together!

"Maybe Larry has been able to get Kevin to cross over to our side," Helene had said while laughing at the very idea.

Natalie took a break to check on dinner and I made a quick call to the Dove, checking with Pierre to assure that Larry and Tom would be at a table where they could have quite an extended conversation. He assured me that he would personally take them in hand. We briefly discussed two private party requests, each from well-established customers. Both events would be the latter part of September, which fit well with Natalie's trip to China. I quickly checked my calendar for possible conflicts. My poker game came up, but I could forgo it. I asked Pierre to book both events and promised to be in touch with both couples early next week.

"I am looking forward to being behind the bar Friday night."

Pierre allowed that would be great. We had a full house booked for the evening.

Natalie announced dinner. To start with, she had made hot-and-sour soup, my favorite! My chef was pleased that I not only tolerated but really enjoyed the spicier dishes she favored. The main dish was shrimp in a Szechuan sauce, accompanied by braised asparagus with garlic. The rice was sprinkled with red pepper flakes. We both enjoyed a cold Chinese beer, Tsingtao, with dinner. While we were eating, the conversation turned to her China project. She voiced her complete satisfaction with her Chinese associate. They were now in touch multiple times through the week, and the planning was moving along very well. Her office enjoyed hearing the frequent conversations, moving so smoothly from English to Mandarin and occasionally to French.

"Chua Lin and I have finalized my dates for the first visit to Beijing. I'll be leaving on the eighth of September and returning the twenty-fourth. We also settled on her first visit to New York, December 5 through 18. The dates are great, and it will give me time to organize myself for Christmas and New Year's Eve."

We looked at the calendar, and Natalie thought her next trip to China would not be until mid-March.

We moved into the living room and settled on the couch. Checking our calendars, we penciled in our Thanksgiving trip to the Cape, our Christmas visit to Brookline, and our New Year's Eve parents' get-together in the city. It became a joke as to which of us was more nervous about meeting the other's parents. Natalie has a bigger challenge, in that she had not only my parents, but brother Patrick, sister Katie, and Shamus O'Leary to meet. I responded to a host of questions Natalie had about all my relatives and Shamus. My advice was very simple: "Be yourself, and they will quickly love you as I do."

Natalie had the advantage of knowing a good deal about each of the people who would be in Brookline. I had always filled her in on my calls and text messages. Turning the table, I had a long list of questions about her parents. I actually know very little about Natalie's folks, other than the basics. While I knew she was close to both, she only occasionally would talk about them. Her father came from a small family with only a single sibling, a sister. Her dad identified as biracial; his father was black, and his mother was white. Mr. Hewitt, an attorney, was the senior partner / managing director in the largest and most prestigious law firm in Chicago. His focus is acquisitions and mergers. While he had always been involved in one big deal or another, Natalie said he was a committed family man and devoted to his family. As a couple, the Hewitts had been involved in Chicago's social scene with a strong interest in the arts. The Hewitts—he being Norton, she being Pei-Ling—frequently entertained at home. At a young age, Natalie developed a great and early ease with an array of different people. Mrs. Hewitt was Chinese and from Hong Kong. Educated in Switzerland and England, she spoke, in addition to English, several other languages, Cantonese, Mandarin, French, and Japanese. Natalie came by her skills in languages naturally. As a child, she and her mother spoke Mandarin and Japanese. Pei-ling's family had had a major international company for several generations. Her mother, CEO and Chairman of the Board, focused her attention on the company's worldwide real-estate investments. Natalie had two uncles, both involved in the family business. While her father had only a sister with one child, the Chinese side of the family had given Natalie four first cousins.

Despite the differences in backgrounds, Natalie and I agreed that our folks would get along just fine. In planning the details for New Year's Eve, there would be time set aside for just the parents to spend time together. With the planning pretty much under control and the family briefings accomplished, we settled into a quiet time of just snuggling. Around ten o'clock, we are off to bed.

Next morning, after a quick breakfast, we were both off to our offices. I was anxious to have my nine o'clock meeting with HSW. In his office, settling in, we spent the better part of an hour discussing the working weekend on the Cape. Without saying so, it was clear that HSW and Larry had already talked.

"I can't tell you how pleased I am with the progress you and Larry have made on the project. Your advanced planning was excellent! I must say that it appears that you and Larry have bonded very well on a personal level. A word of caution, a bit of distance would be advisable."

HSW's tone was very deliberate. I didn't feel a need to respond. The message was *very* clear! We ended the meeting with HSW's offering to be available if I needed his advice.

Back in my office, I settled into my work routine. Around four thirty, Larry called.

"Had a great meeting with Tom Harwood. He has a very impressive background and a quick mind. He finds the concept for my book intriguing, but froth with risk. He sees the same risks you and I have discussed. I am of the mind he will bring great insight and value to the project. I asked him to join our team. He has great regard for you and is aware that Father Murphy is seriously considering joining us. He graciously accepted my invitation and will be coming on board. We discussed timetables, availability, travel plans, suggestions, and the compensation arrangements. We left it that you and he would work out the particulars of an agreement. Thank you, Kevin, for a first-rate suggestion. I hope it works out as well with Father Murphy. I am looking forward to our dinner Friday evening. I'll keep you posted."

I checked with my friend/broker, Kevin Smallwood. A run-through of my accounts showed the market had been very good to me and that Kevin was doing a great job. He asked several questions regarding plans.

"Sounds like a wedding might be in the making."

I laughed. "Not even engaged, although I may be purchasing a ring around Christmastime."

We promised to see each other at the gym the next morning.

I worked through the afternoon and put in several hours that evening, leaving the office around nine. Back at my apartment, I caught up on a bit of mail that had accumulated, placed my weekly food order for delivery, snacked on a small Indian dish I had picked up around the corner, and gathered my laundry for pickup in the morning. With my domestic chores done, I was off to bed by ten thirty.

Wednesday, I arrived to coffee and a bagel, as dutifully arranged by Jane, a job she retained despite her promotion.

The day went very, very smoothly. I couldn't help noticing the real increase in my productivity. It was evident that the team was functioning with great efficiency, and all seemed to be really into the team effort. Wish I could claim it was all due to my superior management skills, fact of the matter, my personnel choices, just happened to be solid.

Wednesday night was my standing pizza night with Annie and Helene. We would, of course, be joined by Natalie. I confirmed the date with Annie.

"We are looking forward to you telling us all about your Cape Cod escapades. See you around seven thirty," she ended with a chuckle.

We had arranged that Natalie would order the pizza and I would pick her up around seven. I left the office and made a quick stop at my apartment to change into casual clothes. Picking Natalie up, we arrived just as the pizza was delivered. Annie served drinks, and we sat down to attack the pizza and get into the week's news and gossip. I sensed my friends were anxious to hear my Cape Cod story. I ended the suspense and went into a detailed and colorful description of the whole experience. There were questions, many questions. There were laughs too. My audience really enjoyed the storytelling. As Natalie had forewarned me, the beach scene drew the most laughs. I reported that I wasn't shocked or traumatized by the experience. I reminded the ladies I had always spent a lot of time at the gym, the locker room, the open showers, where nudity was just a matter of course. I offered that Larry O'Neil's graciousness and entertaining skills are in a class by themselves, the outstanding restaurant meals and those prepared and served at the cottage, Allen Templeton's dinner party, and the near-magical evening of music and poetry on the deck of the cottage, each experience enriched by Larry's circle of friends and the warm regard he was afforded in P-town. Larry's generous offer of the cottage for our Thanksgiving getaway was met with the smallest hint of jealousy. After a fun-filled evening, Natalie and I were back to her apartment. I spent the night as was becoming more the usual.

Thursday morning was devoted to editorial projects and author consultations. As I have mentioned so often, this was the most pleasurable and rewarding aspect of my work. There were times where I turned a project over to one of my fine editors with hesitancy and envy. My world was now managed by the organization of my emails, phone calls, correspondence, and advance review of proposals and manuscript submissions. The overall flow of the operation is concisely tracked and issues flagged for my attention.

I called Tom Harwood to congratulate him on joining our team and to discuss specifics of a formal contractual agreement. He reported that he had spoken with Aloysius Murphy several times. He gave Aloysius a recap of his luncheon meeting with Larry and told Father Murphy that he would be joining the team. Aloysius said he had a continued and growing interest in the project and was looking forward to dinner with O'Neill Friday evening. Tom left it, saying he hoped Father Murphy would be coming on board.

Could it possibly be Friday already? I worked on my weekly report to my boss. I took great care to be timely, accurate, informative, and totally professional in my dealings with Annie. She, in turn, had always been the personification of the professional business manager. I was truly blessed to have a dynamite boss and a very dear friend all in one person!

A call came through from Brother Patrick. He was in Paris for several days on business. He very much found Paris to be the most charming city in all of Europe. All was well with him. He remarked how excited Mom and Dad were for the upcoming holidays. He had arranged for the folks to join him in London for the Thanksgiving holidays; they were hesitant until Pat told them Katie would join them.

"I'm sorry Natalie and I have prior plans, but Christmas is solidly on everyone's calendar."

With that, Pat had to rejoin a meeting. "Be well and love you, little brother."

Late in the afternoon, I had a call from Larry O'Neil with a quick question.

"It just occurred to me; is my relationship with George potentially a problem in dealing with a Catholic priest?"

With no hesitation, I said, "It has absolutely no relevance to your working relationship or for that matter to the project per se. I cannot imagine the subject even being raised. It simply will not be a problem."

A noticeable sigh of relief. "Thanks, I am really looking forward to dinner this evening. I hope it goes as well as my meeting with Tom Harwood."

Larry promised to call Saturday with a report. Natalie and I had planned one of our favorite outings, dinner in Chinatown and great jazz in the Village. I would pick her up around seven.

Natalie had made the restaurant reservations. She delighted in exposing me to the many nuances of Chinese food and cooking styles. Of course, her fluency and knowledge garnered us great service and an outstanding meal. After dinner, we decided to walk to a club noted for its great jazz. We were regulars and knew quite a few people. We joined a table of six. The music, the company, and a nice bottle of wine made for a great evening.

We were back to Natalie's apartment at a reasonable hour, ready to turn in after a very full day.

"I need to start charging you rent," joked Natalie.

I thought about that. "I would be willing to pay half the costs, your apartment is much more comfortable than mine. Logistically, we could save all kinds of time not running back and forth."

I, of course, was being *very* practical. Then, we both arrived at the same moment of truth! Our relationship had reached that point where we were comfortable making the commitment to live together.

Natalie smiled. "Logistics aside, I would love to wake up every morning and have you at my side."

Over breakfast, I said, "If you want to take a few days to think about my moving in, I will understand."

"Sorry, my dear, you made a verbal offer and I accepted. It is binding. Don't forget I am a lawyer by training, and I will sue to enforce our agreement."

Natalie's quick humor was only one of the hundred reasons I loved her!

"I'll check my lease for termination and subleasing possibilities."

As I sat reading and Natalie was busy cleaning up from breakfast, my phone rang.

"We are now two for two! Dinner last night with Aloysius Murphy was one of my best evenings in recent memory. The man is simply fabulous, bright beyond belief, with a span of knowledge as wide as the sea. I am seldom mesmerized with an individual, but a good father is such a rarity. It was very clear that he had invested time in weighing the project. His questions were probing, intense at times, and very interesting. Having a sense of humor, profane at times, coupled with the ability to laugh at himself adds to the aura of the man. He had a major concern, using his position and connections in the church in a commercial venture, appearing to perhaps be questioning the Catholic church's methodology and intentions in the recognition of a person as a saint. I assured him, in absolute terms, that I had no such intentions and would not place the church or him in an embarrassing nor compromising position. This point took more than an hour of our time. At this juncture in our meeting, I was absolutely convinced that Aloysius would add an important and needed dimension to the project. Based on this judgment, I offered to give him an unusual degree of latitude as my consultant and critical reader. He would have complete freedom to vigorously object and argue at any point. Further and in recognition of his status and role in the church, particularly as the advocate in the cause of Fulton J. Sheen, I would not include the late archbishop in my book. After a great dinner, four hours of conversation, and a few brandies after dinner, I asked Father Murphy to join our team. With further dialogue on schedules, travel availability, compensation, etc., everything just came together, and Aloysius happily accepted my offer! Kevin, your preplanning, connections, and suggestions have been superb! Thank you."

With a free morning, Natalie suggested we visit the UN for a hearing on the worldwide plight of refugees. We would occasionally make such visits to the UN. I found the experiences to be very informative. The visits also gave me an appreciation of the high regard afforded Natalie both by staff and any number of diplomats we often encountered. Her breadth of knowledge was impressive and went well beyond her primary area of responsibility. After the hearing, I left for my meetings at the Dove. Natalie had plans to stay on at the UN and would later attend a cocktail party at the Chinese Legation. I planned to sleep at my apartment after work to not disturb Natalie's sleep.

"Why don't we have an early lunch at Tavern on the Green? I'll pick you up around ten, and we can have a brisk walk in the park before lunch. Love you."

I was at the Dove for my meetings as scheduled. My frequent private-party work made each occasion straightforward. Both couples were familiar with the space and possible setups, pricing, staff support, etc. I had consulted the kitchen and had a list of the best available for this time of year. The Dove is highly rated for its food preparations and presentations. Our hors d'oeuvres were things of beauty and literally the talk of the town, anything but the usual. I had ordered a sampler for the meetings with both couples. The wine list recommendations had been made to compliment both occasions. Lastly, I had put together a staffing plan and a suggested layout of the facility. As always, an affair arranged and managed by the Dove would be a huge success.

My meetings with the Connors and the Lanzas went very smoothly. It's great to work with people you truly enjoy and people who value and appreciate your efforts. I wrote up orders for the room layout, table settings, floral arrangements, bar order and setup, staffing requirements, detailed kitchen orders, and asked the business office to give me preliminary cost estimates. Both families have specifically asked me to be present, not really required, but of course, I would accommodate. I copied Pierre, our maître d', adding a few additional points and pointing out noteworthy guests on both lists. I had one open item. The Connors requested live music during dinner. I had suggested classical, a piano and harpist. They loved the idea. The Lanzas would be content with low-key, piped-in music.

I now had time to check in with Father Murphy. I luckily caught him as he was leaving for an engagement.

"I am so pleased that your dinner meeting with Larry O'Neil seems to have gone quite well. He called me this morning and was unusually effusive in reporting how well the two of you connected."

"Right back at him, it was a very in-depth discussion of what I find to be an intriguing project. Larry dealt with my concerns directly and with great respect and awareness of the sensitivities of my position in the church. I also appreciated the unusual latitude he is willing to give me. I am delighted to take the assignment, and I do thank you for the recommendation."

Knowing he was pressed for time, we agreed to talk next week to go over the details, reviewing and finalizing agreements.

It was now time to morph into my role as the bartender extraordinaire. I truly loved being behind the bar and interacting with my customers. It must be the thespian in me. I always had a most appreciative audience at the Dove. Pierre and I had a brief chat about the Connor and Lanza events. It turned out that he knew a marvelous piano player and was sure that he would have professional connections, including a harpist. He offered to check out availability and costs.

The evening, as they always did, went by quickly, with the usual mix of my regulars, new faces, and the out-of-town folks. A fine night, as I estimated my gratuities. I was home by 2:00 a.m. and right off to bed.

I picked up Natalie, as planned, and we were off to the park. I had made reservations at the Tavern on the Green. Sunday mornings were a great time for people watching, and I knew the best table location to see the comings and goings. The table also had the bonus of the best view of the park. We saw Tiger Woods and an attractive lady leaving; later, an important but unidentified Middle Eastern type in flowing robes arrived with what looked like two bodyguards attending. A good day for people watching! After a leisurely breakfast, we took a long walk through the park, just a very pleasant day. With no set plans for the rest of the day, we decided to just hang out at Natalie's apartment. We both had a bit of work to do, so we settled in the comfortable living room. Helene and Annie called, asking if we wanted to do dinner on the fly. Great idea, seven o'clock at Nakamura, the Japanese restaurant we had so enjoyed a few weeks ago. A great way to end what had been a very good week.

*****

Back in the office Monday morning, my focus was on wrapping up the arrangements with both Tom Harwood and Aloysius Murphy. With several phone calls with Larry, Tom, and Aloysius, I had ironed out time commitments, schedules, tentative travel plans, statements of work to be done, compensation, and several other details. There were no issues. I drafted agreements for review, comments, and asked for a quick turnaround. My three good fellows were back to me with minor comments and a few suggestions by late Tuesday. With legal review and sign-off, I was able to turn everything around and have final documents out for signature by Thursday midday. Working with three bright, experienced individuals made my life so much easier. Using courier service, I had fully executed contracts back from all three people by late Friday afternoon.

The staff continued to support me across the spectrum of my responsibilities and greatly contributed to my efficiency. All was well! With the O'Neil project launched, my time was somewhat freed up. The ball was in the author's court, and I was now in the classic editorial support role.

I checked with my landlord on the prospect of my moving, not a problem. The apartment would rent quickly and at a much higher rent. We agreed I would vacate the apartment within two weeks of a tenant signing a lease. I called Natalie with the good news. It would be great if things came together before her trip to China. Luck of the Irish! My landlord had seven quick showings, four prospects ready to sign a lease, a bidding war, a signed lease at 150 percent of the current rent *and* occupancy by August 15. Perfect! I had offered the apartment fully furnished, and the new tenant made a fair offer for literally everything: furniture, rugs, lamps, TV, dishes, pots and pans, microwave, etc. Having to deal only with my computer setup, a few pieces of art, and a few miscellaneous items, the move would be a proverbial piece of cake. The new tenant is a young man, just graduating from the University of Miami and about to begin his career with CBS. He was so pleased to have found the apartment and relieved at being able to buy all its furnishings. I wished him well, shades of a young Kevin Murphy.

Natalie "complained" I was coming into her apartment empty-handed. I knew she was joking, but it gave me an idea. I called Larry.

"You may remember, Natalie is a huge fan of Allen Templeton. I am moving in with her and wondered if a small Templeton piece would be in my reach as a housewarming gift? I can afford up to $25,000."

"Allen's work is usually large scale and sells in the hundreds of thousands. The fewer smaller pieces he paints are also well above your budget. Have you thought about putting those dollars toward an engagement ring, or is that rushing things?"

A great question by Mr. O'Neil!

"I was thinking about proposing while we are on the Cape. I guess I need to wait until I meet her parents and formally ask her father's permission."

Larry agreed. "That's the right thing to do. I am happy for you both."

Dinner with Annie and Helen was, as usual, a mixture of serious discussion, gossip, and laughter, great, good friends! I shared the news that I would be moving into Natalie's apartment, and they offered to help. Helene mentioned an invitation from the Soldatovs for a cocktail party and art show opening; it would preempt our usual Wednesday night pizza get-together.

"That's fine, tonight is a great substitute," said Natalie.

As the new workweek started, I was pleased with wrapping up the contracts for Larry's project and I could move on to a backlog of business. It was hard to believe that summer was winding down. Pierre called with cost quotes for both the piano player and an associate to play the harp. The price was quite reasonable. I asked Pierre to go ahead and book them. I gave Mrs. Connors a quick call, and she was delighted with the arrangement.

I had been giving a lot of thought to Larry's comments on an engagement ring. *If* we could get together with

Natalie's folks *prior* to Thanksgiving, I could have *the* serious conversation with Natalie's father. *If* he gives permission for me to ask Natalie to marry me, *then* I could buy an engagement ring *and* propose to Natalie while we were in Provincetown! Sounded like a great plan!

I called Natalie, and she said, "I've been thinking about our plans for getting together with my family and with your family for Christmas and New Year's. I think the New Year's Eve plan is great *and* can be even better! Your folks and I will have already met at Christmas. The New Year's get- together in New York will be in a more relaxed situation with a focus on the parents getting to know each other. *But* I see a missing element. My father is in town quite frequently for business, and my mother often comes along for her business and to visit friends. It would bring things together nicely *if* you were to meet my parents *before* New Year's and *before* our getaway to the Cape. I think they would be *very* pleased with the idea."

I quickly agreed. "That's a great idea. It would indeed bring things together nicely, and New Year's Eve would be super relaxed."

"Let me see what I can arrange."

Natalie promised to get back to me with a plan.

*****

Mary-Ellen dropped by with several questions on titles in the process. This time of the year, we very often faced the crunch of titles going to press and meeting release plans for the new list. ME summarized: we had fifteen titles due for release on the fall list. Thirteen were on schedule and in pre-press. One title was slightly off schedule; however, the editor involved was excellent and had assured the title going to prepress by Friday. The last title is well off schedule and had already been flagged as missing release on the fall list. The first-time author had been doing reasonably well but encountered a "brick wall" several weeks ago. Our editor could not reach her. ME talked with her agent. With some reluctance, he reported there were mental health issues, a possible nervous breakdown. I was familiar with the author's submitted manuscript to date and thought it showed unusual, good promise for a first novel. We agreed to be supportive and decided to not place the title on the spring list. Hopefully, the reprieve will give the author time to recover.

I left the office around five thirty, which was unusual for me. I hadn't been to the gym for several days. I did a vigorous workout, a massage, and a long hot shower. I felt like a million dollars! I bumped into Mel Goldstein, one of my poker friends. He chided me for missing too many games. I promised to do better. I asked if he happened to know a reliable jeweler. I was going to be in the market for an engagement ring. My luck never seemed to run out! Mel's brother-in-law was a jeweler and a dealer in diamonds.

"In the past, I have sent him referrals and he has taken very good care, excellent quality, *and* very reasonable pricing. If you'd like, I'll give Kaleb a call this evening and introduce you as a close friend, with instructions to give you the very *best* care."

Mel gave me Kaleb's full name, address, phone number, and suggested I give Kaleb a call Thursday to set up a meeting. I thanked Mel and promised to return the favor and lose to him at the next several poker games.

Back at my apartment, I worked up a list of things to do relative to my move, e.g., cancel the newspapers, transfer the utilities to the new tenant, advise my food delivery and laundry services, send out multiple change-of-address notices, cancel my TV service, etc. I scheduled my cleaning service for a total job: rug shampoo, window washing, and the like. I also started to pack my personal items. Everything was in good order.

I snacked on a pasta dish I had ordered in and called Natalie. I gave her a complete report on the organization of my move and jokingly asked if she had any second thoughts. She had just talked with her parents. Of course, they are excited about Natalie's upcoming trip to China and the whole project. They would like to visit and go over the details *and* to meet Mr. Murphy! Her father had a New York City meeting scheduled for October 5 and 6 and could be joined by her mother on the seventh, staying over the weekend.

"That is great, although I will be nervous. Have you told them we will be living together?"

Natalie laughed. "I tell my mother *everything* and I sure she gives my father an edited report. They know that we are in a serious relationship and that I am very much in love with a Kevin Murphy."

"You know I am going to be uptight. What kinds of questions will they ask?"

Laughing as she often did, she said, "You are on your own, my dear, you'll do just fine."

Okay, I would get to meet Natalie's parents and have the "big conversation" with Mr. Hewitt.

"Sir, may I please have your permission to marry your daughter?"

I was so glad I had the conversation with Mel and could work my way through selecting an engagement ring. I would make a point of seeking Mrs. Hewitt's suggestions. With the ring acquisition in motion, I would be able to propose to Natalie during our Thanksgiving holiday on the Cape. A perfect plan!

My move-in date arrived sooner than I could have imagined. All went quite well. The new tenant, Tom Quigley, did the walk-through and complimented me on the neatness of the apartment. I had made several transfers during the week and had pretty much settled in at Natalie's, now our apartment. We celebrated my official occupancy with champagne toasts. I had already done all the tedious work of notifying the world of my change of address. Mom and Dad, Pat and Katie were all super pumped-up to meet Natalie, now assumed to be a future daughter-in-law and sister-in-law.

Natalie was deep into planning for her parents' visit in early October. Friday: cocktails at our apartment with the introduction of Kevin to the parents. Dinner: Chinatown. Saturday: early lunch, Kevin with Mr. Hewitt. Natalie and her mother, shopping. Dinner: Mr. Hewitt's favorite French restaurant. Sunday brunch with parents: Tavern on the Green. Dinner: our Japanese restaurant Nakamura, on Thirty-Seventh Street. We decided that was enough planning, with plenty of open space to play by ear. We briefly looked at the plans for New Year's. All was well in hand. Natalie was great at making all the necessary reservations.

Thursday afternoon, I called Kaleb Leibowitz, Mel's brother-in-law. He would be happy to help me select a diamond for an engagement ring. He told me he had been given specific instructions to take very good care of me. Checking his schedule, he suggested meeting either Monday morning around ten or Tuesday afternoon around two. We agreed on a Monday meeting at his office, located in the Diamond District. I looked at my checking account balance: $10,000 was easily available. I called Kevin to arrange the availability of an additional $30,000 by midweek. Ken was happy for me with the forthcoming engagement and assured me I had more than enough readily available liquid funds.

The weekend was busy with Natalie packing and preparing for her trip. I would be doing my usual Saturday night gig at the Dove. On the sly, I had done a great deal of research on the purchase of a diamond. I think I had a fair understanding of the basics. The four Cs: color, carat, cut, and clarity. The costs of course varied widely, based on the specifics. For example, a white diamond with a good cut, good clarity, up to two carats would price at $4,000 to

$10,000 per carat. A larger stone around three carats, with the same characteristics, would cost $8,000 to $16,000 plus per carat or more. My sense being something in the two to two and a half carats could work. I had a budget of $30,000 to $38,000 for the diamond and a setting.

I arrived at Kaleb's office at one forty-five; I was amazed at the security. I had been pre-listed as a scheduled appointment. The security office cleared me with multiple proofs of identity and a call to Kaleb's office to authorize entry. Kaleb looked to be in his early fifties, short, and very lean, with a nicely trimmed mustache; he wore a yarmulke. After a few minutes of cordial chatter, we settled down to business.

"Do you have something in mind, size, color, cut, clarity, and price?" he asked.

I answered the easier question first, telling him I am working with a budget of $30,000 to $38,000 for the diamond and a setting.

"From there, I am in your hands."

Kaleb opened a drawer and placed several paper wraps on a black display pad; opening each with a diamond enclosed, he arranged the stones in size, left to right.

"For those kinds of dollars, you can expect, about a two-plus carat, a white-colored stone, a round cut, which is the most popular and the most expensive presentation, the cut of the stone would be rated good to very good and in the I/J color range, with a clarity rating of VSI1 or very slightly perceptible imperfections."

Kaleb held up the first and smallest diamond with tweezers and gave me a jeweler's loop and a quick lesson in how to use it. Kaleb commented on what I should be seeing. He then picked up a second stone, the largest, with his tweezers and held it up. "This stone is slightly more than three carats, a round/white stone as you can see. The cut is ideal with the highest rating, with the maximum sparkle or refraction. The color is G rated, which is excellent, and it has a clarity rating of VVS, extremely slight, minimal imperfections. This very fine diamond is priced at $44,500."

He offered me the jeweler's loop and held the stone up for me. It was a stunning diamond! Kaleb then went to another stone.

"Here we have a two and a half carat, round cut, rated fair on the cut, The color is I rated, not bad and the clarity is VS11, some imperfections visible. The price on this diamond is $14,500."

Again, I viewed the stone through the jeweler's loop; the internal flaws were clear.

Kaleb put the first five diamonds aside and laid out several more stones.

"These are called fancy-cut diamonds. We have emerald, oval, marquise, princess, and the pear cuts as the most popular presentations. The primary difference is in the brilliance or refraction being less than a round cut stone. These diamonds range in size from an oval at two and a half carats to the four and a half-carat emerald cut. Price ranges from $12,000 to $39,000."

Kaleb presented each for me to view with the loop, explaining each stone's characteristics. Informative, but my head was beginning to spin!

"Let's approach this from an entirely different perspective," Kaleb suggested. "Does your young lady wear jewelry? Fancy, simple, gold/silver, rings, necklaces, bracelets, color preferences? Does she admire or comment on another woman's jewelry or an engagement ring?"

I thought about it. "Natalie wears very little jewelry, a gold signet ring, on occasions, different jade pieces, pearls when dressing more formally, and she does wear earrings. I don't recall her commenting on someone's jewelry."

"Okay. We have covered a lot of ground. Before we begin to zero in, I would like you to know I will give you a 10 percent discount on the pricing of the stone you select. Additionally, the setting will be priced at the cost of material only. The design of the setting and the mounting of the diamond will be my engagement gift to your young lady."

"With that very generous discount and your excellent guidance, I am leaning toward a round diamond, somewhere between two and a half to three carats, with a very good cut, I or H color with a VS1 clarity rating. The setting should be simple and in 18K gold. I would like to budget around $35,000."

Kaleb slowly took the fancy stones off the table and rearranged the five round stones, smallest to largest. He studied the stones, referring to notations on the wrappers. He pushed stones 1, 2, 3 aside. He picked up stone 4.

"This is a fine two and three-quarter carat diamond with very good cut, H in color, and VS1 in clarity. It would make up into a wonderful engagement ring. It is priced at a list of $32,800." He then picked up stone number 5. "This is a three plus carat, ideal cut, G-rated in color, and

VVS in clarity. This is, in every sense, simply a magnificent diamond. It has a list price of $44,500."

There was a pregnant silence. It was clear that Kaleb was thinking very hard! He reached for his calculator and a pad. With several calculations and referring to notations on each diamond's wrapper, he made notes on his pad.

"Okay. I will sell you the number4 stone in a simple eighteen-karat gold band for $28,965. It will present a wonderful engagement ring." After another prolonged silence, he said, "However, I am recommending the number 5 stone! I gave you a list price of $44,500. Please accept my offer of $36,490 for the diamond set in eighteen-karat gold setting."

I was flabbergasted! That was better than a 10 percent discount by a mile!

"Kaleb, you leave me almost speechless! I accept your very generous pricing for the larger diamond and with great thanks. I will tell Natalie about your wonderful engagement gift. Again, thank you for your excellent advice and your generosity."

We shook hands, and Kaleb said, "This is my mitzvah for this week."

I wrote a check for $10,000 to bind the deal. Kaleb assured me there would not be a problem having the ring ready before Thanksgiving. He would do several preliminary designs for the setting for my review and final selection. I mentioned that I would be consulting with my future mother-in-law on the setting.

"Metz yam, excellent and smart." Kaleb smiled.

The whole process took just about two hours. I was elated and exhausted! As I was on my way back to the apartment, I called Mel.

"Thank you, good friend. Your brother-in-law was great. A straightforward approach, an excellent tutor, and a generous man. I selected a wonderful diamond, and he will be working on the setting design."

Natalie had been super busy, spending long hours at the office, preparing for her trip to China. I likewise was spending long hours in my office, with a focus on developing my long-range plan. Along with work, I also caught up on my social life, the poker game, working out at the gym, and some music with friends. With the rush of things, September 8 was suddenly on our doorstep. Natalie was off to China. We had dinner at home the evening of the seventh and were off to bed quite early. We fell asleep in each other's arms. I wanted to take Natalie to the airport, but she insisted on saying our goodbyes, as the limo picked her up at the apartment early in the morning. We had worked out the time differences and a plan to speak to each other at least twice a week. I wished my sweetheart all the best as she left on her great adventure.

CHAPTER 11

WITH NATALIE OUT OF TOWN, I doubled down on my longer-range staff planning and development initiative. To ensure we had the talent needed to drive the business in the future, I focused on training, identifying promotable candidates, the recruiting needs at several levels, implementing an intern program in cooperation with several universities, and an in-depth review of our salary structure and individual compensation levels. Additionally, I wanted to develop several models of possible reorganization to deal with the group's growing list of titles being managed and the escalation of proposals and manuscript evaluations. Preliminary analysis indicated the overall workflow was being impeded and was less efficient. My immediate concern was in copyediting/ fact-checking.

I initiated group planning meetings, employing the Kepner-Tregoe approach to problem identification and solution. Staff response had been excellent. While a student at Penn, I had looked in-depth at the Japanese success in implementing change. The basis of their success was the slow and methodical involvement of all parties involved and invested in the planned change(s). The process, inviting extensive dialogue, assured both understanding and most important, "buy in" in the organization top to bottom. People understood the problem(s) being identified, the probable cause(s), plausible solutions, and recognized and valued the need for change. People accepted the interdependency of their roles. The net result, all parties took ownership of the change process. When the go button was pressed, the process of change happened smoothly and efficiently.

Annie was aware of my work and asked if she might sit in occasionally on my staff meetings. My staff had the greatest respect and genuine fondness for our managing editor. Her presence was comfortable for all and did not impede staff candor or the openness of the dialogue. Annie was a prodigious note-taker. She seldom interjected herself but would respond to questions directed at her. To my surprise, Annie never brought up the subject of my planning program, in any of our one-on-one meetings.

I missed Natalie and found living in our apartment made the absence tolerable. We did text/email frequently with pithy exchanges. As planned, we managed to talk on the phone, usually once a week, working around the twelve-hour time difference. Her whole experience in Beijing was going very well, stimulating and rewarding. Her relationship with Chrysanthemum (Chua Hua) was both professionally and personally excellent.

Saturday nights at the Dove were busy as people come back to the city from summer holidays and travel. Tourist traffic in the city was showing a noticeable uptick as the cooler weather arrived. The Dove had always been a popular spot for the foreign visitors, and I noticed we were seeing more Asian and Middle Eastern tourists. My bar customers, regulars, and visitors continued to be generous with gratuities. The affairs for the Connors and the Lanzas had gone quite well. They were pleased and very generous!

In my off time, I spent evenings working on finalizing my long-range planning initiative. I was pleased with how it was coming together. I did manage to play a bit of poker and win, lost five or so pounds at the gym, and enjoyed a great evening at the Met's presentation of Verdi's *La Traviata*. Pretty Yende, the South African soprano in the role of Violetta, sung with an impressively warm voice and to rave reviews. Pizza nights with Annie and Helene were as always relaxed and thoroughly enjoyable. I also caught up on my personal correspondence, something I tended to neglect. I did connect with my siblings several times and greatly enjoyed the banter. My folks were just back from their annual getaway to Maine. They reported the prices were reasonable and the lobster excellent.

As always when you were super busy, the time went by quickly. It. was Sunday night of the twenty-ninth. A very tired but happy Natalie returned home! She slept for twelve hours and, after a long hot soak, was almost back to her old self.

I worked Saturday night and Natalie had another long, needed sleep. We spent Sunday tidying up the apartment, which was always immaculate to begin with. Visits to the liquor store, several specialty shops, and the grocery store. We unpacked and then took a nice walk on what was a cool fall evening. We enjoyed an early dinner at a small Italian restaurant around the block from the apartment. Back at the apartment, Natalie admitted to still being jet-lagged and was off to bed by nine thirty.

Natalie's mother's plane arrived Friday around four o'clock, and she took a cab to the Waldorf. Mr. Hewitt had been in town for several very busy days of meetings. I planned to work late, allowing Natalie and her parents some time together to catch up. Her folks took a cab from the Waldorf and were at our apartment with Natalie around six o'clock. I arrived at the apartment around eight o'clock, letting myself in, hearing lots of laughter as I came into the living room.

"Mom and Dad, this is Kevin Murphy. Kevin, I would like you to meet my parents, the Hewitts."

I shook hands with Mr. Hewitt. "I am so pleased to meet you Mr. and Mrs. Hewitt."

Turning to Mrs. Hewitt, she held out her arms in an embrace. "So this is the young man who has stolen my daughter's heart."

"Kevin, please call me Norton and Mrs. Hewitt, Pei Ling."

We sat down and I offered to refresh drinks and poured myself a glass of wine. The Hewitts were great conversationalists and were completely at ease as were Natalie and me. Don't know why I was surprised but Norton had a great sense of humor; we laughed a lot. After a bit, Natalie announced, "I've made reservations at Hwa Yuan, Mom's favorite restaurant in Chinatown. We should be on our way."

The Hewitts were immediately recognized, as we entered the restaurant. Natalie and her mother had a great time discussing/planning dinner with the owner. The style was Szechuan, and the dinner was first rate! As the dialogue before dinner was in Mandarin, Norton and I chatted on the side. To my surprise, he would occasionally ask a question or comment in Mandarin. As I thought about that, it was logical that he would have some fluency as Natalie had told me, she and her mother often spoke Mandarin at home. Natalie chatted more about her project and how well things were progressing. Pei Ling was so pleased that her daughter was connecting with her Chinese heritage with such a unique exposure to its history, arts, and its people.

Norton Hewitt was a tall man, at least six feet and very fit looking. Gray hair was just beginning to appear. I, of course, knew of his mixed heritage. He favored his white mother. As I was to learn later, Norton's dad, who identified as biracial, was also the child of a mixed marriage, a white father / black mother. This explains Natalie's more fair skin coloration. If anything, she was more apparently of Asian descent. Pei Ling was petite with chestnut-colored hair and piercing brown eyes, features Natalie had inherited. As we enjoyed dinner, Natalie and her mother were deep into food talk, and Norton and I continued our chat. It seemed my future father-in-law was very familiar with the publishing industry both in the US and internationally. He seemed to know a good deal about Peters & Wells. Norton had met our CEO, Tom Clarkson, and was acquainted with several of our directors. In his practice, he represented several of the larger European publishers, all with growing interest in the US and worldwide English language markets. He had arranged several transactions over the past couple of years.

As we finished our wonderful meal, Natalie gave her folks the game plan for the next day. They would meet for a light breakfast at the Waldorf around eight o'clock. Natalie and her mother had already planned a shopping expedition. Norton needed to spend the morning wrapping up some business. He and I agreed to have lunch at the Bull and Bear around twelve thirty. Natalie suggested we eat lightly, as we had a seven thirty reservation at Le Veau D'Or. Norton was pleased; it was one of his favorite restaurants in New York. Leaving the restaurant, we took separate cabs. Natalie was super pleased.

"I read my parents quite well. The evening has been a huge success. You have passed muster!"

After Natalie left to meet her mother, I used the morning to do a summary of my long-term planning project. We had achieved all my goals with a strong buy-in by staff. Our solutions were not in any sense radical, but several, involving organizational changes, represented a departure from current company practices. There were also budgetary dimensions: spending more money, focused on staff additions and changes in compensation for current staff. I recognized I would need support from the Personnel Department in developing new job descriptions and drawing a new organizational chart. The compensation point, while financial, will require Personnel support in reevaluating current jobs and establishing salary rates for newly proposed positions. The intern segment of my proposal is innovative, as reflected in the preliminary agreements I had negotiated with both Columbia and Fordham universities. I had developed a very detailed workload analysis: quantitatively expressed in work to be done and staff required, differentiating between current staffing and proposed/ required new hires. Overall, I was pleased and confident of the management's support. With the needed support from Personnel, I would plan to present the proposal to my manager, the managing editor, in late November and, with her approval, to corporate management in December, prior to Christmas.

I left for my luncheon date with Norton Hewitt. I had wrestled with how to approach the question of marrying his daughter. I finally decided it was a straightforward question.

"I love your daughter. I want to spend the rest of my life with her. I want to raise a family with her. I will care for her, protect her, and support her. May I have your permission to ask your daughter to marry me?"

I arrived at Bull and Bear and Norton was already seated. We ordered a drink, and Norton opened the conversation.

"Pei Ling and I are admittedly old-fashioned. We recognize that you and Natalie are responsible adults and are in a serious relationship. I must say, however, that we do not approve of the two of you living together. Having said that, I'd like to know your intentions?"

I could not help laughing, Norton immediately took it the wrong way. Whoops!

"Sir, I am not laughing at you or at what you have said. It was an uncontrolled laugh of nervous relief! Please let me explain. You have made it easier for me to address something I have struggled with for weeks. I love your daughter. I want to spend the rest of my life with her, and I want to raise a family together! I will care, protect, shelter, and support her in every way! May I please have your permission to ask your daughter to marry me?"

The man sat stone silent!

"I have purchased a diamond for an engagement ring, and I would like Mrs. Hewitt to help me in the design of the setting, and I would like to propose to Natalie while we are on the Cape for Thanksgiving."

Norton broke into a huge smile. "As you know, Natalie is our only child, and we love her beyond words. The idea of her marrying and raising a family will be a dream come true for us. While we have just met you, Natalie has told us a great deal about you, your family, your values, your work ethic, and your success in your job at P&W. We know she loves you deeply, and I am sure, she will certainly, and with great joy, accept your proposal. So, my boy, it is with great pleasure that I give you our permission to propose marriage to our daughter."

Norton rose and opened his arms for a hug!

The lunch that followed was filled with great dialogue about the publishing industry. Norton asked many questions, trends, the effects of globalization, my take on several specific leaders in the US publishing industry. On a personal note, he asked where I hoped to be in five years. I kidded him, the question was a standard headhunter probe.

"I am the youngest senior editor at P&W and probably one of the youngest in the business. Basically, in the shorter term, my career path could go in one of two directions: managing editor or having my own imprint. The latter would be a real stretch. Longer term, like every editor, I would aspire to be the CEO of a major publishing house. If I were to ever see this as a real developing possibility, I would move to acquire a solid block of experience in marketing and sales promotion. I am intrigued with the international aspect of publishing and the inevitable globalization we both see developing. My brother Patrick has worked in London for the past seven or so years and travels the world extensively. My sister Katie is just completing her PhD in Ireland and will be marrying an Irish lad and settling there permanently. I speak French fluently, and I will be marrying a truly international woman. My personal global exposure and my vicarious experiences are and will be important to my career advancement. The world is indeed shrinking, and some businesses are intrinsically global. So there is my full spectrum of realistic career expectations all the way to my dreams."

"I find your career plans realistic and well in alignment with where I think the publishing industry is headed. As you talked, you never mentioned money. I understand that you do well at P&W and manage to earn a nice, incremental sum with a side job. Without getting into too much detail, may I ask you if you have independent income, such as a trust fund, or are you in line for a substantial inheritance?"

I laughed. "The simple answer is no on both fronts. My father, as you may know, is a doctor. Our family, can be described as comfortable. I hope my parents live to a ripe old age, spending their accumulated wealth on travel and whatever else pleases them. I have never been cavalier about money. I live quite frugally, I save and invest, my only vice and indulgence is fine wines."

"When you marry, it will important that you have been fully briefed on Natalie's financial situation," advised Norton. "When the time comes, we will insist on having a prenuptial agreement in place. I do hope you'll not have a problem with that."

"Whatever you and Pei Ling decide is in Natalie's best interests and she agrees, I will have no problem having a prenuptial agreement."

"Let's join the ladies up in the suite, I'm sure they are shopped out by now," suggested Norton.

As we arrived that evening at Le Veau D'Or, Catherine Treboux, the owner, greeted us. "So nice to see you again, Mr. Hewitt."

We were shown to a choice table. With a review of the interesting menu, Norton ordered the tripe, his favorite. We all passed on that and ordered sole amandine, the house signature seafood dish. The wine list was outstanding, and I demonstrated my oenophile skills, ordering wines to best complement our dinners. The award-winning dessert, L'ile Flottante, was sinful! The conversation was full of friendly banter. The Hewitts shared stories of Natalie's growing up, with a focus on her teenage years, some to her embarrassment! My future wife and her parents were a fun-loving family, much like my own. We meshed quickly and so well. We had a bit of a do over the dinner check. Natalie had been the host, over my protests, for our Friday night dinner. Norton had signed for lunch at the Waldorf. He then insisted, since this was "his restaurant," he was the host and would take care of the check. Pei Ling decided to join in. Dinner Sunday night at her favorite restaurant, serving Huaiyang-style cuisine from her hometown of Hong Kong, would be her treat. I surrendered to the Hewitts but insisted that I would host brunch Sunday morning. "No argument on that please." We parted company with a round of hugs.

Natalie and I had not had an opportunity to catch up on our individual times with her parents. I knew Pei Ling was very much up-to-date on our relationship as it had developed. She and Natalie spoke at length several times a week. Pie Ling's major concerns centered on the awareness and reaction of my family to Natalie's mixed ethnic background.

"Kevin and I have never discussed it in those terms. It simply is not important to either one of us. Neither of us thought our respective parents would have objections based on race, color, or creed. You and Dad and the Murphys simply are not that kind of people.

"Secondly, Mom and I have discussed what is a sensitive subject. You are aware from several of our casual conversations that my mother and her family have substantial interests both here in the US and in Hong Kong and other countries around the world. As I have shared, Pei Ling is Chairman of the Board/CEO and concerns herself with the company's real estate investments. Let me go into a bit more detail. Mother's two brothers are involved in the management of the company's various businesses. Uncle Shu-Chang is based in London and heads up the investment banking operations. My uncle Ming is the youngest and manages the traditional trading company activities. While based in Hong Kong, he is literally on the road most of the time. I have four cousins who are employed by the corporation: two stationed in Hong Kong, one in London, and one in Dubai. The company is privately held, with all shares held by the family, either individually or through trusts. My mother has a controlling interest. My father's family is of modest means, but as you know, Dad is a very successful lawyer. He is the managing partner of the largest law firm in Chicago employing three hundred attorneys. The firm is well regarded both nationally and internationally.

"The point of all of this, I have a current and substantial income in addition to my UN salary. This has allowed me to accumulate a considerable net worth, deriving from trusts set up for me by my maternal grandparents. As an only child, I will eventually inherit very substantial estates from each of my parents. My parents will insist that if you and I were to marry, we will have executed a prenuptial agreement. I hope that doesn't upset you."

"I've told you briefly, your dad and I had a good and long conversation over lunch. We discussed my career, my prospects and ambitions, and the publishing business worldwide. Your father is very familiar with my world. He knows P&W's CEO and has met several of our directors. The subject of my personal financial situation was raised, basically, asking the question, is there a substantial inheritance likely in my future? The answer was a very simple no. Your father assumes I earn a very good income with my side job, enhancing my excellent salary from P&W. There were questions as to my net worth and my lifestyle. You will be relieved to know your father explained your financial situation in general terms and put the prenuptial agreement on the table. I told him I would have no objections, as long as you agreed to the particulars. The bottom line, I greatly enjoyed meeting your parents. Your father and I get along well, and I believe we are comfortable with each other. Your mother is a woman I can respect and relate to with ease."

Natalie let out a huge sigh of relief! "I hope I pass muster with your family as well as you have done with mine."

Brunch was scheduled for ten thirty at the Tavern on the Green and dinner for eight that evening. I asked Natalie if she would mind if I went back to the apartment after brunch and joined them for cocktails around six o'clock at the Waldorf. She knew I wanted to put the finishing touches on my plan and focus on the presentation.

"Not at all, Kevin, my parents and I will enjoy just sitting around the suite and catching up on family and friends."

Sunday morning was made to order for brunch in the park. We met at Tavern on the Green. I had reserved a table well ahead to ensure seats with a view. It was the best vantage point for people watching. We were not disappointed. With a clear view of the front door, we saw people coming and going. In came Tiger Woods with a lady friend; going out the door I recognized Senator Chuck Shumer and guests; later, we saw Plácido Domingo arrive. Great people watching! The Hewitts were fascinated. Pei Ling commented, "In all of our worldwide travels, there simply isn't another city with the wonderful beat and rhythm of New York City. We love Chicago, but if we ever thought about relocating, in a heartbeat, it would be to New York City."

We spent the better part of an hour comparing the cities, the museums, restaurants, music, theatre, costs, the people, safety concerns, local politics, etc.

Brunch was fine. The Hewitts decided a long walk was in order. As planned, I excused myself and took a cab back to the apartment. My presentation to the executive committee was coming together nicely. I would use a slide presentation and handouts. I am comfortable in front of an audience and preferred an open format, allowing questions and comments from the audience on the fly. I was really pumped up and couldn't wait to have Annie's assessment. I wrapped up, showered, and dressed for dinner. Cocktails and light hors d'oeuvres in the Hewitts' suite, a relaxed family gathering. I needed to get Pei Ling aside for a few minutes to discuss design ideas for Natalie's engagement ring. We managed to chat as Natalie and Norton were out on the balcony checking traffic and the view. I gave Pei Ling a quick briefing on where we were on the engagement ring and asked for her help in selecting the mounting design. She was delighted with my overall plan and so pleased that I had asked for her help and opinion. We agreed I would send her pictures of the diamond and diagrams of suggested ring design as developed by Kaleb.

We left for Chinatown and Wu Ming Ju, Pei Ling's second favorite restaurant. We were warmly welcomed as valued customers. The dialogue was now in Cantonese, with both Natalie and her mother engaging the owner in their usual discussion of choices, preparations, etc. The cuisine of the house was Huaiyang, primarily fish, both sea and freshwater. The seasoning was mild, using a variety of herbs. I was asked if I preferred sea or freshwater fish or other foods from the water.

Growing up just outside Boston and a stone's throw from the ocean and several freshwater lakes and streams, I enjoyed the whole range of what is taken from the water.

The experience of dinner was a visual treat, with an effusion of enticing smells. The food was different from anything I had ever experienced in Chinese dining. The seasonings were subtle and pleasing to the palate. Natalie carefully explained each dish as to origin and preparation. Dining with the Hewitts, I could see, will always be an adventure.

The Hewitts were booked on an early morning flight back to Chicago, so we had planned to have them back to the Waldorf at a reasonable hour. I took leave of Norton and Pei Ling as we left the restaurant. Natalie would ride back to the Waldorf with her folks for a brief goodbye. We parted with a handshake from Norton and a hug from Pei Ling. We were all looking forward to the family gathering for New Year's Eve. Natalie came home after spending an hour or so with her folks.

"Kevin Murphy, you are, to use a fisherman's term, a keeper. Both my parents expressed how happy they were for me and could not be more pleased with you. Thank you!"

Time seemed to be accelerating, which I guess was fine. Natalie and I have settled into a comfortable domestic relationship. We continued to enjoy the good company of Annie and Helene with Larry quite frequently joining us, at art shows, concerts, and social events with mutual friends. Work at the office was also very fast-paced, partially due to the time of the year. I finished my long-range plan, having had excellent input and support from Personnel. I ran several practice presentations with staff, with great feedback for tweaking the final package. I had a commitment from Annie to review my proposal and presentation for feedback and, hopefully, her approval. With our move to new quarters and everyone pretty much settled in, I found the layout to be working quite well. I was seeing less of HSW; he was a very busy man with his expanded responsibilities.

Natalie was fully immersed in the project. She was finding that working from our spacious apartment was more productive without the distractions of the office setting. Chua Hua and Natalie had pretty much worked out effective methods of communicating even with the time differences. The Chinese Legation was very supportive, and Natalie had been warmly received when visiting their embassy in Washington. Progress was good, and both she and Chua Hua felt their work was both meaningful and important to improving relationships between the US and

China. Pei Ling was a constant sounding board for Natalie. Her mother was amazingly well informed on the cultural and historical history of China. Chua Hua's first trip to the US had been booked for December 5 through 18.

As we had arranged, I sent Pei Ling details on the diamond I had selected and the renderings Kaleb had prepared, with several designs for the setting. She complimented me on the diamond selected and assured me Natalie will absolutely love it. With several conversations and a teleconference with Kaleb, we settled on a simple but elegant design to be done in 18k yellow gold. It had been Kaleb's first choice. He assured me the ring would be done well before Thanksgiving, and correctly sized, thanks to information from my future mother-in-law.

My much-enjoyed work at the Dove continued with my Saturday night gigs and more than a few parties and special events. My help at the bar are longtime people, most of whom I had selected and trained. There was an active competition to get on the working list for parties and special events; the gratuities were outstanding! Pierre, the best maître d' in the business, had become a much-valued friend, and we enjoyed each other's company. He constantly worried that with my rapid success at P&W, I would have to leave the Dove. I assured him that money aside, the Dove was an important part of my life.

My folks and siblings were all fine. I kept them up-to-date with my life and with Natalie's China project. When I told them of the introduction planned with Natalie's parents and the plans for New Year's, they all went into overdrive.

"What is going on with you and Natalie?"

The planned Christmas gathering just couldn't happen soon enough! I told Mom and Dad how much the Hewitts were looking forward to the New Year's Eve get-together. They, too, were looking forward to meeting and the time together. All reservations had been made, and we were ready to go.

The date for my presentation to Annie was at hand. I had assumed it would be just the two of us. Her office called and asked me to have materials available for eight people. I called Annie and asked who would be in the meeting: the assistant to the managing editor, the four senior editors, her financial manager, and the personnel director. The meeting was scheduled for two hours, with lunch to follow, for Annie and myself in her office.

I thought the presentation went well. The questions and observations were very much to the point. I was asked by Personnel if the proposed reorganization of my group could/should be replicated across the entire editorial operation. My answer was "maybe." I was obviously comfortable the proposed reorganization would work for my group. I suggested that each editorial group take the question into careful consideration, performing a very detailed analysis of how their group functions and how efficiently work was being performed. The finance manager dug in heavily on the incremental costs associated with both new hires and the significant salary adjustments. I put the argument on the table, the not unsubstantial increase in costs were today's dollars being spent to purchase more productivity and increased profitability for tomorrow. Competition is becoming increasingly global and very aggressive, P&W's differentiation could not be in resources/capital but rather in doing what we do better and more efficiently than our competition. Several of the senior editors and the personnel manager roundly applauded the proposed intern program. The program would be a leg up in dealing with the heavy competition for about-to-graduate talent.

The meeting ran thirty minutes overtime, unusual for one of Annie's meetings. It ended with a round of applause. Annie and I adjourned to her office. Lunch was set up, and we sat down to eat. Annie, during the meeting, had asked few questions and made fewer comments. This was her style. Prodigious in her note-taking, she referred to her pad as we ate. She began by applauding my analytical methodology. One key concern was the restructuring of my group: Was it too personalized? Was it idiosyncratic? Was it possible to replicate in the final analysis? On the matter of costs, Annie observed, she believed the company could absorb my proposed increases in the ongoing cost of doing business, but on a less aggressive timeline. The internship program had her complete support.

"While the basic idea is not new, your approach with Fordham and Columbia is well-thought-out and innovative. I think students will be very attracted to P&W."

Annie had two very specific directives: Rethink and possibly rework the organizational changes. Remove as many impediments as possible to others adopting the basic approach. Make the case from a corporate perspective, not just from the editorial operations point of view. Work with Finance to frame a return-on-investment analysis. Suggest the opportunities for increased productivity and cost savings possible in other areas.

"Kevin, I am pleased with your initiative and the hard work putting this together. The involvement of staff is something I want to introduce throughout the editorial operation. After the first of the year, I'll ask you to do a mini workshop for all our managers. Assuming you will take my suggestions and subject to my review of your rework, I approve your plan and will recommend review and approval at the corporate level. Well done!"

With our planned Thanksgiving getaway clearly insight, I put in very long hours to ensure my long-range plan was revised as per Annie's directives, and it had secured her final sign-off. On reflection, her point on appearing too idiosyncratic was well-founded. With my deep understanding of the core of the editorial process, I retooled the reorganization segment, achieving most, not all of what I wanted. I realized what I hoped for was, in fact, too dependent on me and the very particular people on my team. The revised end product was, in my opinion, generic and could be adopted by all editorial teams. Secondly, the revised end product could not be considered unconventional.

Meetings with the financial manager were a challenge. His contention being my sense of cost savings were just that, not a provable fact. Whereas the incremental costs proposed were substantial, real, and predictable. We went around and around on the point. He was not prepared to budge. I researched the concept of probabilistic forecasting. I worked up numbers as to cost savings in high, low, and most probable modes. I also elongated the generation of cost savings by front-loading the modeled increases in expenses. Analysis showed that the proposal failed at the low end, with savings well below costs in the first four years, breakeven in the sixth year, and positive thereafter. The project was viable at most probable, with estimated cost savings beginning in the third year. Of course, if the high estimated cost savings were realized in year 1, the proposal would be a runaway winner! I reviewed the thinking with our financial manager. He liked my approach and said he would work up the models and cast it in a return-on-investment analysis. I was sure the appeal to him rested with the basic idea that if costs could be controlled by budget and if savings did not happen as projected, the program could be slowed or even cancelled. I was pleased with the end results and had the revised proposal to Annie by mid-November. She and I met, with the finance manager attending. Annie expressed her approval of my revised organization restructuring, and after an in-depth round of numbers crunching, she approved the return-on-investment calculations. She thanked the finance manager, and he left the meeting.

"Kevin, you have proven yourself both resourceful and creative. I asked my finance manager where the probabilistic approach originated. He gave you full credit for the idea. Your thinking processes, initiative, research, and analytical aptitudes are a great addition to your outstanding editorial and overall management/people skills. I will be pleased to recommend your proposal to corporate will my full support."

I thanked Annie for her support and asked, if possible, for a meeting with corporate in December, prior to Christmas. She, of course, knew Natalie and I would be spending Christmas in Brookline.

With my ducks pretty much lined up and in order, I rechecked our car reservations for pickup/drop-off at the Hyannis Airport, our limo reservations to and from La Guardia, reservations for dinner at Les Poissons, and arrangements for Thanksgiving dinner at the cottage prepared by Semmi. I had emailed Allen Templeton asking if he was going to be in Provincetown for the holiday; he knew we would be staying at Larry's cottage. I explained Natalie was a great admirer of his work, and if he had any free time, we would love to have cocktails with him. I had not heard back yet.

Kaleb had emailed, saying the ring would be ready November 14, and requested I call to schedule a pickup. I scheduled Monday the fourteenth for 5:00 p.m. I emailed Kevin at Kidder Peabody to alert him to a drawdown on the fourteenth. Natalie and I decided that we would drive to my parents for our Christmas visit. I confirmed a round-trip reservation for a four-wheel Honda Pilot SUV. Everything was set for New Year's get-together with the Hewitts and my folks. Wow! That's a lot of planning. I hoped we haven't overlooked anything!

Natalie continued to work long hours, thoroughly enjoying her China project. Rather than eating out, we usually had dinner delivered. Fortunately, there were a variety of good restaurants in the immediate neighborhood. We discussed Christmas gifts for various relatives and friends. My choice was always a good bottle of wine. Easy to arrange and to have delivered. We made a list and put together an order. Natalie listed the people for whom she would rather select more personal gifts.

Annie called to confirm pizza night. She asked if we would mind if they invited Larry O'Neil. I happily responded, "Not at all, we haven't seen Larry for several weeks."

Life was just great! The phone rang.

"Kevin, Allen Templeton here. I got your email. You've been looking over my shoulder! Larry mentioned your coming to Provincetown for Thanksgiving. Wonderful! I am just in the process of putting together a Cape Cod Thanksgiving dinner. Please share the festivities with me. I am looking forward to meeting your young lady. I always enjoy spending time with someone who appreciates my work. I am sure the Soldatovs, Phil Arenstein, Alina, and Madam Fontaine will be joining us. My plane is available for you New York people, round trip. We can coordinate all of that later. Please say you will join us?"

I knew that Natalie would be thrilled.

"What a wonderful and kind offer. Thank you, and we will be delighted to have a Cape Cod Thanksgiving with you. The use of your plane is much appreciated."

I heard the joy in his voice.

"I'll assign Phil Arenstein the job of coordinating the travel arrangements. Look forward to seeing you again."

When I was off the phone, I shared the great news with Natalie. She was beside herself!

"Not only do I get to meet Templeton, but I will have dinner with him and several other of Larry's best Cape Cod friends. You've said Allen keeps a lot of his work at home. It will be a private showing!"

I made a list of plans/reservations I would need to shuffle/cancel. With our cancelling Thanksgiving dinner at the cottage, I hoped Tomas and Semmi would not be too disappointed. I called Larry and thanked him for mentioning our visit to the Cape to his good friend Larry Templeton. I'm sure he was completely in on the whole plan.

We had planned to leave the city for the Cape on the twenty-second and returning on the twenty-sixth. Phil Arenstein, in his role as travel coordinator, called with the plan: depart the twenty-second, 7:15 a.m. from the Upper East Side helipad. Leave the Cape Sunday the twenty-seventh 4:15 p.m., arriving back at the NYC helipad around 7:00 p.m. Did that work for us?

"That's perfect and thanks for coordinating the trip."

He would make the helicopter reservations for the party and was looking forward to seeing me again and meeting Natalie.

I called Tomas and explained the change in plans. He understood.

"Semmi will be disappointed, but we are happy that Larry's friends are adopting you."

He would pick us up at Hyannis airport, no need to rent a car, the house vehicle would be available for our use during our visit.

"Thank you, Tomas, looking forward to seeing you and Semmi and introducing you to Natalie."

Back at the office, we were seeing a rich flow of submitted manuscript and book proposals. Clearly, P&W's reputation for success was increasingly drawing authors and agent proposals. On the financial front, the P&W stock, trading on the New York Exchange, was moving up smartly. We were reporting solid earnings growth and were being favorably reviewed by several major analysts.

Annie got back to me. She had given a copy and an overview of my revised proposal to HSW, with her full endorsement, and requested a presentation to corporate management.

"He and I met over lunch yesterday. HSW had several comments/questions, I handled his questions and will send you a note on his pithy and well-made comments. He is more than pleased with the proposal and approved going forward with his full endorsement."

I thanked Annie for her solid support. HSW's office called late that afternoon and advised that the proposal was now an item on the corporate agenda for Monday the twelfth at 10:00 a.m. I was allocated sixty minutes.

I had consulted with Paul, my art and design guru on the presentation, handouts, and slides. His suggestions and comments were great and added punch and comprehension to what was a complex proposal. His creative ideas for presentation of the heavy financial workups made the data easily digestible. With a promise to be back to me by November 28, we would have plenty of time to revise and fine-tune as needed. I had the assistance and support of the best in the business!

Our Wednesday night pizza get-together was a much-welcomed opportunity for both Natalie and me to come down from our frantic pace. Larry was already at the apartment when we arrived. He was becoming a regular at so many of our social gatherings. The friendships he wished for were developing. I thanked Larry for his "behind the scenes" contributions toward making our visit to the Cape so special. He, true to form, smiled and said that he had no idea what I was talking about!

"A little bit of business that I want to share with you and Annie. I have been meeting and otherwise working with Tom Harwood and Aloysius Murphy. The fit is working extremely well! They are two strong, bright, articulate, and well-informed gentlemen. Aloysius's global reach and depth of connections are more than impressive. Our interactions are informative, dynamic, and stimulating. Neither are shy about expressing their opinion. We freely challenge each other. Our planning is moving along to the point that we have tentative but detailed travel plans and agendas laid out and are making appointments for late January."

The attention turned to Natalie's China project. She, of course, was delighted to share the experiences of her recent trip to China. All three of our friends were more than casually aware of China's contributions to the arts over the centuries.

Conversation turned to holiday plans: Thanksgiving, Christmas, and New Year's Eve. Annie and Helene had a full calendar of travel plans, family visits, and of course, the super-busy social scene in the city. Larry and Peter would be in Paris for Thanksgiving, Christmas on the Cape with HSW as a house guest, and New Year's Eve in the city. Natalie shared the New York City introduction of Kevin to Natalie's parents, our Thanksgiving getaway to the Cape, Christmas in Brookline with my family meeting Natalie. They found both families sharing New Year's Eve in the city to be a wonderful idea. A prelude to *something*?

The rest of the evening was spent in sharing the news and gossip from the cultural, political, and social scenes. So much of our private lives overlapped in terms of shared interests and acquaintances. I was sure this was pleasing to Larry. The evening ended with what were now our usual hugs and kisses.

CHAPTER 12

NATALIE AND I BOTH WORKED long hours to ensure nothing would infringe on our getaway plans. We were at the heliport at the scheduled time, joined by Phillip Arenstein and the Soldatovs. Natalie knew the Soldatovs but had not met Phillip. With greetings exchanged, we boarded for the short trip to the airport. Allen's plane was waiting for us, and we took off without delay.

"This is certainly the way to travel," commented Natalie.

The weather was perfect for flying, and we arrived just as scheduled. Tomas greeted us on the ground and handled our luggage. The Soldatovs and Phil were sharing a limo, and we parted. All were looking forward to the Thanksgiving dinner with Allen Templeton.

I had picked up Natalie's ring on the fourteenth as had been scheduled. Words failed me to describe the beauty of the diamond in the setting created by Kaleb. I wrote a check for the balance due and thanked Kaleb for his wonderful assistance and his generosity. We were both very pleased with the product. The setting was simple but very elegant at the same time. I texted Pei Ling, telling her the ring was beyond my expectations, and offered to send her pictures. She declined.

"I would rather see it for the first time on my daughter's hand."

I was a nervous wreck carrying the ring around with me! I had made reservations for dinner Tuesday evening at Madam Fontaine's Les Poissons. I had conspired with Madam with a plan for presenting the ring to Natalie. On our arrival at the restaurant, I would discreetly hand off the ring to Madam. She would personally insert the ring in the dessert to be served at the end of dinner. I would wait until Natalie encountered the ring, fall to one knee, and ask her to marry me. We had arranged for a photographer to be at the ready. I was a nervous wreck, hoping Natalie wouldn't break a tooth or swallow the ring!

After a short drive, Semmi greeted us as we pulled up to the cottage. She was so happy to see me and to meet Natalie. I gave Natalie the grand tour. She loved the house. We went out onto the deck. Larry had "arranged" the weather as well as everything else! It was a great fall day, sunny with a light breeze off the water and a bit of a nip in the air. With the leaves mostly down, we had a splendid view of the water.

After one of Semmi's simple but great lunches, we decided to do a tour of downtown Provincetown and the beaches. We drove to the outermost beach and took a long walk on the sand. Natalie thought the water was a bit too rough for wading, so I set up lounge chairs and we actually both dozed off for a nap. Refreshed, we drove back into town. Traffic was heavy, and the streets were mobbed with tourists. It was a holiday weekend and kind of a last hurrah before the colder weather arrived.

With some difficulty in finding a place to park and paying an outrageous fee, we set off walking up one side of the main street and back down the other side. The shops and galleries were jammed as were the sidewalks. It was a festive scene! Natalie was very interested in the several art galleries and found the works displayed to be well-done, very interesting, and quite reasonably priced. One smaller work was, to her eye, exceptional and more than reasonably priced; she purchased it for the apartment. We realized the season for artists to sell their works is short, and this was the end of the season. An unsold work, left hanging on the wall, did not put bread on the table. Natalie commented, "Artists of Allen Templeton's caliber, of course, do not have that concern. His work is available for viewing in only four or five galleries worldwide, usually by appointment. Just think, I will have a private showing, cocktails, and dinner with the artist himself on Thursday!" Natalie had a huge grin on her face.

We stopped for an early cocktail and indulged in people watching from a street side table. The traffic was a mix of just ordinary folks, younger and older, families with kids, outrageously dressed characters, foreign visitors, and street performers of all sorts, jugglers, poets doing a reading, musicians and singers, even a young lady splendidly performing an operatic piece. With some reluctance, we left our sidewalk theater for our dinner reservation at Les Poissons. Madam Fontaine greeted us warmly as we entered the foyer. She said, in French, how happy she was to see me again. I introduced Natalie, also speaking in French. Madam gave Natalie a kiss on both cheeks and said, in English, how she had been looking forward to meeting her. To Madam's pleasant surprise, Natalie, in her fluent French, thanked Madam for her warm greeting. We are shown to a choice table. As we walked through the room, I managed to slip the ring into Madam's hand.

"Enjoy your dinner, and I'll join you for dessert."

Dinner was, as I expected, just very fine, the food, the presentation, the attentive service, and the warm ambiance. We enjoyed a very fine bottle of wine with dinner and were considering an after-dinner drink as Madam joined us.

"I do hope you enjoyed dinner. May I offer you a brandy? I have asked the kitchen to prepare a very special dessert for the occasion."

Our server brought the brandy and exquisite snifters to the table, and I poured. Shortly after, the waiter appeared with our dessert. The presentation was nothing short of amazing! Several petite castles of whipped cream mounted on individual squares of chocolate cake, decorated with very small strawberries and sour apple cubes. I literally held my breath as Natalie picked up her fork and cut into her cake.

"My goodness, this is marvelous and I'm sure very fattening."

Natalie had not noticed the photographer I had hired to capture the moment. She took a second portion. God, I hope she didn't swallow the damn ring! As she was about to put the fork into her mouth, she paused.

"What is this?"

As she began to wipe the chocolate and cream from the ring, I jumped up and sank to one knee. Natalie looked at me as if I had lost my mind. Wiping the ring clean, she let out a very loud scream!

"Natalie, I love you and want to spend the rest of my life with you, will you marry me?"

The photographer moved into place and captured the moment. Madam clapped and the room erupted in cheers. Natalie put the ring on her finger, smiled, and with tears streaming down her face, said, "Kevin, I love you so much and can't wait to be your wife."

People came over to our table offering congratulations and a smiling elderly couple sent over a bottle of champagne. They all added to making the evening so special. We thanked Madam profusely. She smiled, offering our dinner experience as her engagement gift. We left with hugs all around and said how much we were all looking forward to Allen Templeton's Thanksgiving dinner. I drove back to the cottage with great care; several martinis, a bottle of wine, brandy, and champagne had me on the edge. Tomas and Semmi were still up, waiting for us to come home. Natalie rushed to show Semmi her ring.

"Oh my goodness, is that a real diamond?" Semmi asked in awe.

Tomas offered his warmest congratulations and suggested a celebratory toast.

"I have been so nervous most of this night, I already have had one too many! What I really need is to fall into bed!"

We all had a good laugh and bid each other good night.

The bed had been turned down, our bags unpacked, nightclothes laid out on the bed, and a fire burning in the fireplace. I said to myself, "Thank you, Larry."

We dressed for bed and sat by the fire. Natalie was mesmerized with the fire and its light reflecting off her diamond. We eventually made our way to bed, made love, and fell asleep in each other's arms.

The sun streaming through the windows woke us early, but we just rolled over and snoozed for another hour or so. Natalie was first up, showered and dressed for the day.

After my usual long hot shower, I dressed, and we made our way downstairs. Semmi was on duty, ready to prepare our breakfast. Semmi asked to admire the ring again, holding Natalie's hand.

"I have never seen anything so beautiful. We are so happy for you both. God bless!"

We had planned a quiet day at the cottage, simply relaxing with a good book. Semmi and Tomas knew our plans for the day and had dinner planned for the evening. We were both prepared to be surprised. Semmi, of course, knew of my love for seafood, and I had assured her that Natalie shared that liking. We opted for breakfast in the kitchen, chatting with Semmi as she cooked. The weather promised to be a more typical November day on the Cape. The early sunshine would give way to rain and a heavy fog later in the day. Perfect day to curl up with a book in front of a fireplace. After a great and hardy breakfast, we adjourned to the family room. Tomas anticipated where we would settle and had a nice fire burning. Natalie excused herself to share the *big* news with her parents. I decided to hold off and surprise my folks, Pat, and Katie, until we were all together for the Christmas holidays. While Natalie was on the phone with her parents, I made just a few calls. I had promised Natalie that business would not intrude on our holiday.

I selected a book from the Larry's great library, went back to the kitchen for another cup of Semmi's fine blended coffee, and returned to a very big and comfortable chair next to the fireplace. Natalie came back into the room, beaming.

"You sneak! You had my parents in on your whole plan. They were so pleased that you formally asked my father's permission to propose. Mom is delighted to have been asked her suggestions on my ring and cannot wait to see it on my hand. You are ten feet tall in their book and probably are capable of walking on water too."

Tomas came in with a tray and fresh coffee.

"Would you mind if I do a bit of work-related reading?" asked Natalie.

"Not at all, so long as it isn't work you feel compelled to do."

The day drifted along. We enjoyed lunch by the fire, and I actually drifted into a light nap for an hour or so. Tomas brought in the *New York Times*, the *Wall Street Journal*, and the local paper. I switched from my book, which was quite good, to catch up on world events. Natalie and I exchanged views and our opinions on several items in the news. We were both basically conservative with a bit of liberal leaning in social matters. After I had read the *Journal* and we discussed the market, interest rates, and the like, we had our first in-depth conversation about our finances. I was surprised at just how well Natalie was being paid at the UN, $225,000, plus a very generous cost-of-living allowance. An interesting note, all of this was exempt from federal, state, and local taxes! In addition to all of that, the

UN provided wonderful benefits, including an excellent pension plan, a rarity these days. Natalie then disclosed her income from her trust, while variable, would comfortably average $600,000 to $1,000,000 or more a year. Natalie, as I know, lived relatively frugally. Her investment accounts included a significant block of stock in the family corporation, generating reliable and substantial dividends. I was thunderstruck when Natalie said that her investment accounts, Roth IRA, cash, and real estate amounted to a net worth well in excess of twenty-eight million dollars! As her father had indicated, Natalie would inherit very substantial estates from her parents *and* her maternal grandparents. She will eventually be the largest shareholder in the family business.

I was almost embarrassed to discuss what, in comparison, was my meager financials. My current income at P&W was better than $75,000 with a move to $90,000 very shortly. I was now eligible for both incentive compensation and stock options, which in time could be significant. The cash awards under the IC plan could be in the range of $45,000 in the next year or so. P&W benefits are excellent, and I too have a fine pension plan. As Natalie knew, I lived a lively but relatively modest lifestyle. My only vice being a taste for fine wines. In addition to my income from P&W, I regularly earn $5,000 to $8,000 a month from my activities at the Dove. Thanks to Kevin Smallwood's sound advice and good management, my Edward Jones account balance was in the neighborhood of $450,000. I am completely debt free and have an excellent credit rating. I noted I had paid cash for Natalie's ring. While I was taken aback at Natalie's finances, she was not at all surprised nor dismayed at mine! After a pause, I asked Natalie a question, "Now that I know you are an extremely wealthy young lady with an excellent job, good future prospects, and an heiress to *another* sizable fortune, would you please marry me?"

Natalie almost fell out of her chair laughing.

"Hopefully, it will be a long way into the future, but yes, I will inherit very sizable estates from my parents and from my maternal grandparents. You see why my parents are insistent we have a prenuptial in place before we marry. I have become comfortable with my wealth, both the current and what it will be in the future. My mother has given me a good and balanced perspective. I accept wealth as a challenge to do good. I have lived my life thus far, pretty much on my own earnings and would prefer that we do that as a couple, living on our combined earnings."

I didn't need to think too long before replying. "I could not agree more. We will build our life together based on our own initiatives. When we are blessed with a family, you may very well opt to be full-time stay-at-home mom. That will be your choice. Providing for our children's needs, educational and otherwise, might involve drawing on your piggy bank. That's a discussion we will have at the time. If you would like, I will be happy to discuss and advise on your philanthropic activities. The way I look at it, we will join the ranks of most other young married couples, having money problems, our problem, having too much, not too little!"

This brought a huge laugh from Natalie.

We bundled up to take a long walk before cocktails. Despite a dense fog and a bit of a chill in the air, the walk was invigorating.

"I would love for us to have a getaway on the Cape. More modest than Larry's cottage."

"Our children could spend a large part of the summer out of the city and the grandparents, and our extended circle of friends and family would have a wonderful place to visit."

"I couldn't agree more," I responded.

Our walk took us down to the water; the sound of the waves crashing, and the smell of the sea were magical. The exercise and the stimulation of the senses created an appetite. We were both hungry! Not surprising, Tomas and Semmi had hors d'oeuvres and cocktails prepared as we returned.

"Dinner at seven thirty if that will be okay, and we'll serve in the dining room."

"That will be just perfect, thank you."

As we were enjoying our cocktails, the house phone rang. Tomas answered and brought the phone to me. "It's Mr. O'Neil, he would like to speak to you both."

I put the phone on speaker.

"A quick call to wish you both a happy Thanksgiving. There is a rumor going around, something special happened as you were having dinner last night at Les Poissons. Congratulations and much happiness!"

We expressed our deep appreciation and wished both he and George a happy holiday.

I was running out of superlatives. The dinner prepared by Semmi was off the charts! It was a fall version of the best from the sea. Striped bass were coming down to the

Cape waters from Canada as they do every year. Bay scallops were still being harvested, the limited season was just ending, and lobsters were still in good supply. I learned later on, Semmi had consulted with Madam Fontaine as to what we had eaten the night before, avoiding duplication. Planning, planning!

Tomas, for his part, had consulted with Larry, discussed the planned menu, and was directed to serve a lightly chilled Montrachet from the cottage wine cellar, a Grand Cru Criots-Batard 2016. Did I mention, *planning*! With a wonderful sense of humor, Semmi had replicated the castle dessert from the prior evening. She told Natalie not to expect another diamond ring! We thanked Tomas and Semmi for a wonderful dinner. They beamed and wished us much happiness.

Thanksgiving Day arrived. We both reached out to family. My folks were in London with Patrick and Katie; Pei Ling and Norton were joining his sister and family in Chicago for the holiday meal. Patrick, Katie, and my folks were out and about when we called, so we left a message: "Could you find a turkey in London?" We called Annie and Helene. They would be having dinner with their family at the Dove. I ended the call with a tease.

"We'll have something to show you when we are back in town."

I sent off a number of emails to friends, office people, and my associates at the Dove.

Anticipating dinner at Allen Templeton's would be an extraordinary affair, we ate a very light lunch. The day was sunny and brisk. We took another walk, exploring the neighborhood. There were just a few cottages/homes in the entire area, all on very sizable lots, measured in acres according to Larry. Very few were visible from the road. Those we could partially see seemed to be done in the traditional Cape Cod style and, as with Larry's, gave the impression of being modest. We did manage to have a closer look at one home. It was of considerable size! We met a couple as we were strolling and exchanged cordial holiday greetings. After our walk and with several hours until we were expected at Allen's home, I suggested that we do more exploring of the general area. Traffic was light, people already at their holiday destinations. I had googled the locations of Phil's home as well as the Soldatovs. The doctor's home was on a road leading down to the Bay. As a departure from the traditional Cape style, most of the homes were very contemporary. Phil's house sat well back from the road, on a rise that would give a splendid view of the Bay. While not overly large, it was a dramatic, soaring design with huge expanses of windows. Facing east, the morning sun would flood the interior. Back out to Route 6, we traveled several miles to the outer limits of Provincetown. The unpaved road to the Soldatovs ran to the west and the ocean. The topography was dunes and scrub pines. There were not many homes visible. Driving along, we came to a barrier marking a private beach. We parked the car and walked the beach. At one point, we were able to make out two spectacular homes, high on a bluff affording an unimpeded view of the ocean. I ventured a guess that one would be the Soldatovs' Cape home.

Returning to the cottage, we had a bit of time to relax and dress before cocktails and dinner at Allen's home. I asked Tomas to fire up the hot tub and Natalie opted for a short nap. After our relaxation, we dressed and were on our way to the Templeton home. I remembered the way. I brought a good wine, appropriate to the holiday, a 2017 Napa Valley Cabernet Sauvignon. As we arrived, there were two cars in the driveway. Allen answered the door and greeted us warmly.

"So good to see you again, Kevin, and I have been looking forward to meeting this lovely young lady."

As we made our way into the very large living room, Natalie could not take her eyes off the several major pieces of art on the walls. The Soldatovs and Phillip were already enjoying cocktails and greeted us. Shortly after, Madam

Fontaine and Alina arrived. What a wonderful group of people! I again said to myself, "Thank you, Larry!"

With a cocktail in hand, Madam raised her hand and proposed a toast.

"As always, good health to our host and good friends gathered here. I am pleased to announce the engagement of Kevin Murphy and Natalie Hewitt. It happened just last night at Les Poissons. Much happiness to the young couple!"

There followed a big round of applause, hugs, and handshakes. Madam invited Theresa Soldatov to inspect Natalie's engagement ring.

"That is so beautiful, I love the setting. Kevin, you have excellent taste!"

Allen came over and gave us his best wishes. "I understand, Natalie, you find my work to be interesting. Let me give you a brief tour of what I have here in the house. As you can see, I display my work where I can enjoy it every day. Come along, let's start with my studio."

Allen took Natalie by the hand, and the two of them went off, already in deep conversation. Drinks were refreshed by the attentive staff, and we settled into light but interesting conversations.

Just as I was beginning to wonder where Natalie and Allen might be, they came back into the living room. Allen guided her to the several heroic works hung in the room. Overhearing their conversation, I was very impressed with how Natalie was engaging the artist. Her questions focused on technique, the introduction of texture, how certain colors were achieved, scale, and the framing perfectly matched to the work itself. With the announcement that dinner was about to be served, Allen and Natalie were drawn back into the group.

As I remembered from my earlier visit, the dining room was unique, large, and at the same time, intimate. The table was set with three to a side with Allen at the head of the table, Natalie between Alina and Sergei, and I shared Theresa with Phil. As promised, this was to be a traditional Cape Cod Thanksgiving dinner. The turkey was carved and served at the table with the precision of a surgeon. This tour de force earned the carver a round of applause. As dinner progressed, Natalie shared her China project with the group, with a very interesting overview of her recent trip to China.

"I assume you have some fluency with Chinese," asked Theresa.

"Well, the long answer to your question is my mother is Chinese from Hong Kong. As a child, I grew up speaking both Mandarin and Cantonese, and I am fluent in both. I majored in Asian Cultures in undergraduate school, and so my interest in sharing our cultures, American and Chinese, was developed early on. My family has business interests in China, Japan, the Koreas, Taiwan, Dubai, England, the US, and the Philippines. I have been fortunate to have traveled extensively with my family."

Natalie was engaging, witty and obviously very bright. She held her audience in the palm of her hand right through dinner.

Sergei and Theresa were well-known movers and shakers in the worldwide art community. Sergei had apparently overheard Natalie's fascinating discussion with Allen on his work.

"How did you come by your great insights into contemporary art?" he asked Natalie.

"Thank you for that compliment. As I had said, I majored in Asian Cultures, but I have a strong minor in contemporary art of the twenty-first century. My maternal grandparents have an excellent and extensive collection and are, as are you and Theresa, very involved and supportive of several major art museums. I greatly enjoyed time with them, visiting museums, art shows, and auctions. In traveling, we had the opportunity to visit with other collectors and enjoy their holdings."

Allen raised his hand. "Just as a matter of course, I have many questions put to me about my work in general and heavy probing on occasion on a particular piece. As I see it, part of my job as an artist is to answer these probes with candor and in a way that encourages, even invites people to enjoy and understand what it is that I am trying to achieve. In all honesty, I am also selling. I need to rationalize a person spending the outrageous prices I ask for my paintings."

This drew an extended round of laughter.

"Natalie has an unusual eye, married to a keen understanding of technique. There hasn't been a need to invite her to enjoy my work nor to labor over my techniques. Her sensitivities match Theresa's. I enjoyed the hour we just shared. Thank you, Natalie."

After a fine dessert, pumpkin pie or blueberry pie or ice cream, we all adjourned to the living room. Madam wanted to discuss wedding plans with Natalie. The conversation started in English but quickly moved to French. Natalie had said she wanted to practice. Being a natural linguist, she never missed a beat. Theresa joined in; girls loved to discuss wedding plans, the number of bridesmaids, color of gowns, menu for the reception, cake ideas, church or other sites, etc. The gentlemen covered the usual: the stock market, world peace or lack thereof, climate control, inflation, politics, etc. While I would guess we were all Republicans, there was a general consensus: our political scene was, at best, chaotic!

I was truly happy the evening had gone so well, particularly for Natalie. I got Allen aside and told him how much I appreciated his bringing us into his circle of friends with his wonderful holiday dinner.

"You know that Larry O'Neil and I are the very best of friends. He and I both have many acquaintances the world over but very few people we consider as friends. Madam, Theresa, Sergei, Phillip, Alina, and Thomas are in that small group. I must tell you confidentially, I worry about

Larry's choice of other friends. When he is here on the Cape, he is very much at peace. The people in this room are enriched by our friendships. When I first met you, my instinct told me you could be a true friend to Larry. Over the past months, he and I have talked about your evolving relationship, both professional and personal. We've also talked about your small group of friends, Natalie, Annie, and Helene. I hope you understand that while Larry is gay, his personal feelings for you are totally asexual. He would very much value your friendship and a closer association with your circle of charming, bright, and delightful ladies. I would like you to know that a person who is a true friend to Larry O'Neil is a friend of the people in this room, Allen Templeton included!"

The evening ended at a reasonable hour, and we parted company with warm wishes all around. In the car, Natalie was beside herself!

"We are moving to Provincetown! I cannot remember another evening where I have so enjoyed myself. These people are twenty-four karat! Bright, informed, articulate, witty, and so genuine! I can't thank you and Larry enough. This will always be an incredibly special memory."

CHAPTER 13

FRIDAY AND SATURDAY WERE, BY design, devoted to each other. The day started with an indulgent sleep-in, a great breakfast in the kitchen, chatting with Tomas and Semmi and then off to wander and explore the Cape. We took Route 6 and stopped in Chatham. We both remembered prior visits to what was considered the prettiest town on the Cape. We spent time window-shopping and then had a late lunch at the Chatham Bars Inn. Probably the best clam chowder on the Cape, after Semmi's, of course. We wandered into Hyannis, and as expected, the streets were crowded. We decided to skip the long lines at the Kennedy compound. Driving back toward Provincetown on Route 28 provided more than a few reasons to stop and explore. Next to lobsters, art seemed to be the second most popular commodity for sale. Possibly tied with saltwater taffy.

We were back to the cottage just as the cocktail hour arrived. To their great disappointment, we had told Tomas and Semmi that we would be eating out both Friday and Saturday evenings. Last week, I had asked Larry to recommend an Italian restaurant and had made a reservation. It took some name-dropping to secure a table.

We had our pre-dinner cocktails on the deck. Tomas had started a fire, perfect for a brisk evening. Allowing for heavier traffic, we left for Bell Italia. The restaurant was somewhat off the beaten path. Parking looked like a real problem, solved with a $20 bill to an enterprising young man with a long driveway, just down the street from our destination. What the restaurant lacked in not having a view was more than made up by its intimate charm. Avoiding Chianti bottles, repurposed as candle holders; the small dining room tables were covered in white cloth, not red-checkered plastic; a small, fresh flower arrangement, also not plastic, and real candles in painted porcelain candlesticks. We were greeted by the maître d' and immediately seated. Our waiter, an elderly gentleman, with a heavy Italian accent arrived and lit the candles.

"I am Anthony, and it will be my pleasure to serve you this evening."

Being the foodies we were, we had more than the usual questions. Anthony could have been the head chef. He answered each of our questions, with a great understanding of foods, sauces, spices, and cooking techniques from the different regions of Italy. With all of that to consider, we ordered cocktails and asked for the house wine list. We discussed the menu and specials for the evening, selected our entrees, and turned to the wine list for ideas. Natalie had decided on veal Marsala with a side of creamy polenta. With so many dishes I liked, Anthony helped me by recommending a special of the evening, eggplant Parmigiana-Reggiano over lobster-stuffed ravioli. For starters, Anthony spoke highly of the house-fried calamari. We ordered a serving. Next, we discussed Anthony's thoughts on a wine complementing our entree selections. He supported my thoughts, Opus One, a Cabernet from the Napa Valley (2017). After we had ordered, the maître d' came to the table and, with profound apologies, informed us that Opus One Cabernet was out of stock. He suggested a Lorenzo Accomasso (2014), a Barolo Rocche.

Dinner more than lived up to our expectations. Portion size was not overwhelming, as could happen in some Italian restaurants. Anthony's service was more than attentive. I must say that the acidity and tannins of the Barolo Rocche blended nicely with Natalie's creamy veal Marsala sauce and my mild red sauce over the eggplant. With Anthony's continued excellent guidance, we ordered strawberries Zabaglione along with espresso. We were served anisette, compliments of the maître d'. Leaving a more than generous gratuity for Anthony, I made a point of thanking the maître d' for his kind attention.

Despite telling Tomas and Semmi not to wait up for us, they were on duty as we came home. We were both ready to turn in after a delightful day. Semmi and Tomas had, of course, set a fire, turned down the bed, and laid out our nightclothes.

We awoke to the sound of rain, rolled over, and snoozed for an hour or so. We roused ourselves, showered, dressed, and joined Tomas and Semmi in the kitchen. We enjoyed chatting with them as Semmi prepared our breakfast. Tomas gave us the weather report, raining all day and into the evening, very heavy at times.

After breakfast, we settled in the den, in the very comfortable chairs, Natalie with her casual work-related reading and me with the newspapers. The fire, laid in by Tomas, was perfect for such a gloomy day.

"I think I've gained at least five pounds in the last few days," complained Natalie.

"I can top that! How about we skip dining out this evening and ask Semmi for a simple and early dinner?"

Natalie thought that was a great idea and went off to the kitchen to consult with Semmi. Semmi and Tomas were delighted!

The day drifted by with the only interruption being an occasional phone call. Pei Li called, as did Annie and Helene. Natalie fended off questions from our friends as to "What is going on?" They reported they were hearing rumors. I had calls from both Patrick and Katie. All was well with the family gathering in London. Mom and Dad really enjoyed the visit and shared Patrick's love of the city.

All were looking forward to the Christmas gathering of the family and our guests.

Lunch was simple, as we had requested. Semmi's clam chowder, grilled cheese sandwiches on home-baked bread. Around five, we went upstairs to pack for the trip home. All our clothes were laid out on the bed, washed/pressed! Leaving out our travel outfits, we packed, ready for an early departure.

"We need to do something special for Tomas and Semmi. Their care and attention made the getaway so relaxed and enjoyable."

I agreed and suggested we consult with Larry when we were back in town. We joined Tomas and Semmi in the kitchen.

Semmi's idea of a light and simple dinner came out as a wonderful roast chicken, served with baby potatoes and carrots. We had skipped cocktails. I asked Tomas if we happened to have any beer in the house. Silly question, he gave us a choice of several! We very much enjoyed dinner and were off to bed by nine thirty.

We were up and ready to leave by around six. Our car rental, as arranged, had been delivered that morning. We thanked Tomas and Semmi for their great care and for making our getaway such a treat. We had said we would not be having breakfast in the morning. Semmi had prepared a thermos of coffee and several home-baked bagels with cream cheese for us to munch on as we drove. They never stopped planning! The drive from the Cape to the city was uneventful, and traffic was relatively light. Making great time, we were back to the city, unloaded the car, and returned it to the rental agency. I dressed for work and was in the office by noon.

My whole focus is now on my upcoming presentation to the executive committee. Meeting with Paul, my art and design guru, we reviewed the slides and the handouts. Great job and with a few minor changes, we had an excellent finished product.

"Outstanding job, my friend." I applauded my associate.

Late the next day, he delivered the finished product, slides, handouts, audio support. Paul assured me he would personally set up the room for my presentation. I called Annie and told her I had the finished product, and would she like me to run through it with her? She declined. I offered to send up a copy of the handouts for her review prior to the meeting.

"Not necessary Kevin, I have every confidence in you and your work. I want to see/hear it as you present it to the executive committee."

I was pleased that she will be in the meeting.

That evening, I gave Natalie the full presentation, inviting her comments and critical feedback. I also wanted to get my timing down, remembering I had been allocated sixty minutes. As I concluded the run-through, Natalie gave the following assessment: "First, the visual aspect is excellent. Complex material is diagrammatically presented with good use of color for differentiation. Content-wise, your underlying rationale for the proposed reorganization, while conceptually sound, could become argumentative, with what I see as an overemphasis on compensation. I would step back from that a bit and not open it up to comments/objections that could detract from the overall concept. The intern program is strong, made so much the better, by having already developed a detailed plan with Fordham and Columbia. The probabilistic approach to the financials recognizes predictions of future events are reasonable across a range of possibilities. It is a sophisticated approach. The executive committee should recognize and appreciate it. Overall, the presentation is solid. Your style of presentation, while acutely focused, comes off as relaxed. This projects confidence. The pace is good. I would suggest inviting questions as you go through the presentation. I find that senior people do not want to hold their comments/questions. Keep your eye on the clock. Do not over-run your time!"

Natalie's comments were excellent, a fine-tuning to my presentation.

*****

The time had arrived. I was quite relaxed as I took the elevator up to the corporate offices. I arrived ten minutes before the appointed time. The secretary at the conference room door invited me to have a seat. At a bit after ten, HSW came out of the room, smiled, and invited me to join the executive committee meeting. I had arranged for Paul to have access to the room prior to the meeting to set up my presentation. There were six men and three women around the table. I know five of the six men: Mr. Conroy, the CEO; Arthur Black, the executive vice president; George Sanders, vice president–finance; Thomas Long, legal counsel; and of course, the vice president–publishing, HSW. The sixth gentleman was introduced as George Kincaid, a senior member of the Board of Directors. The three women at the table were Mary Ellen Connors, vice president–employee relations; Annie, managing editor; and MaryAnn Push, Mr. Conroy's administrative assistant, serving as secretary to the committee.

HSW introduced me and outlined what I would be presenting to the committee. He indicated, "Mr. Murphy's proposal has been intensely reviewed by his supervisor, Ann Hopkins, managing editor, and by me. We both find the proposal to be an excellent, well-reasoned piece of work and it has our full endorsement. I would like the committee to be aware that Mr. Murphy undertook the study and prepared the proposal at his own initiative." HSW said, "With your permission, I give the floor to Mr. Murphy."

Mr. Conroy gestured and said, "Kevin, the floor is yours."

"Thank you, Ms. Hopkins and HSW, for your support and thank you, Mr. Conroy, for the opportunity to address the executive committee. Ladies and gentlemen, please feel free to ask questions or make comments as we move through the presentation."

With that, I distributed the handouts, lowered the lights, and pulled up the opening slide. An immediate question came from our board member. "Why do you feel, your proposal is timely and meets unmet needs or addresses critical issues?"

I gave Mr. Kincaid a tight answer. I explained what I considered the critical issues needing to be addressed. He seemed satisfied. As Natalie had anticipated, the compensation points drew both questions and a few very pointed observations from both the VP of Employee Relations and the VP of Finance.

"Admittedly, I have perhaps put too much emphasis on the compensation element of the proposal. While important, it is not the essence of the proposal and is open to modification."

Once over that hump, the presentation went quite smoothly. The questions were focused and good, the comments supportive. As I had hoped, the VP of Finance was very complimentary on the approach taken to develop the return on investment calculations. Our board member joined him in commenting that it put the proposal in an excellent perspective.

I had managed the presentation is just minutes under the hour allocated.

"If there are no further questions or comments, I'd like to thank Mr. Murphy for a fine job. Senior editorial support and endorsement for the proposal is noted. Thank you."

Annie and I rose and started to leave the room.

"Ms. Hopkins, please stay with us for a few more minutes," asked Mr. Conroy.

What transpired in the room after would become clear soon.

*****

Natalie had called Helene and invited her and Annie for drinks. I had been home just a few minutes before our friends arrived.

"Okay, you two, what happened at the Cape?" asked Helene.

Natalie laughed and extended her hand!

"Kevin, you have excellent taste in a bride-to-be and in diamond rings. You are also great at keeping secrets. Congratulations," said a beaming Annie.

Following Chua Hua's very productive time in New York in early December, Natalie and I were off to Brookline for the Christmas holidays. Patrick, Katie, and Shamus had already arrived and were settled in at the family homestead. To not overwhelm Natalie and Shamus, my mother had planned just a small family dinner. There was a lot of news to be shared. Patrick announced he had just received a substantial promotion and would be relocating back to the States, working in New York City. Hoorah! Katie and Shamus announced their plans to marry sometime in the fall of next year. Shamus had followed the proper protocol and had asked my father's permission to marry Katie the very evening they arrived in Brookline. Plans were still in the making, but the wedding would be in Ireland. Now it was my turn. Mom and Katie had both noticed Natalie's engagement ring, but neither had commented.

"Well, I have some great news to share, while Natalie and I were visiting Cape Cod over the Thanksgiving holiday, I proposed, and thank God, she accepted! Mom and Dad will be meeting Natalie's folks over New Year's Eve in New York City. We haven't settled on a wedding date, but rest assured, you are all invited!" To say that the mood was super joyful would be an understatement. There were lots of questions for both Shamus and Natalie. The next days were filled with meeting my fun-loving, sometimes raucous Boston Irish family. Including my grandmother, uncles, aunts, and cousins by the dozen. Natalie and Shamus fitted right in. It could not have gone any better!

The next big event, the meeting of the parents, followed hard on the heels of our visit to Brookline. My parents arrived midday on the thirtieth and checked into the suite we had reserved at the Waldorf. The Hewitts arrived around five and check into their regular suite. It was a wonderful New York City winter evening, with light but steady snowfall. The plans called for cocktails in the Hewitt suite, with dinner downstairs in the Bull and Bear dining room. Both my father and Norton Hewitt were fond of steak. A house specialty of the restaurant was Satsuma Wagyu steak, imported from Japan and regarded as the best steak in the world. Natalie and I arrived at the Waldorf. She went directly to her parent's suite, and I went to fetch my parents. Natalie and I had no reservations about our parents getting along; both sets were very social creatures, interesting conversationalists with broad areas of interest. The Murphy family arrived at the Hewitt suite and were greeted with hugs and kisses from Natalie. I exchanged the same with Norton and Pei Ling. Natalie and I had briefed our respective parents on the other couple. With the introductions made, we all settled into relaxed conversations over cocktails. The dialogue was animated, and conversations sometimes happened simultaneously. Getting to know you flowed easily. As the dinner hour rolled around, it was clear that the group chemistry was just fine. Natalie and I shared a knowing smile as we made our way down to the Bull and Bear. Suffice to say, dinner was just great. Norton and my dad gave the steak rave reviews. The parents shared stories of our growing up, often to our mild embarrassment. As we left the restaurant, Pei Ling invited everyone to their suite for an after-dinner drink. Natalie and I begged off. We were concerned with traffic and the snowstorm.

Sunday morning, the parents came to our apartment, for a light brunch around noon. The afternoon was spent with family news and gossip, Natalie's travel plans, our preliminary thoughts on a wedding date, location, and such. As the evening celebrations at the Dove would go into the early morning hours, our parents wanted to have a have brief nap before dinner and the evening festivities, they left for the hotel around 4:00 p.m. The plan was to rendezvous at the Dove. Our reservation was set for 7:30. The evening was formal. My darling fiancée Natalie was stunning in a soft gold gown, accented by a remarkable jade jewelry ensemble. She remarked how well I looked in my tuxedo. I'll avoid my usual blow-by-blow description of the evening. It was the Dove at its very best! Outstanding start to finish! More than a few of my regulars stopped by our table with best wishes for the New Year. Pierre had been super attentive. The owners of the Dove each stopped by the table with best wishes; several bottles of the very best champagne arrived at our table with their compliments.

CHAPTER 14

Allow me to develop perspective. I am now going to move quickly through several major happenings, leading up to the moment of my *crisis!* Natalie and Chua Hua wrapped up their study and wrote a very detailed analysis of the cultural scenes in the United States and China. Their analysis had both present and historical dimensions. The study covered literally all art forms with excellent photography, illustrations, and an audio library. Areas of cultural uniqueness were noted as were commonalities. The paper was well received, in China, the US, and worldwide. The authors received critical acclaim for the scholarship of their work. The UN reprinted the paper in fifteen languages and made a worldwide distribution. Letters of commendation were received from the governments of China and the United States along with other governments and major universities. The project was viewed as a major contribution to sharing the rich cultural heritages of China and the US.

In early February, I was called to Mr. Conroy's office, already seated were HSW and Annie.

"Kevin, I want you to know that the executive committee has met with Ms. Hopkins and HSW several times to review in-depth their sense of how best to move forward with your proposal. The committee has fully approved your plan. We recognize that the plan is bold with far-reaching implications for P&W. The committee, with HSW's and Ms. Hopkins's approval, would like the proposed plan implemented across the entire editorial operation.

Recognizing the importance of the initiative and the need for dedicated management to ensure success, we have approved creating a new position in the management chain of the company's editorial operations. The new position, reporting to the managing editor, is that of associate managing editor. Kevin, we are pleased to announce your promotion to the position. Congratulations!"

Patrick happily arrived in New York City, found a great apartment, joined my gym and the poker group, and quickly assimilated into our broad circle of friends. It was just great having him home.

In early September, the extended Murphy clan was off to Ireland for Katie's marriage to Shamus. Kathleen has taken the Gaelic name Caitlin. Katie had asked Natalie to be her maid of honor. This pleased Natalie no end. The trip included the required pub crawls, rounds of golf, multiple dinners and cocktail parties, dove shoots, and a great deal of laughter. Shamus's family were as fun-loving as the Murphy clan. A great time was had by all!

We saw less of Larry, although he and I talked frequently. He was totally immersed in his book and traveled extensively with Tom Harwood and/or Father Murphy. Aloysius was now Monsignor Murphy, having been elevated directly by the Holy Father at the recommendation of the Archbishop of New York. Aloysius was now an apostolic protonotary, the highest ranked of monsignori. Larry was extremely pleased with the progress they were making and notes how impressed he was with Monsignor Murphy's connections and access within the Catholic church, in the US, Rome, and worldwide. As the editor on the project, I couldn't be more pleased.

Natalie and I had set our wedding date for mid-November, about a year after our engagement. With much thought and discussion along with needed research, we had settled on Cape Cod for a destination wedding. A great stroke of good luck, we were able to book the very much in-demand, Chatham Bars Inn. The three-day affair involved the coming and going of 182 guests: family, of course, along with our New York City and Provincetown friends, work associates, a goodly number of guests and relatives from Hong Kong and China, and several distinguished guests from the UN. Patrick of course, was my best man, assisted by Shamus and Larry O'Neil. Natalie had Katie as her maid of honor and Annie and Helene as her bridesmaids. We made a point of insisting that the reluctant Tomas and Semmi attend. The weather cooperated, and the day was sunny with 60 degrees, warm for mid-November. Monsignor Murphy officiated; he had arranged for and gave us a special Papal Blessing. The Inn did an outstanding job.

We received a bounty of great and unique wedding gifts. We were surprised and stunned to receive not one but two Templeton paintings. The first, from Annie and

Helene, was a smaller work Natalie had admired at Allen's home last fall. A larger painting from our Provincetown friends: Allen Templeton, Phillip, the Soldatovs, Alina, and Madam Fontaine. Tom Harper's gift was his wonderful music. His chamber group played for the wedding service. Tom sang and played the piano at the reception. Chua Hua's joint gift with the government of China was a delicate and magnificent fifth-century carved piece of jadeite. Larry O'Neil's wedding gift was over-the-top and outrageous. He had carved out a buildable plot from his considerable acreage and an adjoining neighbor's substantial property to form a three-acre homesite. He has deeded the lot to us for our future cottage in Provincetown! We will be neighbors, to our mutual delight.

The next year found us both very busy with work and frequent travel. With the greatest reluctance, I had to face being able to continue my work at the Dove. My association, spanning nearly ten years, was not just about the income, which had always been great, that was now incidental. The fact of the matter was those times behind the bar and managing special events for my regular customers represented a very important part of my life. I had developed a range of wonderful friendships, with customers, the management, and the staff. Very simply, I totally enjoyed my time at the Dove. It met so many of my social and emotional needs, I could *not* wean myself completely from the association. I had several conversations with Pierre, seeking his guidance. We agreed that my time behind the bar was where I was of the most value to the Dove. A commitment of two Saturday nights per month seemed to be feasible, to be scheduled with great flexibility to accommodate my P&W work needs. The planning and management of special events could be adequately handled by staff I had trained and worked with over the years. Covering the Saturday nights when I was not available would also be more than adequately tended to by staff I had selected and trained. Pierre commented that there would be fierce competition to get the assignment! Management fully understood, appreciated my continued loyalty, and approved the plan.

Natalie and I had begun preliminary discussion about a larger home. She had purchased the coop unit when she first arrived in New York. At the time, the market was down, and the purchase price was more than reasonable. Today, the market was right on the sell side. Prices were also definitely up substantially on the buy side. The inventory was ample. Despite higher prices, all cash offers, which we would do, gave us some leverage. When we casually mentioned the idea to Patrick over drinks, he said he would definitely want to purchase Natalie's apartment. As a part of these conversations, Natalie and I discussed a future family. We both agreed that three children seemed just right.

The first part of March, Larry submitted the first installment of his novel, the four opening chapters. I read the manuscript quickly for first impressions and then reread with my critical editor's eye. The author clearly laid out his proposition, the thesis for the work. His intent was straightforward. The lives of several people, some of whom have been declared saints by the Catholic church, would be rigorously examined, searching to understand the rationale for their life choices. Saint Francis of Assisi, Saint Teresa of Calcutta, and Mahatma Gandhi, an ordinary mortal, were those selected. It was already apparent from the opening chapters, considerable research had already been done on all three, looking at their lives and putting them in perspective as to the times they lived in. The manuscript was rich in detail. The author had been physically "in touch" with Francis, Mother Teresa, and Gandhi, visiting multiple sites in Italy and India.

The delicate process of declaring sainthood was treated with an objective discussion of the complex and protracted process. She was a rare exception to the norm. She was a fast-track saint. I was particularly pleased; the author had included a discussion of the cause of Pope Pius XII. There had been resistance/reluctance to declare him a saint based largely on the Vatican's poor defense of Italian Jews and a disinclination, to challenge and condemn Hitler and Germany for their deadly anti-Semitism and the Holocaust. It being alleged, the Pope's decisions had been largely political.

Larry's treatment of the pending cause of Pope Pius XII focused on the very deliberative and rigorous process employed by the church. Monsignor Murphy, Tom Hardwood, and Larry had been granted a very rare, open access to the Vatican Library. This openness gave great credibility to the integrity of the process of making a saint.

Following his past practice, Larry generated manuscript at a prodigious pace. Our copyediting/fact-checking was made easier by the clear evidence of the excellent, ongoing involvement of Dr. Harwood and Monsignor Murphy.

Their contributions were substantial. There was evident, subtle, but significant change in the author's approach. The shift would only be apparent to those of us involved from the very beginning. The absence of any adversarial posture was significant. Monsignor Murphy had initially been deeply concerned with the matter. First, he worried about aggressive questioning of the subject's intentions or motivations in choosing the lifestyle and values embraced. Secondly, there was a deep concern about questioning the purpose saints served for the institutional church. None of this cynical probing was at all evident. Unless an unanticipated roadblock occurred, Larry's third book would be on our fall list, keeping to the very rare two-year start-to-finish pattern so peculiar to Larry O'Neil.

In my new position as associate managing editor, my time was substantially devoted to bringing our large editorial operations on board with the reorganization plan. I used the Japanese methodology for instituting change. I had utilized it very successfully with my own staff. It would be a slow and in-depth process of explaining and achieving the buy-in of all involved. Implementation per se was meticulously planned in digestible stages; resistance was nominal. Some rethinking and modifications were dealt with quickly and effectively. I was optimistic we would be operational under the new structure by year-end. While I missed the involvement in day-to-day editorial work, I found pure management to be stimulating, and it gave me a great sense of achievement.

As I had expected, we were able to release Larry O'Neil's book to prepress for placement on the fall list. The book met with huge success right out of the box. Sales far exceeded our expectations. As a footnote, Paul, my Art and Design guru, had produced a riveting cover design. The eye was not drawn but pulled to the book on display! Early reviews lauded the Catholic church for providing edifying lives for the world to emulate, absent any evidence of feeding crass institutional needs. The reviewers praised the rigor with which the author examined the subject's life and motivations for choosing commitment to the poor, hungry, sick, and underprivileged. We had a bestseller!

With the release of his new book, Larry took all by complete surprise, with the exception of Monsignor Murphy, with a startling set of profound life-altering decisions. First, Larry formally became a Roman Catholic. Secondly, as an apparent separate decision from his conversion, he terminated his long relationship with Peter Cordillion. Peter angrily blamed me in cahoots with Monsignor Murphy and the Catholic church for Larry's decisions. We had the genesis of my crisis; the fuse was lit!

CHAPTER 15

I WAS ATTENDING A RECEPTION, CELEBRATING the hugely successful launch of the O'Neil title, joined by Natalie. It was a large gathering, with the usual industry types, the press of course, and a substantial number of clergy, including, the cardinal archbishop of New York in the good company of Monsignor Murphy. As the publisher, we were the host for the gathering. The affair was catered with elaborate hors d'oeuvres passed and an open bar. Our CEO and senior executives were in attendance.

Well into the evening, Natalie and I were chatting with Monsignor Murphy when Peter Cordillion approached.

"Well, here we have the two bastards who stole Larry from me."

His voice was very loud, and he was obviously drunk. His comments were widely overheard.

"The fucking Catholic church is nothing more than a money machine for the asshole sitting on his throne in the Vatican."

Natalie tried to calm Peter down and took hold of his arm.

"Don't touch me, you slant-eye bitch," he screamed, shoving her aside.

She fell to the floor. With the violent attack on my wife, I landed a solid knockout punch to Peter's chin! The room was in an uproar. The press was feverishly taking notes, and two photographers were snapping pictures. Thankfully, security arrived and removed Cordillion. It was suggested I leave the hall.

The aftermath was ugly! The press had a field day! Pictures included, with Peter on the floor and me being escorted out of the hall by security. The cardinal was asked for comment on the Cordillion attack on the Catholic church. Mr. Conroy was asked to comment on a senior corporate P&W employee engaging in fisticuffs with a guest. Neither were happy with the attention; being skilled at dealing with the press, each declined to comment. Both were on the other side of the room and were only aware there was some kind of problem. HSW was also on the other side of the room, but somehow was quickly made aware of the violent verbal and physical exchange between Cordillion and me. HSW was asked to comment. He called for the immediate termination of the P&W employee who had violently struck a guest.

"His conduct is simply not acceptable for a corporate executive of P&W. He has exposed the company to a serious legal liability."

Of course, HSW was too far removed to have heard the exchange nor to see Cordillion physically assault Natalie. But remember, he and Cordillion were very close, having been in a relationship in prior years.

The press cornered Larry.

"Did you know the people involved in the altercation? What did Mr. Cordillion mean when he accused the monsignor and Mr. Murphy of stealing you? Do you think Mr. Cordillion was drunk?"

Larry was more than angry. Mr. Conroy approached him and apologized for the incident.

"I don't like how P&W runs its author receptions," growled Larry as he stormed out of the hall.

That evening, Annie called and very bluntly told me to *not* come into the office for several days and to have no contact with my staff or any company employee. No explanation! She ended the call with "Trust me, Kevin."

I debated calling Larry. Natalie advised waiting a few days until things calmed down. With the press coverage, it didn't take long for the phone calls to start. My Provincetown friends all called. To a person, knowing Peter very well, his drinking problems and his volatility, they were in complete support of Natalie and me. Each promised to talk to Larry and express their distaste for Cordillion and their support for me. Allen Templeton was particularly distressed when I told him of Cordillion's physical and verbal assault on Natalie and that my job, thanks to HSW, was in jeopardy. Helene comforted Natalie who remained deeply upset by Cordillion's ethnic slur. I learned much after the fact that Monsignor Murphy had immediately sat down with the cardinal and explained, in detail, what had transpired and why. The cardinal subsequently called Larry to discuss his book. He had already read it; peace with the church was achieved! My good friend Aloysius asked the cardinal to call Mr. Conroy, clearing up any possible misunderstanding and congratulating P&W for having published a fine book.

News traveled fast. Bad news moved with the speed of lightning. Patrick knew all about the fracas, he had been at the reception and, of course, read the papers. My parents and the Hewitts were beside themselves. Norton called and, while obviously containing his anger, suggested that we might want to take legal action against Cordillion. He was outraged that my job was in serious jeopardy. He said he would immediately call his contacts on the P&W board and the CEO. I asked him not to do that.

After two days, an eternity, I was summoned back to the office by Mr. Conroy's administrative assistant. We were to meet in the executive conference room at 10:00 a.m. I was informed that the attendees would be Mr. Conroy, Thomas Long, Mary Ellen Connors, Arthur Black, HSW, and Annie. The CEO, Exec VP, VP Legal, VP Employee Relations, VP Publishing, and the managing editor. I am rarely nervous, but I was terrified as I entered the conference room! Was my *perfect life* about to end? Greetings were minimal, and Mr. Conroy immediately called the meeting to order.

"This meeting has a singular purpose. You are all painfully aware of the horrific mess caused by the fracas at the reception for Mr. O'Neil. Press coverage has unmercifully focused on the sorted exchange between Mr. Peter Cordillion, Monsignor Murphy, Kevin Murphy, and the treatment of Mrs. Murphy by Mr. Cordillion. You need to be aware that Mr. Cordillion has been Mr. O'Neil's partner and is a longtime friend of Mr. Weathersbee."

I thought it was interesting that HSW was referred to by his full name. The CEO continued, "I want to inform you, Mr. Cordillion's attorney has contacted our legal counsel, indicating their intent to file suit against Mr. Murphy personally and against the company. Mr. Long will discuss the merits of their case at a latter point in the meeting. Our Board of Directors is extremely disturbed by the very negative press. With that as background, Mr. Weathersbee, Vice President Publishing, is the senior Corporate Officer responsible in this matter. I will turn the meeting over to him."

"Thank you, Mr. Conroy. As you all know, I have spent my entire professional career, some thirty-four-plus years, with P&W. The company has been and is the singular focus of my life! Modesty aside, I have built, developed, and nurtured what is recognized as the finest editorial operation in the business. P&W can rightly claim to be the finest publishing house in the country and is recognized as one of the best worldwide. My standards are exacting and cannot be compromised. As you all know, I have considered Anne Hopkins and Kevin Murphy to be the best of the best. I have devoted a great deal of attention to mentoring both and have enjoyed both our professional and personal relationships. Today, with deep regret, I acknowledge failure. Mr. Murphy has allowed his personal feelings to override the best interests of the company. His actions at the O'Neil book signing are simply unacceptable. He embarrassed the company, our CEO, the cardinal archbishop of New York, the featured author, and numerous distinguished guests. He viciously and physically assaulted both a friend of mine and a dear friend of Mr. O'Neil. Mr. Cordillion had perhaps, indelicately and too forcefully, expressed his personal opinions. P&W is now exposed to legal actions that could be negatively impactful to the company. I would advise this committee that P&W is at risk of losing Larry O'Neil as an author. The dollar implications of that loss would be considerable." HSW paused. "In my considered opinion and judgment, Mr. Murphy has demonstrated a lack of good judgment, personal discipline, and maturity. He no longer has my confidence and support. I am asking the executive committee to terminate his employment immediately and for cause."

Mr. Conroy had received a note from his assistant. He asked for a brief adjournment and left the conference room. The group sat through a very awkward silence. The CEO returned and reconvened the meeting. HSW stood and said, "Mr. Conroy, before we move ahead, I would like the committee to fully appreciate how strongly I feel on this matter. I have recommended a severe action in response to the most challenging personnel issue I have ever faced. It is well-known that I do not take corporate matters lightly. To acknowledge a personal failure and publicly face up to it is extremely difficult for me and frankly very humbling. That said, please know that I cannot nor will not compromise. Should the committee fail to act on my recommendation, I will immediately submit my resignation from the company."

The committee members looked at each other with dismay.

"Mr. Conroy, may I please address the committee?" asked Annie.

"Of course, Ms. Hopkins, you have the floor."

Annie stood as she spoke and walked around the table. "As with HSW, I have spent my entire professional career with P&W, some fifteen years. I have been most fortunate to have had HSW as my supervisor, mentor, and friend. He is, in my judgment, the finest editor in the business. His claim to have built the company's editorial excellence is not an exaggeration. As to Kevin Murphy, you all know that he has been under my supervision since first joining the company, some nine years ago. In the past, I have applauded his performance, dedication, insight, and sheer brilliance and have wholly supported his rapid progression up through the editorial structure. I have *never* had reason to question his judgment, maturity, nor his total commitment to the best interests of the company. His work with Larry O'Neil has been textbook perfect, in fact, brilliant! P&W now has in hand a superb novel, which, without a doubt, will reach the bestseller list. This result positively reflects on the excellent relationship between author and editor.

"It is with the greatest of reluctance that I simply cannot support HSW's recommendation in this matter. If you will allow me, HSW, I honestly think you are too emotionally involved with the people in this situation. I implore you to reconsider and withdraw your recommendation or with understandable reluctance accept the decision of this committee, without resigning. Intellectually, I do not like the very idea of ultimatums. However, to add a level of gravity to my opinions, as you have done with your recommendation, I will immediately submit my resignation, should the executive committee choose to adopt your recommendations to terminate Mr. Murphy."

Mr. Conroy spoke. "As with Ms. Hopkins, I find that ultimatums rarely should be put on the table. My first reaction is to suggest the committee simply not accept either.

However, on reflection, I value the integrity of both individuals and conclude our decision must accept one and reject the other. When I left the room a few moments ago, it was to return a call from Larry O'Neil. He has a good sense of what the committee is dealing with this morning. He has requested permission to address the committee and feels he can assist us in reaching the best decision. He will be here in fifteen minutes. I believe he will be of great help to the committee in sorting through this matter. Before Mr. O'Neil arrives, I want to share with the committee several conversations I have had over the past few days. Cardinal O'Leary called me to discuss the situation. He had met with Monsignor Murphy, an individual he holds in the highest regard. With the permission of several people directly involved, Monsignor Murphy explained the personal dynamics underlying Mr. Cordillion's heated and violent confrontation with himself and Mr. Murphy. The monsignor being a firsthand witness was able to give

417

the cardinal a complete verbatim report on the one-sided exchange. Not only was the language vulgar but also offensive to the Catholic church and to Kevin Murphy and Monsignor Murphy. As Mrs. Murphy attempted to calm Cordillion down, he referred to her as a slant-eyed bitch and shoved her aside with such force that she fell to the floor. The treatment of his wife, Cordillion's drunken state and his growing hostility and aggression, explains, if not justifies Kevin's physical reaction. I also had a call from Allen Templeton, the well-known artist and a very close friend to Larry O'Neil. The two have homes in Provincetown on Cape Cod. He is very well acquainted with Peter Cordillion. On too many occasions, he has witnessed Cordillion's inclination to drink to excess. There is, in his opinion, a direct correlation between Peter's drinking problem and his tendency to become aggressive, if not hostile in social settings. It is a given in the small community of Provincetown to simply avoid Cordillion when he is drinking heavily." Mr.

Conroy turned to HSW. "Are Mr. Templeton's observations and opinion accurate?"

HSW looked perplexed, and he weakly responded, "We all on occasion have had too much to drink. Peter is by nature very bright and can be intolerant and perhaps aggressive."

There was a knock on the door, and the secretary ushered Larry O'Neil into the room. Mr. Conroy welcomed him.

"Thank you for joining us. As you seem to be aware, we are dealing with a complicated personnel situation. A result of the misfortunate turn of events at your reception. We all deeply regret the ugly affair and the stress it has caused you. To put the matter squarely on the table, Mr. Weathersbee has asked the committee to essentially find Mr. Murphy at fault and to terminate his employment for cause, charging, extreme poor judgment, embarrassment to the Catholic church, P&W, and of course, to you. Additionally, Mr. Cordillion has initiated legal action against the company and Mr. Murphy personally. Lastly, Mr. Weathersbee has suggested your displeasure with the whole situation is likely to cause you to void your contract with P&W. Ms. Hopkins, Mr. Murphy's immediate supervisor, has taken strong exception to Mr. Weathersbee's assessment of Mr. Murphy and has forcefully requested this committee to reject Mr. Weathersbee's recommendation. We have had what we accept as credible commentary on Mr. Cordillion's drinking habits and how it can affect his interactions with…people."

Larry thanked Mr. Conroy and the committee for allowing him to attend and to offer his perspective on the situation.

"There is no question that I was deeply distressed and angry with how my reception deteriorated into an ugly and very public fiasco. At the time, I was not aware of exactly who was doing what to whom nor did I know the specifics of the words exchanged. I was not aware of the physical attack on Mrs. Murphy. My first awareness of the situation came with seeing Peter Cordillion on the floor, the press and photographers swarming all over the scene. All hell had broken loose! There is no question that Peter Cordillion has a serious drinking problem. His natural assertiveness can become truly hostile when he has had too much to drink. Unfortunately, Peter's drinking problem is increasingly more pronounced. I also want the committee to be fully aware that Mr. Cordillion and I had been in a personal relationship for the past five years.

"In the process of researching the lives of Saint Francis of Assisi and the recently declared Saint Mother Teresa along with developing a deep and profound understanding of how and why the Catholic church goes about the process of declaring an individual to be a saint, I was increasingly drawn to the church. As you know, I worked very closely with Monsignor Murphy on my novel. Over the past several years, in our time together, here and traveling, we often found the time to discuss the Catholic faith. I very quietly became a convert to Catholicism. Independently, I have elected to terminate my relationship with Peter Cordillion. Peter simply could not, nor would not accept, using his term, my abandonment of him. He placed the blame squarely on Monsignor Murphy, Kevin, and the Catholic church. His unforgivable verbal and physical attack on Mrs. Murphy arise from his deep-seated prejudices against minorities.

"Kevin Murphy's role as my editor, has been performed with intelligence, skill, and sound advice. My work as an author has been enriched by his being there when I needed him. I also, by way of disclosure, want the committee to know that over time, Natalie and Kevin Murphy have become my dear friends. I look forward to having Kevin as my editor as I work on future novels under the P&W imprint.

"I hope I have clarified any misconceptions and made my position clear. P&W is very fortunate to have Kevin Murphy in their employment. Thank you."

Mr. Conroy thanked Larry for his candid presentation.

"I'll allow questions of Mr. Weathersbee, Ms. Hopkins, or Mr. Murphy before we go into executive session."

With no questions, Mr. Conroy asked us four to leave the room but to remain in the general area, awaiting being recalled once the committee had reached a decision. With the committee now in executive session, the CEO asked for comment. Tom Long reported that in his studied opinion, the lawsuits threatened by Cordillion were without merit and posed no financial threat to the company or to Kevin Murphy personally.

Mary Ellen Connors commented, "I accept HSW's ultimatum as very real, he will resign if we fail to terminate Kevin Murphy. I believe there is little or no chance of a compromise. HSW is now around sixty. If he were to retire at sixty-five, P&W would benefit from his continued employment for another few years. Can we risk getting by without his incredible experience and admitted talents?"

Art Black raised a hand and commented, "Ann Hopkins is around thirty-seven, Kevin Murphy is just thirty-one. They are both exceptional and can give P&W sixty years of combined service before retiring. They both have a demonstrated talent for recruiting and developing both editors and authors. The internship program, with Fordham and Columbia, should provide us with a fine stream of entry-level editorial talent over the years ahead. The real risk, as I see it, is our competitors attempting to lure Ms. Hopkins and/or Mr. Murphy away in the immediate years ahead. We *cannot* afford to lose them in this situation."

"If we were to reject HSW's proposal and he resigns, what happens next?" asked the CEO.

"I would be prepared to promote Ms. Hopkins to the position of vice president–publishing and Mr. Murphy to the position of managing editor," suggested Arthur Black. "They have worked together successfully for the past nine years. Both are super bright, have excellent track records, are held in very high regard internally, in the industry, and are committed to excellence and to P&W. We have a deep bench in the editorial operations to support them. Are they apt to make mistakes in their youth and relative shortness of experience? Possibly, but I am sure the company will survive. I think our employees would accept the situation in a supportive and positive way. The impact on morale, I predict, will be positive."

Mr. Conroy addressed the committee, "I believe we may have reached the point of reaching a decision, three in fact. HSW has made a straightforward motion, the company should immediately terminate Kevin Murphy, associate managing editor, for cause, relative to the debacle occurring at the recent O'Neil reception. It is clearly understood by the committee, a rejection of this proposal will result in the immediate resignation of Mr. Weathersbee as vice president–publishing and his voluntary termination of employment with P&W. I suggest that the committee reject his proposal for the termination of Mr. Murphy, further, we acknowledge and accept his resignation without any attempt to change his position. The committee understands that if we were to accept HSW's proposal, P&W would immediately lose both Mr. Murphy and Ms. Hopkins as employees. Secondly, there has been a suggestion and generally supportive dialogue as to promoting Ms. Hopkins to the position of vice president–publishing, and the concurrent promotion of Mr. Murphy to the position of managing editor in the event of HSW's resignation. I would ask that each of these actions be made as separate motions, seconded, and voted as such by the committee."

Mary Ellen Connors moved to reject Weathersbee's proposal to dismiss Kevin Murphy and further moved the committee immediately accept Mr. Weathersbee's resignation. Mr. Conroy seconded the motion. Discussion by Mr. Conroy stated his support of the motion with the deepest regrets. The motion was unanimously approved by the committee. Arthur Black made a motion to elect Ms. Anne Hopkins to the position of vice president–publishing, with the resignation of the incumbent. The motion was seconded by Mary Ellen Connors; no discussion followed, and the motion passed unanimously. Mr. Conroy moved that Kevin Murphy be promoted to the position of managing editor, in the event the position was vacated with the promotion of the incumbent. The motion was seconded by Mr. Black. There was no discussion and the motion passed unanimously.

The CEO addressed the committee. "I suggest another brief recess, after which I am going to place a call to Mr. Chandler, chairman of our Board of Directors. I would like all of you in the room for that conversation. Mr. Chandler has been fully briefed and is standing by for our call. He is very aware of the real possibility of HSW's resignation. He has assured me he would personally support the final decisions of the executive committee and has assured me the entire board would also support the decisions of this committee."

The call was placed after a fifteen-minute break, and Mr. Chandler immediately came on the open line. Mr. Conroy gave the chairman of the board a concise summary of where the committee had been, the discussions, including the input that Ms. Hopkins had offered her resignation if Mr. Murphy were terminated. Tom Long assured the chairman that the potential lawsuit against the company was completely without merit and did not represent a risk of financial impact on the company. The promotions of Ms. Hopkins and Kevin Murphy garnered a very positive reaction from Mr. Chandler.

"I know this has been a very trying experience for the committee. We all are saddened by the loss of Mr. Weathersbee both professionally and personally. Rest assured I have complete confidence in your judgments as will the full Board of Directors. Thank you."

Mr. Conroy then asked Ms. Hopkins and HSW to rejoin the committee. Addressing HSW, "The executive committee has discussed your proposal and the comments made by Ms. Hopkins and Mr. O'Neil. A motion to reject your proposal was made, seconded, and unanimously approved by the executive committee. The committee, with great reluctance, acknowledges your resignation and accepts it forthwith."

HSW rose to his feet, his face beet red. "That is outrageous. I will take this to the Board of Directors."

Mr. Conroy spoke in a soft voice, "HSW you need to be aware, our actions have been taken with the *full* knowledge of the chairman of our board. Just a few minutes ago, the committee held a teleconference with Mr. Chandler. He was given a *full* briefing on our meeting today. The chairman has assured the executive committee that we have his full support and further assures us, we will be completely supported by the entire board."

With that, HSW stormed out of the room.

Larry O'Neil and Kevin Murphy were invited to rejoin the executive committee. Addressing the two, "The executive committee has totally rejected HSW's proposed termination of Kevin Murphy's employment. Further, with sadness, we have recognized his resignation and accepted it effective immediately. With the office of vice president–publishing now vacant, we announce the election of Anne Hopkins to that position. Concurrently, with the position of managing editor vacant with the promotion of the incumbent, Kevin Murphy is appointed managing editor. The executive committee has every confidence you will both fill these very large shoes and take P&W to new horizons. Congratulations to you both!"

Mr. Conroy rose to his feet and led a round of extended applause. Larry embraced Annie and shook hands warmly with me. Annie and I shook hands and could not resist a warm embrace.

My god! After the intense emotions of the past week, I was absolutely spent. Leaving the conference room, I rushed to my office to call Natalie. I told her in detail what had transpired. We were both deeply moved by the support of Annie and Larry and the unanimous support of the executive committee. My promotion was right out of the blue. Beyond my imagination.

"I very much need to make several calls. I'll try to be home early."

In succession, I called Mr. Conroy and the individual members of the executive committee to express my appreciation for their support and confidence. I called Annie and simply said, "Thank you, dear friend!"

My call to Larry involved my thanking him for his support and for willingly discussing his personal life in making his case. I called Monsignor Murphy and had to leave a message. I thanked him for his intervention and support. I asked him to convey my deep appreciation to the cardinal for his support. With all that taken care of, I turned to family. I had asked Natalie to pass the good news on to her parents. I texted Katie and Shamus, called my parents, and was so proud sharing all the news with Patrick. All were relieved, pleased, and so proud of me! Last, I called friends. I called Helene, although I knew Annie would have already given her a full report. She was doubly pleased. For the two of us! I next called Allen Templeton.

"Your support was powerful and deeply appreciated, thank you."

I composed an email and sent it off to friends and close associates, thanking all for their moral support through a most difficult time. I shared the dual promotions of Annie and myself. Last on my list and with trepidation, I called HSW. He had given his assistant directions for shutting down his office and immediately left the building. I tried his cell phone, but no answer. I then wrote a note by hand and sent it to his home address.

"I understand and forgive your actions in the meeting with the executive committee. I want you to know I hold no animosity toward you. I deeply appreciate your mentorship and guidance over the past nine years. I hope someday, we can recapture our friendship. It is something I very much value."

Natalie called. Her parents were so relieved and pleased. They offered their very best congratulations and wanted you to know how proud they were of their son-in-law! Helene had called Natalie; she was putting "something" together at their apartment for around seven thirty. Let the good times roll! Natalie checked if I would be free over the weekend; her parents want to come to the city to celebrate. My calendar was clear, and I asked Natalie to call and asked my parents to join in the celebrations.

Within an hour, the news, via an effective grapevine, had been widely disseminated. The phone rang, people stopped by, the emails flooded in. I joyfully basked in all the good wishes. I was surprised to receive a direct call from the chairman of the Board of Directors.

"Kevin, I want to add my personal congratulations on your promotion. The board has been aware for some time of your outstanding contributions to the company. I have just recently become aware of your relationship to Norton Hewitt, which of course had nothing to do with recent events. Your father-in-law and several of our board members are well acquainted. Norton Hewitt is highly regarded within the publishing world, and he is very well informed and on top of developments worldwide. He is known to and knows the key players. I'm sure you will find ample opportunity to learn from him, I encourage you to take full advantage of the opportunity."

I thanked him for his support.

We arrived at our dear friends' apartment to the sound of several guests who had already arrived. Using her much practiced skills, Helene once again had put together a wonderful evening. Among the throng of people, we found Monsignor Murphy, Larry O'Neil, my brother Patrick and his wife, Theresa and Sergei Soldatov, Phil Arenstein, Jane McFarland, Ken Smallwood, Tom Harwood, Pierre from the Dove and a host of others from P&W, the publishing world of New York, my gym, and even a few of my poker buddies. How did Helene do it? We were joined by phone with Madam Fontaine, Allen Templeton, Alina, and with Tom Hopper in Boston. The evening was a literal love feast among good and dear friends. Natalie and I couldn't say thank you enough times to our dear hostess.

In the weeks following, Annie and I were closeted with staffing decisions, budget reviews, our author roster, the master publishing plan going forward, the advertising and sales promotion program, the status of the reorganization plan, and a review of the intern program. Our first and a key staffing decision addressed replacing me as the associate managing editor. We indeed had a deep bench as had been observed. We had several excellent candidates on our roster of senior editors. The choice was difficult, we were looking less at experience per se and more on compatibility and personality. The choice was mine, but I valued Annie's input. I chose Nancy Laterna, the most experienced of the senior editors. She was highly organized and very well regarded across the board, her editors, authors, staff, and the other senior editors. The choice was supported by Annie.

"Nancy will require very little direct management."

We also reviewed in depth the staff reporting to the managing editor. Finance and Personnel were doing a good job. The current administrative assistant to the managing editor was outstanding. However, I wanted to bring Jane McFarland along with me, filling that position. That all worked out just fine. Admin assistants were required to always be one step ahead of a given situation. Etienne, the current admin assistant to the managing editor had worked with Annie for a number of years, Annie very much wanted to bring her along as the admin assistant to the VP Editorial.

The reorganization plan I had developed and which the executive committee had approved was implemented within weeks of my promotion. I was personally excited to develop and deliver a series of workshops on the plan, the underlying rationale, and the methodology for implementation. Using the Japanese model of achieving full buy-in, the slow adoption proved to be hugely successful.

I am amazed at how smoothly and quickly everything settled into place. To the credit of the exemplary people employed by the company, the solid and consistent support of our executive office and the Board of Directors, and the fine work of our established and our new authors, P&W continued to be held in the highest regard worldwide. In a nutshell: we managed to create and foster a team of superior employees, coupled with a growing and deep bench of outstanding authors, committed to producing excellent books. The consumer market, based on excellent reviews and outstanding marketing, bought our product. The financial community awarded the company outstanding evaluations on the company's performance, and Wall Street was extremely kind to our stock.

CHAPTER 16

HAVING SURVIVED THE ACUTE TRAUMA of the Cordillion affair of several years ago *and* my perfect life having not come unraveled, I moved on with life! I continued to be blessed in my work, in my relationships, and in my family life. Let me summarize the major events of the past years in the life of the Kevin and Natalie Murphy family. The joy and the sorrow.

The biggest and most important event(s) had been the arrival of our children. We had been blessed with three: Brian Patrick Murphy, Margaret Pei Murphy, and Natalie

Ling Murphy. With the growth of our family, we sold Natalie's co-op to Brother Patrick and purchased a three-story brownstone on the Upper East Side. It had been considered a cosmetic fixer-upper reportedly a steal at $3.2 million. With assists from Pei Ling and dear friends Annie and Helene, it was transformed into the perfect home for our family. As we had discussed and agreed prior to our marriage and as reflected in our prenuptial agreement, we could, by mutual agreement, tap into Natalie's trust, particularly for the benefit of our children. Real estate purchases/investments were specifically allowed if the proposition was prudent and a financially sound investment for the trust. We arrived at a 60/40 joint ownership, with the trust owning the larger share. Norton Hewitt, as the trustee approved and as a lawyer, handled all those issues connected with buying and selling real estate. The cost of his services was, of course, nominal. We were very *comfortably,* living on our combined earnings, and we were debt free.

Natalie continued her work at the UN. She had been promoted twice in the last five years and was now a senior vice president and earning a *very* handsome salary. Her work and responsibilities allowed her to work remotely a good bit of the time. With my promotions, stock options, and incentive compensation, I was now earning a substantial income, even exceeding Natalie earned income. With the deepest regrets, I withdrew from my limited involvement at the Dove. The demands of my job and the considerable demands of having young active children left me no option. Management and the owners fully understood, as did my dear friend Pierre. Natalie and I were hosted at a wonderful retirement dinner at the restaurant. I was given a gold Rolex watch. Natalie and I visited frequently for cocktails and dinner, staying in touch with the friends we have developed over the years.

Provincetown was now our home away from home. We had been spending at least one month in a rental each summer and many long weekends with Uncle Larry, to his absolute delight. Tomas and Semmi couldn't wait for our visits. They all spoiled the kids! With great excitement, we started the construction of our own cottage.

Brother Patrick met and married Susan Osborne, a very lovely young English woman, an associate of Natalie's at the UN. They were happy at home in Natalie's former apartment. Susan had been a wonderful addition to the family, and they were enjoying their first child, Kevin Shamus Murphy.

Sister Caitlin (née Katie) and brother-in-law Shamus were both teaching and had managed to produce three sons: Shamus, Keegan, and Aiden. They visited the States most summers for a month. Mom and Dad had been making frequent trips to Ireland: holidays, birthdays, and each time Katie was about to give birth.

Sadly, several years ago and within months of each other, we lost both of Natalie's maternal grandparents. I also lost my paternal grandmother, the last of my grandparents, at the age of ninety-six! Very unexpectedly, my father also passed away, with a rapid onset of cancer of the pancreas. We all had a very difficult time dealing with the loss of Dad. Mom was devastated and dealt with her grief by being the super grandmother to her growing herd of grandchildren.

You may remember a conversation Natalie and I had with her parents over brunch at the Tavern on the Green about their love of New York City. With the arrival of the first grandchild, Natalie's parents rented a condo in the city. With the arrival of number two, Pei Ling had to be in New York most of the time. Norton's firm had maintained a New York office for years, so my father-in-law found it quite easy to shift the bulk of his personal practice to the city. The Hewitts eventually sold their Chicago home and purchased a co-op on the Upper East Side, just two blocks away. They were now New Yorkers! Pei Ling was now a full-time Loa Loa, a Chinese grandmother.

Both Peter Cordillion and HSW were gone. Peter drank himself to death several years ago. HSW committed suicide just a few months ago, with an overdose of pills. His passing hit me very hard. I hadn't heard from him after his departure from P&W. He never acknowledged my note. I was absolutely taken aback, deeply moved, and very sad when I received notification from his attorney; I was the sole beneficiary of HSW's sizable estate. In his will, he had written. "I leave my estate, in its entirety and without exception to Kevin Murphy. I have spent the last years of my life profoundly regretting the pain I caused him. He is the son I never had. I am so proud of him and hold him close in my heart."

Monsignor Aloysius Murphy had been installed as the auxiliary bishop of Brooklyn, appointed by the Holy Father, at the request of the cardinal archbishop of New York. The appointment required a dispensation from the Aloysius's Jesuit superior. The bishop had baptized all our children. We enjoyed his company when he can get away for a quiet dinner or a rare long weekend at the Cape.

Larry O'Neil continued as an award-winning author producing a new title every two or three years. With the huge accorded given to his novel *Saints and Other Noble People*, the Holy Father, John Paul II, named him a Knight of the Order of Pius IX. The book had remained on best-seller lists and had been translated into eight languages. It was named the Book of the Year by the American Library Association. Larry's new titles were always received with huge success worldwide.

Allen Templeton still resided in Provincetown. Unfortunately, he suffered a major stroke and was no longer able to paint. We have added two Templeton works to our collection. We spent many happy hours with him when we visit Provincetown.

Madam Fontaine, now retired, was devoted to caring for Allen Templeton's needs: medical appointments, attending various local events, etc. She too was an honorary aunt to our children. They loved practicing their French with their *la tante*.

My dear friend Pierre retired from the Dove after a minor heart attack. He and Larry O'Neil enjoyed being honorary uncles to our kids. Pierre often took Brian for walks in Central Park. According to Brian, he and Uncle Pierre were the best of friends with several ducks!

Annie and Helene were just okay. Helene struggled with breast cancer, a too frequent problem for an Ashkenazi woman. She had one breast removed and was dealing with a reoccurrence of malignancy in the second breast. Our dear friends were honorary aunties to our children, the source of too many toys, bikes, dolls, clothes, etc.

With the too soon an arrival, the next decade of my life had been inevitably filled with both joy and sorrow; we lost too many dear ones, my mother, dear friends, Pierre, Allen Templeton, and Helene.

Our children, parental bias aside, were perfect! Thus far, we had survived having two teenagers, Brian and Margaret, both of whom were excelling in school. Brian showed great promise on the tennis court and Margaret played the violin, sang beautifully, and was a perfect junior mom to her sister Natalie. The teenagers were popular, and our home was always full of their friends. Our youngest Natalie was a proverbial piece of work. Precocious, energetic beyond belief, spoiled but adorable nonetheless. All three kids spoke Mandarin and French with excellent fluency. We joyfully welcomed several new cousins: Fiona O'Leary, Genevieve and Michael Murphy, and have another O'Leary due in a couple of months.

The cottage in Provincetown, finished nine years ago, was our piece of paradise. Thank you, Uncle Larry O'Neil! Natalie and the kids spend most of the summer months on the Cape. Family and friends were welcomed, and they came! Katie, Shamus, and their crew spent about a month each summer. Patrick and his family were frequent one week and holiday visitors. Norton and Pei Ling spent as much time as possible with us, given that Norton still maintained a very active practice. We enjoyed weekend visits, out of season, with a broad range of friends. Uncle Larry and Tomas and Semmi are a loving part of our family. Our children are such a part of their lives, and they are a very important part of my children's lives. Our Provincetown friends were a joy, Madam Fontaine, Alina, Phillip, Sergio and Theresa, Tom Hopper. Chu Hau, when she was in the States, had visited several times.

Since Helene's death, Annie and Larry had become quite close. Annie visited Provincetown frequently; she had a very special relationship with our little Natalie. Dear friend Larry O'Neil continued to produce great novels for P&W; we were the best of friends. Our mutual friend, Aloysius Murphy, was called to Rome several years ago. With the special permission of his Jesuit superior, he was now an archbishop in the Vatican Curia, with the Dicastery for the Cause of Saints. Additionally, Aloysius served as general counselor to the superior general of the Jesuit Order. He tries to see us when he has reasons to be in the States.

Three years ago, Natalie reached the decision that her role of mother to three growing children required more and more of her time. She recognized the competing, growing demands of her senior position in the UN, and reverted to a consultant position. The adjustment went surprisingly well. Pei Ling was bringing Natalie more and more on board with the responsibilities of being the Chairman of the Board, a position Natalie will someday assume. They were traveling worldwide, which also placed demands on Natalie's time and energy.

My world at P&W was the source of pride, contentment, challenge, and reward. The company continued to do very well. Annie and I enjoyed continued success in our endeavors; we were a team. We had both been approached by several major publishing houses with attractive propositions. Our CEO and the board were aware of these approaches and had designed golden handcuffs to bind us to the company. We had each been given new challenges and opportunities. Our individual success in dealing with these challenges and opportunities had earned each of us substantial financial rewards: salary increases, incentive compensation awards, and significant stock options. Annie had been promoted to executive vice president and was seen as a major contender to succeed our current CEO. With Annie's election as executive VP, I was elected vice president–publishing.

CHAPTER 17

I HAD SAID, EVERYTHING SEEMED TO accelerate as time passed, so very true! Let me share with you how events and life had unfolded for my family, my friends, and myself, as yet another decade unfolded. Our personal/family life was a joy. I ask you to recall the joke I made when Natalie and I first discussed her financial situation. We would be joining lots of young couples in having money problems; ours being having too much, not too little! This had sent Natalie into uncontrolled laughing for twenty minutes! Natalie had continued in her role of a consultant at the UN earning (tax-free) nearly $300,000. With the press of the business, the children's needs, the need to manage her philanthropic activities, and her increasing involvement in the family business, two years ago, she reluctantly withdrew completely. With the death of her grandparents several years ago, she inherited a substantial block of equity in the family corporation, a really substantial position, adding to her already major holdings. The company continued its long-running success and paid out very handsome dividends each year. Last year, this amounted to $2.9 million paid into Natalie's account. Natalie's portfolio, which had always been conservative, earned a whopping $4.9 million last year. When we first discussed Natalie's finances prior to our marriage, her net worth was slightly more than $26 million. In the last twenty-five years, despite dispensing many generous grants and outright gifts, it had grown to just about $287 million! I now earn, with incentive compensation, just north of $675,000. Additionally, with very generous stock options, I own 150,000 shares and have options on another 250,000 shares. My inheritance from HSW was a pleasant surprise of nearly $5 million. With continued excellent advice and management from good friend Kevin at Edward Jones, my investments had done quite well, to the point that my net worth was now in excess of $38 million. Wow, aren't the Murphies fortunate? That joke of years ago had come true! All that money was a problem. With a great deal of advice from Patrick and my father-in-law's law firm partners, specializing in wealth management, we established a family office to manage the incredible complexities of our situation. Natalie was very focused on increasing her philanthropic activities.

Our children were a total joy. Brian was approaching fifteen. He was not quite a scholar but did well in school. He had an eye on Harvard and showed a great interest in the family business. He had, at his request, accompanied Pei Ling and his mother on several trips. He found China fascinating. Margaret, thirteen, on the other hand, was a true scholar. Academically, she was, with ease, a straight A student. Musically, she is gifted with a marvelous voice and gave an accomplished performance on the violin. She and Tom Hopper were soulmates. He had invited her to perform on several occasions with his chamber music group. She showed a great interest in her mother's philanthropic activities, particularly relating to the arts. Margaret had developed a deep understanding and appreciation for the family's art holdings through her grandmother, Pei Ling. We welcomed her to our meetings and in discussing grants. Then there was Natalie. At age nine, she was the princess. Everyone—Mom, Dad, brother, sister, grandfather, grandmothers, aunts, uncles, and family friends—existed for her pleasure and to meet her every need! Precocious, energetic, spoiled, bright, engaging, funny, and a joy to be around. As with her siblings, school came easy to her. She had friends by the busload. Where she was headed in life was a mystery at this point. All three kids enjoyed time with their cousins, our time at the Cape, our friends, and being with their grandparents.

Aside from our P&W involvement, we frequently saw our dear friends, Annie and Larry, socially with relaxed dinners and cookouts, even our traditional pizza nights, and attending musical events and out an about on the social scene. They were almost always in the audience for an event involving the kids. A tennis match, a musical performance, a play, or whatever. While they had been friends for a good number of years, their bond had grown since the passing of Helene. Our Cape Cod friends, living in the city were a continuing pleasure. Sergei Soldatov was not aging well and suffered several limiting issues. Theresa remained a doyenne of the Museum of Modern Art and a highly regarded and prodigious poetria. The Soldatovs traveled less frequently but continued to entertain at home. An invitation to one of their soirees was still highly prized. Phillip

Arenstein was semiretired and was spending more time at his home in Provincetown. He saw himself fully retiring in a few years and moving to the Cape year-round. We see him more on the Cape than in the city. Madam Fontaine was a wonder. Well on in years, no one knew how many, she was still out and about. Alina, with her enormous talents, took over the restaurant as Madam retired. Les Poissons continued as a highly rated dining experience under her excellent management. We had the joy of frequently dining there when we were in Provincetown. Tomas and Semmi refused to retire. At Larry's insistence, they were now supported by a younger couple, Tomas's nephew and his wife, who were natives of Provincetown. Semmi and Tomas were devoted to Larry and enjoyed being another set of grandparents to our children. Semmi remained a chef beyond compare. A highlight of any visit to Provincetown was a meal prepared by her. Aloysius Murphy was now embedded in Rome. Rumor had it that the current Pope held him in the highest regard. We saw him less frequently but remained in close touch.

My world at P&W provided me with not just financial rewards, but more importantly, an enormous sense of satisfaction and fulfillment. I had the pleasure of working with people who were bright, committed to excellence, and loved what they are doing. Our authors were, as they had always been for me, stimulating and a delight to work with. As a senior member of management, I found the corporate experience to be intellectually challenging. The team was just that, a team. We approached problems, challenges, opportunities with a joint focus. The benefits of a stable team cannot be overstated. Of course, Annie and I were joined at the hip, and we were ribbed by fellow members of the executive committee that we could read each other's minds. Which, by the way, was not far from the truth. Annie made a point of exposing me to other major aspects of the business, marketing, finance, strategic planning.

How blessed I was to have had her as a mentor all these years. This broadening was, as I was to learn, by careful design. Let me explain. Tom Conroy, the longtime CEO of P&W, had met with Annie eighteen months earlier. He indicated that he and the board had been in discussions, at his suggestion, relative to a succession plan. At the time, the CEO was sixty-nine years old and expressed a wish to retire at seventy-one. With vigorous weighing of the pros and cons and considering alternatives, the board unanimously accepted the CEO's recommendation for Anne Hopkins to be, in pectore, designated the next CEO of P&W. Follow-on meetings between Annie and the CEO involved a rigorous review of the current senior officers of the corporation. Designating needed replacements over the next five years would result in identifying prospective internal candidates and the need for external search for qualified prospects. The position currently held by Annie, executive vice president, found Tom Clarkson and Annie in complete agreement as to a successor. I was the apparent choice. A concrete plan had been developed, in order to expose me, in- depth, to the broader areas of corporate management. The CEO and Annie met with the board and reviewed their analysis of corporate staffing going forward. The specific recommendation for replacing Annie as executive vice president met with enthusiastic approval of the board. With their approval of the plan for broadening my understanding of corporate management, the chairman of the board suggested that I begin attending all board meetings going forward.

Following that Board meeting, I was asked to join the CEO and Annie in Mr. Clarkson's office. Tom Clarkson indicated that the board was convinced that I should not continue as VP of publishing. The issue needed to be addressed immediately. I was taken aback, not knowing what to say. Silence! It seemed an eternity. Then, I remembered being exposed to Tom's sense of humor years ago.

With a studied pause and a sober delivery, I said, "I agree with the board. I need additional challenge, and I am now considering a very attractive offer from a European publisher with extensive interests in the United States."

The look on both Tom's and Annie's faces was one of pure shock! I simply could not hold back laughing. "Got you!"

We all nearly fell out of our seats laughing.

"I deserve that, you obviously have a long memory of our luncheon years ago when HSW proposed you as Larry O'Neil's editor," Tom said, as he continued to laugh.

After we all calmed down, the CEO explained: the board had approved a transition plan. With Tom having a planned retirement, some eighteen months hence, Annie would be elected president/CEO, and Kevin Murphy would be elected executive vice president. Annie introduced the plan to expand my familiarity with corporate management, to include attending all future Board of

Directors' meetings. I could not thank them both enough for the opportunity and their support.

My in-laws were well. Norton, at seventy-five, was still incredible busy with his law practice. His only distraction from work being his immersion in the role of Grandpa! Norton was especially close to Brian, encouraging his interests in the family business and suggesting law school (Harvard, of course) as an excellent background. With Margaret, he saw her filling a much-needed role and involvement in the family office as it relates to its philanthropic efforts and the management of the family trust's substantial art collection, developed by her great-grandparents. He, as with us, had no idea where our darling Natalie was headed. That aside, they enjoyed each other's company, frequently over lunch or visits to his office.

Pei Ling continued as the super-involved grandmother. She, at seventy-three, was in excellent shape and was handling the increasing demands of her job as CEO/

chairman of the board of the family corporation. She especially encouraged Brian's interest in the company and was so pleased with his fascination with China. Natalie's increasing involvement found her and her mother traveling frequently both domestically and abroad.

My mother was dramatically slowing down at age seventy-nine. Patrick and I made a point of frequently visiting her in Brookline, and we tried to get her to the Cape during our summers. Traveling to Ireland was simply no longer feasible. Katie, of course, stayed very much in touch, with phone- calls and frequent pop-in visits to Brookline. We were lucky to have a loving and caring family in the Brookline area. Nieces and nephews took the best of care of Aunt Peg.

The O'Leary family of Ireland were thriving, now with four boys and two girls. A joyful handful for sister Katie. Good brother-in-law Shamus was now head of his department at the University of Dublin and was a recognized scholar. Seats in his classroom were highly sought after. We greatly enjoyed their summer visits to Provincetown. Caitlin (née Katherine) was no longer teaching in the classroom, with her household duties taking priority. However, she did find the time to research and write. I've lost track of the number of scholarly books and papers she had written. Like Shamus, Caitlin was considered a scholar of note.

Brother Patrick was getting on in years, as I liked to tease him. He was now about to shortly enter his sixties! He and his lovely English wife, Susan, had added three children to the Murphy family tree, two boys and a darling daughter. We frequently consult with him on financial matters dealing with the company and our family office. Patrick, career-wise, had done very well. He was now a senior executive vice president and on the Board of Directors of one of the major financial houses on Wall Street. Patrick remained my best friend, and we found the time to be together and share life's joys, troubles, and challenges. His family visited

Provincetown as often as possible year-round. Our children were close, as you might guess.

We now moved into yet another decade. Accepting the realities of the passage of time, with great sadness, we dealt with the loss of my mother. She never really recovered from the loss of my father. Additionally, we lost dear friends, Sergei Soldatov, Madam Fontaine, and Tom Harwood. Jane McFarland also passed away in retirement. I never stopped missing her in the office. All these passings were in the normal course of time. I was shocked and dismayed to lose, too soon, Kevin Smallwood to a sudden heart attack. Natalie had to deal with the loss of Dr. Nu, her longtime associate at the UN and her dear friend Chrysanthemum (Chu Hua). Annie and I were saddened with the passing of our advocate, Tom Clarkson, the retired CEO of P&W. A particularly sad event for my family and for Larry O'Neil came with the passing of both Tomas and Semmi, just a year apart. Both had become, over the years, an integral part of our family.

The family office was up and running smoothly. As we had hoped, Margaret, following her graduation from Yale, with a BA in Art History, joined the family office with a focus on grants in support of the arts. Margaret also was immersed in the trust holding the family art collection. Natalie and Pei Ling were delighted with her being so involved. Margaret married her longtime boyfriend from her college days. Son-in-law, Adam Boyer, also a graduate of Yale, was from San Francisco. He is an architect employed by a top firm in the City. He is fun to be around and was a dynamite golfer. Margaret and Adam gave us our first grandchild, Adam Boyer III.

Brian, with an accelerated undergraduate degree in Finance from Penn University, enrolled and graduated with honors from Harvard Law School. Again, to the delight of his father and mother, Norton, and Pei Ling, he joined the family business as an assistant to the chairman of the board. While at Harvard, through his Hong Kong cousins, Brian was introduced to a young lady, Chun Hua, also studying at Harvard. Chun Hua's family were well acquainted with Pei Ling and her family. While Chun Hua was fluent in English, she was delighted that Brian spoke Mandarin fluently, enjoyed Chinese cuisine, and took immense pride in his Chinese heritage. The two dated for two years while at Harvard. With her graduation, Chun returned to Hong Kong. Brian found many business reasons to visit frequently. The young lady's family initially were not warm to Brian as a prospective son-in-law. Over time, Brian's deep understanding and love for all things Chinese became clear. The deep affection between the two young people was evident. Coming up on two years of a long-distance courtship, with parental approval, Brian proposed to Chun Hua. The couple were married in Hong Kong and settled in New York City. Chun Hua and Brian gave the Murphy's grandchildren number two and three in short order. The first, a beautiful girl, Chung Ling, our first granddaughter.

Our second grandson came along just a year later, a healthy nine-pound boy, our second grandson, Chau Hauyo. Brian was promoted to vice president of planning, reporting to the chairman of the board.

Pei Ling's brothers asked for a conference in New York with Pei Ling and Natalie. The subject, planning the next generation of management of the corporation and consideration of a change in distribution of equity in the firm. Both uncles were and had been involved in the management of the business as were their children, Natalie's four cousins. The brothers were getting on in years, the older brother, Shu Chang was in his mid-eighties and Ming, the younger brother, is seventy-six years old. Both were in good health. The entire family is dedicated, hardworking, and each performed their jobs with excellent results. Their children, based in Hong Kong, London, and Dubai, contemporaries of Natalie, were all in their late forties and early fifties. The cousins had been with the company since graduating from college. The investment banking business, headquartered in London, was managed by Shu Chang. Brother Ming, based in Hong Kong, managed the traditional trading company. Both brothers were quite wealthy. Shu Chang held approximately 20 percent of the Corporation's B shares; Ming 10 percent, and their children collectively approximately 5 percent. Natalie owns 14 percent, and Pei Ling holds 51 percent. The class A shares, with sole voting rights, were held partially in the trust established by Pei Ling's parents, 40 percent (Trustee Pei Ling) and directly by Pei Ling, 40 percent, and Natalie with 20 percent. The Class A shares were not paid a regular dividend. Pei Ling, now eighty-four, managed the real estate investment side of the corporation and remained the corporate CEO and chairman of the board. Family relationships were cordial, open, and very traditional.

The brothers arrived late on a Sunday afternoon. Allowing for jet lag, the first meeting was scheduled for six o'clock Monday evening with dinner at the Hewitts' home. Attendees were only Pei Ling, Norton, Shu Chang, Ming, and Natalie. The lavish meal was catered by the Hwa Yuan restaurant. Dinner was leisurely executed, with conversation all about family and no discussion of business. The formal meeting was scheduled for Tuesday morning at 9:30 a.m. at the corporation's office on Fifth Avenue. It was agreed the brothers would propose the agenda. Attendees would be the brothers, Pei Ling, Natalie, Norton Hewitt, and Brian Murphy.

The meeting began promptly at nine thirty. Shu Chang distributed an agenda.

A. Financials for the corporation: three years. Actual and a five-year forecast by operating entity.

B. Equity positions by individual.

C. Dividend pay-out by individual for the past five years; forecast of dividend payout by individual for next five years.

D. Compensation paid to all family members: five years actual.

E. Discussion of the trust: origin, assets, management, duration.

F. Management succession plan.

G. Discussion of the viability and possible approaches to changes in equity positions.

The financials were impressive. The corporation was growing at a steady and significant rate. Profitability was excellent, although uneven by business. Cash flow, particularly critical to supporting the investment banking business, remained strong overall, with a growing weakness in the trading business, more than offset by excellent cash flow from real estate investments. The forecasts going forward recognized the global political dynamics having significant impact on the trading business. Additionally, real estate investments were increasingly being restricted by regional instabilities. However, the US continued to be an attractive market of opportunity. On the personal level, compensation via dividend payments and other compensation had been and will continue to provide excellent opportunity for all members of the family involved in the business.

Discussion, centered on the trust, did provide some concerns. Both Shu Chang and Ming expressed a degree of concern/resentment that only Pei Ling and her heirs benefit from the trust established by their parents. It wasn't so much a matter of financial dimensions per se; rather it dealt with control of the corporation by way of restricting all voting rights to the A shares. At the end of the day, after a healthy dialogue, it was recognized that the matter is what it is, as it had been decided by their long-deceased parents. The focus then turned to the duration/expiration of the trust and the series of possible consequences. The trust had been established nearly sixty-five years ago. With amendments, the expiration is now set at seventy-five years.

Basically, about ten years from the present. Pei Ling, anticipating the subject being of major concern to her brothers, had given the matter considerable thought. Following several in-depth discussions with Norton, Patrick Murphy, and Brian, she and Natalie developed an approach. Pei Ling presented the core of the proposal: A shares held by the trust could be purchased by any B shareholder for a price per share, equal to 2.0 times the cumulative B class stock dividend paid over the prior two years. Over-subscription will be resolved by proportional allocation. A shares held by individuals *may*, at their sole discretion, be sold to B shareholders at a mutually acceptable price. Funds derived from the sale of A shares held by the trust (40 percent) will be deposited in a new trust to be established along with the art collection held by the original trust. The original trust allowed for its termination by the mutual agreement of both the A shareholders (100 percent) and a majority of the B shareholders. The newly established trust would be chartered as a philanthropic endeavor promoting the awareness and appreciation of modern art with an emphasis on Chinese and other Asian works. The trust would be managed by Pei Ling and a board of her choosing. The proposed approach, after many questions and good dialogue, was approved. Shu Chang and Ming were very pleased.

The attention then turned to the succession of management. Each of the principals had given the matter some great thought. Shu Chang proposed his eldest daughter Jing Li, fifty-two years old and based in London, to eventually succeed him. Jing Li was married with three children, two of whom are employed by the corporation. With degrees in accounting and strategic planning, she had been involved in the investing banking operations for nearly thirty-two years. Ming proposed his second son Xiang, aged fifty, as his replacement. Xiang had also been with the trading company since graduating from college with a degree in economics. Xiang's only son was also employed by the company. Xiang is stationed in Dubai and traveled extensively throughout the Middle East. Both Jing Li and Xiang were multilingual, speaking English and French, and Xiang was fluent in Arabic. Pei Ling proposed Natalie as her successor. Natalie was now fifty-two, and her background and credentials were well-known to her uncles. There was quick consensus on the recommendations and follow-on conversation focused on the depth of the bench in the next tier of management. There existed general agreement that there was excellent depth with experienced, well-educated young people already on board. Brian Murphy is acknowledged as a prime example. All three of the principals indicated an intent and desire to continue in place, health permitting, with immediately putting in place a phase-in for their designated successor.

The highly successful meeting ended at five thirty. With dinner planned for 8:00 p.m. at Wu Ming Gu, preceded by cocktails at the Murphy residence. Several comments were made during the evening at how cordial the meeting had been and the pleasure the older generation found in the family continuity through many generations. Natalie and I were so pleased that Brian represented the tenth generation of the family involved in the business. The original trading company dates to the early 1700s. In deference to me, the conversations were mostly in English. My son received the highest compliments for his fluency in both Mandarin and Cantonese. Interesting that I understood Mandarin quite well when it was spoken. Remember, I lived in a household where my wife and children often spoke in Chinese.

Our youngest, Natalie, still a ball of fire, finished college with a degree in philosophy from Smith College. She encamped to Provincetown and quickly settled in, becoming best friends with Alina. She enjoyed working at Les Poissons and quickly demonstrated a knack for the business both up front and in the kitchen. She came by a taste for fine wines and with a more in-depth knowledge than most, apparently by being around her father. She and Alina had many in-depth conversations about wines in general and in its cultivation. With Alina's family ownership of several first-rate vineyards in Italy, it was a natural for the two of them to make several visits. Natalie was in the vineyards, poking in the soil, trimming vines, picking grapes, and processing the juice. She carefully observed the barrel selection and preparation, the critical blending and aging processes and sampling the end product. France was next on her learning curve with several months of study in the primary regions. Germany, Spain, and Portugal followed, consuming a whole year of travel and study. The emerging vineyards of South Africa also warranted a brief but highly informative visit of several months.

With the equivalent of a master's degree in Viticulture and Enology, our darling Natalie returned home. Working with her mother, Brian, and staff, she explored vineyards for sale worldwide and land availability, specifically in the California wine country. Following several months of research and travel, she settled on a two-hundred-acre-plus piece of undeveloped land in the prime California wine belt. Brian handled the negotiations and arranged financing. The deal was closed on the land at a good price per acre, $78,000. Equipment, land preparation, and buildings brought the investment to $15.6 million. Norton and Pei Ling gifted Natalie $2.5 million; Natalie and I also provided a $3 million gift. Brian and Uncle Patrick each provided $1 in low-cost loans, which were forgiven on their due dates. Natalie provided $1,600,000 from her personal account. The balance of $6 million was provided 50 percent through a loan from the company's investment banking business at market rate and 50 percent as an investment by the property management operations. Natalie encamped to California, built a charming house on the property, and went to work.

The variables in wine growing/producing a fine wine are many and complex. Climate, moderate temperatures. Soil, rocky with a high mineral content. Fertility, lower fertility "controlling" the vigor of growth, balancing between leaves and the fruit. Minerality, high pH soils result in lower pH wines with enhanced fruit aromas and a structured acidity. Drainage, the most desirable soil would be friable or crumbly, allowing water to seep deeply into the soil and foster roots to grow deeply in search of the water. The roots will be healthier and less vulnerable to extremes of dry or cold weather. Heat retention, higher rock content in the soil allows for greater retention of heat. Absorbed during sunlight, heat is used at night to keep the root system warm and encourage the ripening of the grape.

Starting a new vineyard most often began with raw material from a nursery, providing certified virus/disease-free plants which are usually one year old. At this point, field grafting, after a year in the ground, mates *vinifera* species cuttings to the rooted American root stock. Alternatively, one can elect to purchase and plant one-year-old bench-grafted vines from a nursery.

Increasing the density of plantings per acre and controlling growth with different trellising systems had introduced greater control over the variables contributing to both yield and quality. Vineyard management attempts to keep most of their vines in the twelve- to twenty-five-year-old range. This establishes the longer-range replanting program. The pruning program, following harvest, is also important to the sustainability and quality of the grapes grown. We had seen a strong migration of American vineyards, particularly in the US western states, to sustainable and organic agriculture, biodynamics, and integrated pest control.

There were several years of intense labor, developing the vineyard and waiting for the vines to mature, about four years. The vineyard plantings take up about 150 acres. All had gone well, and Natalie will have her first limited production bottled ready for the market next year. I had placed a "future order" for four cases! Once the initial years of intense efforts lessened a bit, Natalie found time to develop a relationship. Her partner, Jean-Andre Boussard, a transplant from France, was a sixth generation viticulturalist. He worked with Natalie as a paid consultant in the early years of establishing the vineyard. They had been a couple for the past six years. Was there a marriage in the future? As was always the case with Natalie, you never know!

In my world at P&W, Tom Clarkson retired as planned, and the board elected Ms. Ann Hopkins (my dear Annie) as president and CEO of P&W. Concurrently, I was elected as executive vice president. The years melted away as we continued to produce fine novels to take to market. Forewarned by my father-in-law, our company was on the radar of several large international publishers. We very much wanted to retain our independence. However, the reality was the board had a fiduciary responsibility to the company's shareholders. Annie and I were given "golden parachutes." I was now approaching sixty, and Annie would soon be sixty-six. I had mentioned that Larry and Annie had developed a very close personal relationship following the death of Helene. Larry was still writing, although his books were now three or four years in development. He too was approaching sixty-six. Larry had a lifelong passion to travel, although now less frequently, spending time with Annie in Provincetown. Very quietly, several years ago, Larry had sold his apartment and moved into Annie's much larger home. They were a couple! Natalie and I were very much taken by surprise, with Larry and Annie announcing over a casual dinner, they were going to be married! As if that weren't enough, Annie said that she intended to retire in about six months. Wow! The wedding plans were already made with a very small, private, and remote wedding. Aloysius Murphy, now his Eminence Aloysius Cardinal Murphy, would marry them in Rome. Would Natalie and I stand with them as the bridesmaid and best man? The wedding date was about two months hence. Their plan was to travel, spend lots of time on the Cape, and maintain a pied-à-terre in the city. We were so happy for them.

As she had planned, Annie introduced her intent to retire to the board at their next meeting. Members of the board were taken aback. They said they would put on the table whatever was needed to change her mind. Annie simply said, "I have given forty-two years of my life to P&W. I have been fully rewarded in every conceivable way. The company has been my life. I am comfortable in knowing that I can leave with the company I love in good and able hands and move on to a new chapter in my life. Confidentially at this point, I will be marrying Larry O'Neil in the very near future, and we will embark on a life of travel and spending lots of time at our home in Provincetown."

The chairman of the board graciously said, "Anne, we are of course delighted with the news of your marriage and wish you and Larry O'Neil all the happiness in the world. We thank you for your forty-two years of service to the company and for bringing us to our preeminent position in the publishing world. I agree with you that you are leaving us well prepared to meet the challenges of the future."

As the meeting adjourned, the chairman asked me to remain. We were joined by the vice chair of the board.

"Kevin, we want you to know there is no question that the board will unanimously elect you as CEO/president of the company, succeeding Anne Hopkins. The board knows how you are perceived in the industry. We have attempted to bind you to the company with stock options, golden handcuffs, and a golden parachute. We are aware, as I am sure you are also, of several international companies sniffing around. The board will handle any approach as basically a hostile takeover. Remaining independent is our objective. However, the board has a fiduciary responsibility, and we must act in the best interests of our shareholders. The board would very much appreciate your continued commitment to the company and your assurance that you will be willing to, in the near future, take on the responsibilities of president/CEO of P&W."

I paused before I answered. "I have had the pleasure and good fortune to have worked with our CEO, Anne Hopkins, for my entire career, some thirty-seven years here at P&W. Words fail me to articulate what these years have meant to me on every front. I have been challenged, stimulated, richly rewarded, and have worked with an incredible group of people. I would be deeply honored to serve as the next president/CEO of this company. It would be the fulfillment of a life's dream."

We parted with warm handshakes.

Our trip to Rome several weeks later was an exciting and wonderful experience. The cardinal laid out the proverbial red carpet, including a private audience with the Holy Father. The wedding service took place in an intimate side chapel in St. Peter's Basilica. Aloysius hosted a splendid dinner reception for the five of us. In addition to the food, the wine was the very best Italy has to offer. The evening was full of recalling great times spent together. Our stay was short but gave all of us more great memories of good friends. Natalie had arranged a reception for the newlyweds following our return to the city. One hundred eighty-four guests attended, with the Dove doing its usual outstanding job.

Several weeks later, Annie's retirement was announced along with the news of the election of Kevin Murphy, president/CEO of P&W!

EPILOGUE

HAPPY, BLESSED, PROSPERING. I ENJOY good health, cared for by a loving and supportive wife, thriving on being the father of three wonderful children and grandfather to five grandchildren, with the prospects of more to come. I am enveloped by the love and support of my extended family.

Added to this richness, I have an incredible wealth of friends, and I completely and passionately love my work.

I occasionally wonder why the Good Lord granted me this *perfect life*. I don't know if I will ever figure that out. I

have tried in small ways, hopefully sometimes in meaningful ways, to help those where their life is less than perfect.

It occurs to me, Shakespeare summarized it so well:
"All's well that ends well!"

ABOUT THE AUTHOR

**F**RANK FARRELL WAS BORN IN 1936 and grew up in upstate New York. After college (Siena, Loudonville, New York), a tour in the US Army, and graduate school (University of Illinois), Frank married Janet L. Starr and entered the "real world" of work.

Over the span of six years, Frank worked in four different states: New York, Oklahoma, Arizona, and New Jersey. At the last stop in New Jersey, Frank joined a GE/Time

Inc. joint venture, General Learning Corporation. It was here that he formed a lifelong love of publishing. In the years following, the author worked with some of the very best: Silver Burdett, Western Publishing, and Grolier Inc. Frank cofounded the Millbrook Press as the capstone of his publishing career.

Melding his interest in educational materials and issues facing children, Frank has been heavily involved, for many years, in matters relating to their well-being. He has served as a court-appointed guardian ad litem and educational advocate. He also served as an elected member of school boards in Connecticut and Florida, as a board member of Voices for Children, the Book Industry Study Group, and as the founding board chairman of the Center for the Book in Connecticut.

Frank and Janet, his wife of sixty-three years, are parents to a daughter and two sons. The Farrell family tree now includes nine grandchildren and six great-grandchildren and counting. The Farrells make their home in Brookfield, Connecticut. Frank is an avid bridge player, golfer, pool shark, voracious reader, and community volunteer, and he spends his "idle time" painting abstract art.

Printed in the USA
CPSIA information can be obtained
at www.ICGtesting.com
LVHW041600110324
774162LV00005B/19